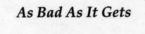

As Bad As It Gets

As Bad As It Gets

JULIAN RATHBONE

This edition published in Great Britain in 2004 by
Allison & Busby Limited
Bon Marche Centre
241-251 Ferndale Road
Brixton, London SW9 8BJ
http://www.allisonandbusby.com

A catalogue record for this book is available from the British
Library

ISBN 0 7490 0679 X

Printed and bound in Spain
by Liberduplex, sl

JULIAN RATHBONE's first book was published in 1967 and has been followed by more than thirty novels and one work of non-fiction. He has been translated into fifteen languages. Twice nominated for the Booker Prize, he has been awarded the Deutsches Krimi Preis and the prestigious Crime Writers' Association Macallan Short Story Award.

A contributor to various newspapers, magazines and periodicals, he is also a successful television and film scriptwriter whose work has been broadcast in over forty countries. After long spells in Turkey, France and Spain, he currently lives in Hampshire.

Chapter One

You don't want to know why I was in Mombasa, but I'll tell you anyway. Normally I hang out in Bournemouth, where I earn my crust as an enquiry agent. Bournemouth – you may not know this if you're not a Brit – is the UK's premier seaside resort, great club-scene, casinos, lap-dancing bars, an h and c town, and I don't mean the plumbing. Four miles to the west you come to Canford Cliffs and then Sandbanks which are enclaves for the seriously rich, very nouveau rich. Two of these, a Mr and Mrs Margeon, had employed me to go to a beach club hotel, one of those all-inclusive jobs, about fifty miles up the coast from Mombasa, to check out that their twenty-year-old son Arnold had indeed died in a scuba accident and that there were no suspicious circs.

Some years back Jimmy Margeon invented a soft drink, a soda: two thirds conventional cola cut with one third non-alcoholic ginger beer. It didn't go too well. Then, one day, finding herself fresh out of tonic, Tina Margeon used it as a mixer with one-third vodka. They called it Jinjapep. 'Have a drink on the margin – Go to the edge with a Jinjapep' was the slogan. Two years later Jimmy sold out to a global food and drink conglomerate for twenty million quid.

My one visit to them (they took my name from the Yellow Pages) was, at that time, one of the saddest experiences of my life. Imagine: elegantly curved art deco style picture windows overlooking Brownsea Island with the Purbeck hills blue on the horizon beyond, the parquet floors like pale gold ice, the drinks trolley as well as the bar in the corner, the white kid sofas, the kitsch paintings of nudes (no fig-leaves), the out-of-season peonies in a Waterford bowl with gold mountings, Jimmy in white slacks, an Armani pull and Gucci shoes, Tina in Westwood Lycra pants that hugged lipo-ed buttocks as if they were madly in love with them, Enya from the *Lord of the Rings* on the Bang and Olufsen, all this and sorrow. Real misery.

They paid me a couple of grand plus expenses. "Money don't mean a thing no more, Chris – fly Club, hire limos, kit yourself out if you haven't got the right clothes, just bring us back peace of mind that we done all we could, OK?" On the flight out I read up on the coroner's report, and Scuba for Beginners, spent three days at the hotel talking it all through with the manager, the Scuba instructor and so forth, and came to the same conclusion the Coroner had: Arnold drowned in his own vomit having filled his mask, and all this in the hotel swimming pool during his second half-hour of beginners' instruction. Yes, he had been told not to eat for two hours before the lesson, yes he had had a very late buffet-lunch because he'd spent the morning as well as the early afternoon going round the golf course in one hundred and nine which was also what the temperature was. He'd had a couple of girls with him, who'd gone long before I turned up, and they'd said he'd had diarrhoea the night before.

So much for that. I faxed my findings to Sandbanks using the hotel's business centre, and added that I'd call on the Margeons when I got back, if they wanted me to. Meanwhile, I thought I might take two or three days even a week out – after all I was two grand ahead of the game – and have a look at Kenya. Maybe try and get a late booking on a safari tour, that sort of thing. This may seem a daft way of doing things but there were factors: I live on my own and can do what I like; it was my first time ever in real Africa; any money I spent was money the Child Support Agency, aided and abetted by my ex, would not get its claws on.

So there I was, and that's why I was there, sitting in the departure lounge at President Moi, Mombasa's glassy, gleaming airport, waiting for the evening flight back to Nairobi, watching the sunset and feeding the crows.

There were two of them – big and black, but with white collars and bibs, pied crows, they're called – strutting their stuff over the tables and floor, wherever there were crumbs or even lumps of food returning trippers had given them while they waited for the inevitably delayed flight. The wall of the cafeteria was glass and faced west, but expanses of it were kept open for coolness which is how the crows got in. The area inside was big and airy with high corniches they could perch on before swooping down for scraps. I guess the airport authority was still trying to figure out what to do about them.

Just as the blood-orange sun dipped below tree-tops and a low rise of hills on the far side of the air-field, and the 737 from Nairobi that we were all waiting for touched down with a scream of tyres on the runway, I became aware of a presence at my shoulder, a large hand on the back of the plastic chair next to mine, and a voice that was deep, musical, and somehow went with the hand, which was strong, tanned brown, and with black hair almost to the knuckles.

"May I join you?"

My first instinct was to take a slow meaningful look at the tables around us, unoccupied since most of our fellow-travellers were sitting in the rows of seats between the shops in the mall behind the cafeteria, but I took a look up at him, decided he looked interesting.

"Of course."

He pulled the chair away from the table, sat in it, placed a buttercup yellow camel-hide bag with push-button catches, a bit like a Gladstone but designer, close beside him and floated that hairy hand in front of my chest. I gave him a second before I took it to let him know I'm no push-over. Dry palm. Firm squeeze but not demanding. I returned it likewise.

"Ludwig Holly," he said.

"Chris Shovelin," I replied.

Holly was shortish, thick-set, bow-legged, deep-chested, arms that looked longer than they were. Short-cropped thinning white hair above a broad face, small nose slightly squashed, his lips thick. In short, a touch simian, an impression strengthened by the hair on his wrists and the white hair that was visible where he had left the top button of his maroon piqué shirt open, but coloured, no. Maybe Levantine, Egyptian perhaps, even gypsy, but who am I to say? His eyes, behind gold-framed, slightly tinted specs, were deep-set and very dark, with bloodshot yellowish whites. When they weren't smiling with an open friendliness they had the melancholic appearance of mountain tarns. His clothes were old-fashioned – cream linen jacket a touch crumpled, unlined, the shirt, baggy cotton trousers with turn-ups. Somerset Maugham would not have been surprised to meet him in Mombasa, Conrad would have recognised him and Graham Greene would have bought him a drink.

He was about my age, which is a lot older than I care to admit to, but not yet sixty.

"Nairobi?" he asked, pushing the sides of his jacket apart as he relaxed into the chair.

"Is there anywhere else I can go at this time of night?"

For night it was already. Only the merest aquamarine glow above the hills was all that was left of the day. Holly laughed.

"Not unless you have a private plane. Or know someone who does." His accent was vaguely but not genuinely American. Berlitz American you could call it. We exchanged the usual chat for the forty minutes it took the ground staff to turn the plane round, he giving out rather less than I... which is unusual. I make my living asking questions – answers, I charge for. By the time the flight was called he knew why I was there and in what capacity, that I was going to stop over in Nairobi for at least three or four nights, I might even try to get on a safari trip, that the Serena Hotel was holding a room for me, no problem.

"Everywhere businessmen go, or tourists, is underbooked," Holly commented. "Bin Laden must be a happy man. Just about everything he could have hoped for has happened. I hope you bargained with them. They'd rather let a room go at half-price than keep it empty."

Of course I'd done nothing of the sort. Englishmen of my age and class – lower-middle pretending to be middle – don't bargain, not when we're buying. Not that I was of course. It was the Margeons' money I was using.

He also had a basinful of my reactions to my few days on the Kenyan coast, what I felt about the wonderful green lush fertility, the wide brown rivers, the atrocious roads, the contrasts between glitzy wealth and mud-hut poverty, the small-holdings with a stand of bananas and the huge prairie-like fields of sorghum, pineapples and sisal presumably owned by the giants of international agri-business. Perhaps, if the concept was familiar to him, he recognised a streak of knee-jerk, uninformed Old Leftism in my discourse; certainly he knew I was by profession an enquiry agent or, in the inevitable gloss everyone puts on the job description, a private eye.

"Ah," he said, and his eyes twinkled with a slightly mocking smile, "that explains your head-gear."

And he picked my hat up from the table where I had put it, and turned it over. It's a fairly wide-brimmed felt fedora.

"Genuine Stetson, I see."

I couldn't resist spilling the beans.

"I bought it in San Francisco," I said. "Seemed appropriate, though it was very expensive. I've owned suits that cost less."

"But worth every cent. Hammet had one, as well as Sam Spade."

"Precisely."

About him I learned bugger all.

One thing I did learn though was that here was a man who knew his way round. He followed me up the steps into the 737, leaving the twenty or so mostly elderly Brits and Germans on the tarmac, and upgraded himself into Club by offering the senior steward a twenty-dollar note folded behind his boarding card.

My chief memory of the flight, and I'm still grateful to him for it since he pointed it out and I might otherwise have missed it, is the sight of Kilimanjaro seen in the light of a just risen full moon, as big and gibbous and bright as they come, out of the left hand window. We were the only customers in Club and the cabin lights were out. It looked as if it was just below us, rising out of a flat sea of nacreous mist or lowish cloud that reflected the moonlight. Then he got me over to the other side of the plane to look out of the window opposite.

"Sometimes," he said, his voice soft now, almost reverent, "you can make out the summit of Mount Kenya to the north-east. They say if you get to the top of either on a clear day and you can see the other, then that is the longest view you can get on Planet Earth."

I couldn't swear I saw it, but I like to pretend I did.

"Wonderful to see snow so close to the equator," I commented.

"Make the most of it. It's thinning out. Probably be gone and the glacier with it in a decade or so."

"Global warming?"

He shrugged.

"Of course. But not necessarily caused by greenhouse gases. Could be part of the global cycle that brought and took away the Ice."

He said it as if he knew what he was talking about.

Once the big mountain had slipped by we settled back into our wide seats, stretched our legs and continued to chat for the half hour or so that was left. He refused the South African champagne-style the stewardess offered and had a Tusker beer which he span out for most of the trip. I don't drink alcohol so

I had a tomato juice. With Lea and Perrins. Amazing. I guess every airline with any pretensions at all carries Lea and Perrins on its planes. He spent most of the time talking about Nairobi, or rather warning me about it.

"You go to Rio, Jo'burg, Kingston, San Francisco, Mombasa even, and the concierge in the good hotel gives you a street map and marks it up for you. Don't go here or here, or even there. The rest is safe. Not in Nairobi. Not in Nairobbery. In daylight you're relatively safe inside Moi Avenue, between Moi and Uhuru Park. But not if you're carrying a camera, or wearing jewellery..." He glanced at my rings. I wear three or four, more than most men do. "Don't stand around, keep moving as if you know where you're going. At night you take a taxi and you order it from the hotel desk and you keep it until you get back. Maybe it cost you? Ten of your pounds, fifteen? So what? Better than a broken head and everything gone, even your shoes. And if the worst does happen keep away from the police. They'll take anything the muggers left, lock you up, and make you pay them to let you go."

Lots of lights, but with black, blank patches, scrolling into the leading edge of the wing, then it tipped against the moon-full sky and we heard the rumble of the undercart going down. Only four days since I had landed here first, in my first African dawn, over a grey ochreish plain dotted exactly as it should be with the etiolated acacias you see on all the posters, and wildebeest and buffalo – we were coming in over the Nairobi National Park. Tower blocks on the horizon, rumble and bump of wheels on the imperfect tarmac. That time, of course, I'd been in transit with a four hour wait in the crummiest transit lounge I've ever been in, before flying on to Mombasa. This time I was to get the full Jomo Kenyatta Airport experience.

Not too much hassle since we were coming off a domestic flight, then a long wide concrete bunker-style corridor with closed gift, souvenir and jewellery shops set incongruously in the walls at either end, leading into a big barn-like concourse. More shops, cafeterias closed apart from a kiosk or two, exchange booths, guys with placards, taxi-touts. Fairly crowded even at that time of night, black faces, very black, everywhere. The coast is part Arab, part Indian, as well as African, whereas Nairobi is pure Africa. The deep ebony blackness was, what shall I say?, noticeable, faintly disturbing at first. But after a day or two you get used to it. Even more surprising to me was the presence everywhere of armed black police, surprising because they treated the ordinary guys and women around with a ready rudeness and roughness that made you think 'redneck'. But I guess pigs are pigs whatever their colour.

Holly walked beside me, went with me to the baggage reclaim where I had a hold-all to pick up.

"I'll leave you now," he said. "If the Serena knows what flight you're on there'll be a car for you. If not I think there's a shuttle covers the four or five best downtown hotels. If you have any problems while you're here that you think I might be able to help you with, give me a buzz." And he slipped a thin sliver of paste-board into my palm. "And here's a thing…"

He paused, and a sort of speculative but distant look came into his eye.

"… I know where you are so if I need a private eye, and I might, I'll get in touch."

This was an odd thing to say under the circs, but before I could say anything he'd moved on from me to something else. My eyes followed him and I saw him met by a Greek God. Tall, athletic body, early thirties, powder blue shirt with the sleeves of a cashmere sweater loosely knotted at the neck, immaculate ivory-coloured chinos, tightly waved sun-bleached blond hair, complexion a pale terra-cotta, six-foot-three, not more than one seventy pounds, moving with a natural, animal elegance as he took Holly's bag and put an arm round his shoulder. Gay? Gay couple? Perhaps. But it's not something you wear ostentatiously in President Moi's Kenya. Those big black policemen beat queers to a pulp and then eat them. Greek God? That's a silly cliché. This guy was nordic, Scandinavian, Swedish maybe. Looked like he could have stepped out of one of those Third Reich posters advertising the *herrenvolk*. Then the conveyor belt jolted into motion, and I forgot about both of them. I didn't even give the card more than a cursory glance as I slipped it into my top pocket. Ludwig Holly in copperplate,

an address. Two lines, a number and the name of a
street, and the one word Nairobi beneath it. In the
left bottom corner an email address, in the right a
telephone number, both in tiny print.

My canvas hold-all came round, I scooped it up
and headed for the taxi-rank.

Chapter Two

Eight o'clock in the morning and I was looking out of my hotel window. Maybe I was paying more than I need have done, but certainly I had one of the best or better views. In front of me, under the window, a neat hotel garden with a couple of guys in uniform cotton jackets, scouring lush cropped grass for litter or fallen leaves. To the left a swimming pool. Then a high hedge with, to the right, a narrow gate where a couple of security guards were checking in the day-staff, cleaners and the like. They had clipboards and the workers had IDs with photos. Beyond the hedge a park – grey grass, pine trees and eucalyptus, an avenue of jacaranda along the perimeter road, but not in bloom, and beyond them the high-rises, some of them big enough to be called skyscrapers, glitzy and glassy, of downtown Nairobi. To the right, at right-angles to the hotel which was on a loop off it, a main thoroughfare cut through the park. It was busy. Traffic streamed into town, cars and buses, but the most common vehicles were bicycles and *mata-tus*, the clapped-out mini-buses discarded by the safari companies and now carrying as many as twenty-five passengers in spaces designed for eight. The sidewalk was busy too, hundreds of men and a few women streaming into town. Most of the men wore western jackets and trousers that didn't match and carried battered looking document cases; the women wore conventional, definitely non-sexy sweaters and dull skirts apart from a few who were wrapped in multi-coloured printed cotton or fine woollen sheets.

In the park itself sacred ibises walked on black stilts and stabbed the ground with long curved beaks – sacred maybe, but they looked scruffy, ill-kempt; around them pied crows squabbled over scraps. Men gathered in groups. They looked shabby, ill, poor. Some seemed to be at collection points where they hoped to be picked for a day's work, but others were settling in for the day with cigarettes and booze. Later I worked it out for myself, and confirmed it in a copy of the English language *Daily Nation* – they were on the edge of the more debilitating stages of AIDS and occasionally, come evening, there would be those who had dozed off and didn't wake up. The sky was overcast but not solidly so. Within an hour much of the cloud broke up and the sun shone with what felt more like a burn than warmth.

I turned from the window, and the thought crossed my mind that maybe this wasn't after all the room with the best view.

Breakfast was the full five star international buffet: tropical fruits, waffles, omelettes, the cooked 'English', croissants, fresh rolls, toast machine, the lot. Left me feeling bloated but ready for anything, and worryingly unbothered by the poor starving sods outside. They crossed my mind, give me some

credit, but what could I do? Fill a doggy-bag? While
I ate I had a look at the other punters: trippers on a
pre-safari night-stop or, done that, and now waiting
to be bussed to the airport for a week on the coast,
and three or four top, and I mean very top businessmen. You know how I know they were top? They
were old: the silver waved hair, the thousand quid
suits, and most of all because they had underlings,
male and female, in tow, who made notes in elec-
tronic notebooks while the Masters of the Universe
tucked into their guavas and passion-fruit.

It was a conference of course. At ten o'clock on the
dot, just as I was going through the foyer and out
under the marquee, six large black BMWs, top of the
range, flags on their wings, cruised in off the main
road and swung round the flower-filled roundabout.
Men in black, black men in black, were getting out of
the front passenger doors before they had properly
stopped, unbuttoning their jackets, eyes sweeping
over the shrubberies, eyeing up the hotel frontage,
and, bloody hell, wondering who the fuck I was. I
turned my back on them, grinned at the doorman in
a you-know-I'm-a-guest-don't-let-them-shoot-me
sort of way and sidled off towards the main road.
But I glanced back and saw Kenya's rulers, in a
human capsule of secretaries and bodyguards, moving as if on wheels through the glass doors.

So who were the Masters of the Universe at
breakfast? Arms dealers? The Pharma-industry?
Mineral Extraction? Agri-business? No point in
wondering – no one was going to tell me.

I strolled down Kenyatta Avenue, with the park I had seen from my window on my left and another on the right, to the big intersection where Uhuru (Freedom) Highway crosses it. Downtown Nairobi now rose in front of me in the shape of the usual gleaming forest of banks, hotels, and regional HQs of the bigger global corporations that you see at the centre of every major conurbation the world over. But first there was a maelstrom of flesh and storming metal to get across. Police whistles shrilled, brakes screamed, distressed engines spewed black smoke, women who appeared to be moving house with their belongings on their heads sailed past like clippers, sumps clanged as vehicles were squeezed by their neighbours into potholes at least a foot deep. I hovered on the edge like a cowardly swimmer, braving not cold rapids but the possibility of being mangled alive between hurtling hunks of hot metal. Somewhere a light changed, or a policeman blew a whistle those around me understood, and I was almost carried to a central reservation marked by broken kerb-stones. The flow of metal resumed in front of me but now, by and large, going in the opposite direction. Again an almost momentary pause in the screaming cascade of rusty metal, peeling chrome, whirling fumes, allowed a surge across; as part of it I was buffeted by the crowd coming from the other side. Sidestepping, weaving, challenged and knocked sideways by a shoulder charge I tripped on a loose lump of concrete and almost fell on to the sidewalk as a matatu clipped my heels.

Well, I was in culture shock and maybe it wasn't quite as bad as that. Invigorated rather than intimidated, I made my way on up Kenyatta, past the new General Post Office, and almost immediately I was brushing aside just about every blandishment and threat aimed at getting anything valuable I might have on me, off me. Babes wrapped tight and lying in the crooks of the arms of healthy, indeed beautiful young girls could win a fifty-shilling note off me so long as they looked happy and smiled, the maudlin ones I rejected. Small boys dragging at my sleeves and gawping up at me with tragic eyes imbued with suffering I could handle. I made myself a rule: if I could get that soulful look to change to a complicit grin I was prepared to part with ten Kenyan shillings, ten pence. Older hustlers I tried to ignore, kept my eyes fixed above their heads, shrugged off any physical contact with unaggressive determination. But once or twice I was frightened: a young man would try to engage me in conversation: "Where you staying, man?", "You English, man?" and so forth while others slowly closed in round me, one or two on each side, a couple behind, edging up closer. I began to feel glad I'd taken those rings off, that I wasn't carrying a camera. All I had was a wad of K shillings, about thirty quids' worth, held in a roll in my jacket pocket, and I was quite ready to part with them if things began to look seriously physical. I'm a coward. Believe me.

Then suddenly they were gone, melting away like scavenger gulls behind a ship which has crossed an invisible border. I glanced over my shoulder. A family maybe twenty yards behind me, two adults, two adolescent kids, clearly looked likely to provide better or easier pickings. And suddenly it really hit me how we stood out, me as well as that family, how we were different, how we were the ethnic minority now, this was their city, not ours.

Less bothered, I began to take in something of my surroundings. Above me the sky was now almost clear of cloud, the sunlight was hot if you stood in it, black kites swirled like those paper planes one used to make, not the darts but the delta-shaped ones with tails, at five hundred feet or so above the avenue; then came the big blocks, some upended shoe-boxes, several newer, post-modern – ziggurats or with curved, bent frontages of coloured mirrored glass: Barclays, Deutschebank, AFI with its corncob, green and gold, for the 'I', the Mercedes star, BA, the logos one sees in every developing conurbation from Lima to Macao, from China to Peru. The contrast came at street level. The pavement was cracked, the kerbstones fell away round deep holes, some with a snakepit of cables at the bottom, gaping without warning or protection. The trees looked as if they were dying and the flowers in the neglected beds rattled in the fumes and slipstreams of the traffic. Shops were boarded-up or half empty, often they were just open spaces between concrete piles filled with litter, trash and garbage. Every now and then pedestrians were forced into narrow files where an older building was being demolished in a confused racket of falling masonry, drills, bulldozers and dumper trucks. The big glass doors of the corporations were inches thick, with uniformed police, para-militaries and security guards on both sides, the harsh black hardware of H and K MPs or Berettas swinging at their sides or from their belts. But between blocks sidestreets ran into areas where the buildings were lower and older and at the end of one on the far side I could see a sunlit square with palms and the impressive frontage of a mosque. There were market stalls too.

Near the top of Kenyatta, a hundred yards or so short of the junction with Moi, I found a bookshop with quite a large stock in English: the usual Grishams and Clancys, TEFL textbooks, and guides. You'll have guessed by now that I'm a bit of a birdie and I bought the *Collins Guide to Birds of East Africa* for only a little more than I would have paid in England. Then, mindful of Holly's warning that the bad lands lay on the far side of Moi, I retraced my steps a short way, found a more or less official crossing and got to the other side with no rush of adrenalin at all. Easy-peezy.

Street markets don't vary any more than downtown skyscrapers, yet they all have their own quirks and even if the aubergines glow as richly purple in Cape Town as they do in Cairo, and the heaped chilli peppers and judias beans are as lushly green, the music blaring from sound-systems varies, and so do the knick-knacks for tourists, and anyway, they're always fun and every now and then you have to stop and look, usually at a food-stall, and ask yourself 'What the hell is that?' And while the 'Calvin Klein' knickers, 'Tommy Hilfiger' tops and 'Reebok' trainers are the same, the local clothing is not.

From the street market I strolled into a big oblong, partly enclosed, galleried courtyard filled with the tourist stuff, everything you could possibly make from ebony, ivory and soapstone, from troupes of serried elephants to beetles, from chessmen to croc-odiles; there were baskets made from sisal, jute and cane, and decorated with African motifs; masks, feathered head-dresses, assegais, elliptical shields, fly whisks made from the tails of colobus monkeys or antelopes (bone-in), knobkerries and huge collars consisting of thousands of bright beads. If you stopped for more than ten seconds the cry went up: 'Seeing is free, come in and look, you are my first customer today, kind sir, I can see you are a connois-seur, have a shufti,' but all done with an open friendliness, cheery fatalism, and little apparent resentment when you moved on with a shrug and a dismissive wave of the hand. There were so many tiny shops, so many potential customers – you might buy elsewhere but the next one along might buy here.

But then I found myself in the meat and fish-mar-ket. This was something else. All right it was nearly lunch-time, the best produce no doubt had gone while I was still having my breakfast, but what was left, offal, heads and tripes, attracted flies like William

Golding never imagined, the smashed remains looked like Waterloo two days after the battle, the smell was something Dante never thought of. I staggered out into a side street, handkerchief to my mouth, on a corner by a cinema (Tom Cruise, *Mission Impossible 2*) and made it back on to Kenyatta.

Never mind that market, I was peckish by now. I looked up and down. Behind me a cyber café, but not the sort that actually sells coffee, just rough plaster walls, flaking paint, tatty posters, a booth where you got your ticket, and stalls set up on tables with screens and keyboards. The latest thing? Yet somehow it contrived to look older and shabbier than the professional letter-writers with their typewriters it no doubt replaced. But across the road, in a gap between two blocks, there was a space, a rectangle of sunlight with tables and chairs and a glass frontage set back on the side – Simmers Restaurant. Again I crossed the cataract, quite the old Nairobi hand by now.

Simmers was what I wanted. 'The Answer on a Plate' was its English slogan. Not smart, not a McDonalds either, but an ordinary place where the local office workers were already having their lunches. The tables outside were all taken but I found one inside. OK, it was not a diner, it was grubby and busy, but cheerful too with a counter at one end where cooks fried and grilled and big pots, yes, simmered on bottled-gas rings. The menu was in whatever brand of Swahili was the common language but English too. I chose Kuku

Choma – fried chicken – and out of the choice of
manioc or chips, chickened out and went for chips.
It was OK, you know? And with a Coke cost about
one pound fifty.

What now, I thought, as I pushed back my chair
and stood. The national museum seemed worth a
visit, according to the Lonely Planet guide. Huge
collection of stuffed birds. Casts of footprints made
by our ancestors four million years ago. But again I
remembered the warnings. So... go back to the
Serena, get them to call up a taxi. And maybe use
the swimming pool first. I made my way back on to
the main drag.

They closed in round me straight away. Perhaps,
I thought, one of them had been in Simmers and
had seen the wad of shillings I peeled notes from to
pay.

There was one on each side of me, and I sensed
another behind. But it was the one in front I had a
proper look at. Black baseball cap with the white
NYPD logo, pocked skin, yellow teeth, breath like
sewage overlaid with garlic and raw spirit. Shabby
black leather bomber, GAP t-shirt, white on black.
Big boots like DMs. I took a step forward, hand in
front.

"Don't be raising your hand at me, Mister," and
he lashed out with his right boot at my left shin and
then took advantage of my reaction to knee me in
the balls. As my head came forward his hands came
up in a double fisted blow that caught my upper lip
and nose. I sat down, very heavily, on a corner of

broken concrete. All four began to kick me. I blacked out. My last thought was, hell, I'm no longer just a tourist, I'm a victim.

Chapter Three

I wasn't out for long. I came to as strong hands in my armpits lifted my torso, and another pair hooked under my knees. They tried to be gentle but it was an awkward business getting me onto the floor of the back of a Land Rover. Once in, I looked up between the spread knees of a big strong policeman who was sitting on the sideways facing bench above me, and he looked down and grinned. A slight jolt, enough to lift and bump my head on the floor, and we were off. A siren wailed, loud enough to shut out the traffic noise. Good, I thought. If they get me to A&E, Nairobi Hospital, in five minutes, I may not die, I may not even wet myself. I felt the blood trickle down the inside of my chin and on to my neck. I might, though, bleed to death.

A&E? Apparently not. It was at the Central Police HQ at the north end of Moi that they unloaded me. Worse than that, the two policemen in the back with me expected me to walk, though when there were steps to get up they were kind enough to hook an arm or two round my waist. They smelled of fresh sweat and their bodies felt hard. As the shock wore off I was beginning to hurt, my face especially and my shin when I put any weight on my left foot. Enough to make me wonder if there was a fracture, a crack anyway. I squealed, moaned and groaned, just to let them know. And because I'm a cry-baby.

They took me into a communal toilet; pools on the cracked tiles, one of the basins coming off the wall, only held there by the pipes. In a doorless cubicle they sat me on the pedestal above caked shit and tried to sponge my face down with coarse paper towelling. I yelped again as any scabs that had begun to form were scraped off and I bled worse than before. One of them, the fatter of the two – they were both pretty bulky – pushed more paper into my hand. I got the message and held it to my mouth and nose, then pulled it away. The blood looked dark. I went on dabbing, they went on handing me paper towels, some of them soaked in water. They looked down at me, and at each other, muttered at each other in Swahili or Kikuyu or whatever. They looked worried, then the fatter one leant towards me. He looked concerned and that made me want to cry again.

"How you feel? You feel OK?"

"You can walk. Can you talk?" his mate chimed in.

I ran my tongue round my teeth. Neither tongue nor teeth were damaged, only my lips. The top one had swollen into what felt like a ballooning blister.

"Yeth, I gun dawk," I said, but was already wondering why it was important that I should.

They nodded at each other, got me to my feet, headed towards the door.

"I godda pee."

They carried on.

"Your-In-Ate."

They got the message, changed course for the urinals. Armitage Shanks. So do I. But although the feeling became a pain, I couldn't get anything to come. I farted. They helped me back to the cubicle. Sitting down again, this time with my trousers round my ankles, and the company politely out of my vision, I peed a bit, not much, farted a lot more, then I turned myself round and vomited. Chicken and chips and some blood – internal bleeding or just what I'd swallowed? More paper towels, then we tried again, down some stairs, along a corridor, a knock on a door, into an office.

A cheap desk, filing cabinets, a couple of telephones, and a guy behind the desk, one shoulder part hidden by a bulky looking monitor sitting on top of its computer, could have been the first IBM compatible Amstrad, or even older, the sort that took floppies that were floppy. One of my friends let go of me, pulled up a chair, the other dropped me in it. Then they took up positions behind me, against the door, arms folded, legs apart. I tried to get the guy behind the desk into focus.

"I am Commander Tom Komen and it is my job to find out what happened to you and with your help bring your assailants to justice."

I managed to nod. Against the dirty window and in the general gloom, and not forgetting vision that was blurred with tears, I was still only getting an impression, not much more. Greying hair, cut short, a bony face with highish cheekbones, a pale brown suit, more a taupe I suppose; not, I thought, a uniform.

"And you are?"

"Christopher Shovelin."

Name, rank and number. But hell, forget what I'd read about the police, this was the law, on my side, surely? Don't call me Shirley. I shook my head. A mistake.

"Staying at...?"

"The Serena."

"Tourist?"

"Sort of."

He made a note on a pad or note-book. A moment's silence disturbed by the cliché of a buzzing fly.

"Explain yourself."

I sighed, pulled in breath. It didn't increase the pain, but it didn't help any either.

"I came to Kenya on business. When it was done I decided to stay for a few days. As a tourist."

"And what happened just now?"

His accent was educated, sort of Oxbridgey the way some Africans are. Brisk, got a job to do, not sympathetic.

"I was just walking back to the Serena..."

"You'd finished what you had come here to do?"

"No, no. That had been at the Turtle Paradise Shoreline Club, up the coast from Mombasa. I flew in from Mombasa last night."

"You were at the Turtle Paradise Shoreline

Club…" he was reading off the note he had made on his pad, "on *business*?"

"Yes."

"So what were you doing this morning?"

"Just going for a walk. Looking around."

Why was this guy giving me a hard time? I was the bloody victim, for chrissake.

"And then?"

"Like I said. On my way back to the Serena these… thugs set on me. Four of them I think."

"Did you get a good look at them at all?"

"Just the one in front. Black New York Police Department baseball cap, pocked face, one point seven five metres, seventy kilos. That's five-eight, eleven stone."

I wasn't too sure how metric Kenya is.

"You'd recognise him again?"

"Yes."

"You're very sure."

"Yes."

"Why? Isn't it the case that to whites all blacks look alike?"

'Blex' is what he said.

"Professional training."

"Really?"

"I'm an enquiry agent."

Silence. Did he look a touch smug? Maybe. Good technique, trust me, I know, the way he'd led me to give him my occupation without him having to ask. Or was there more to it than that? Had I confirmed what he already knew? We were both experts at this game, I thought, enjoying a little exploratory foreplay. Then, come on, I told myself, you're drifting into paranoia.

"Let me be sure I've got this right. You were at the Turtle Paradise Shoreline Club as a private investigator, a PI?"

"Yes. My client's son died there in a scuba diving accident. The client sent me out to check the facts."

He thought for a moment, made a note.

"This morning. Did they take anything? Did they rob you?"

"I don't think so." I felt in my jacket pockets. Bird book still in the left hand one, the right one empty. "No, I'm wrong. About two thousand shillings."

"Not your passport? Travellers' cheques? Camera?"

"No. I followed the guide book's advice. Left all that in the hotel."

"Very sensible." Komen leant back, fiddled with his pen, held at each end by each hand in front of his face. Even so I got a better look at him. Older than I had thought. Skin slightly greyish beneath the darkness, deep lines running down the sides of the cheek-bones to the corners of his mouth. The suit looked a good one, maybe with some cashmere or silk in the mix.

He put the ballpoint down.

"Mr Shovelin, tourism is of vital importance to our economy. We have to do everything we can to make sure incidents like this are cleared up and the perpetrators properly punished, as a deterrent to others. If we pick up these hooligans we might want to ask you to identify the ring-leader. So I am asking you for how long you are expecting to remain in Nairobi. At the Serena."

Well, that's a thought. I had to admit to myself that the town had lost what appeal it had had in the last half hour or so. Nevertheless, I felt no urgency about getting back to Bournemouth.

"I really haven't decided. Look, right now I'd like to have a doctor or whatever check out the damage, and then just sleep it all off at the hotel."

"Of course. There's a doctor on call at the Serena. No need for the hospital unless he advises it. My boys will run you back there."

He pulled in a second pad and scribbled on it.

"Here's a number," he said. "Ring it when you have decided about your departure." He added an afterthought. "And if you should see the man who led your attackers."

The same guys as before helped me up on to the front bench of the Land Rover and I sat between them. I glanced back as we pulled out of the yard in front of the Central Police Station. There were several vehicles parked there: four by fours like the one we were in, riot control vehicles like the old Pyrene water cannon on a Foden chassis and the usual patrol cars. I saw a baseball cap moving above them. Black. Then its owner stooped and let himself into the sort of souped-up Cortina Dorset police used ten years ago or more. Excuse me, I should have said, do you mind stopping and letting me have a close look at that guy over there. In the cap. Before he steals one of your cars. But then… black baseball caps are almost as common these days, in Nairobi like everywhere else, as trilbies or bowlers used to be.

Dr Sanjit Ray, well, something like that, was part at least Indian, youngish and cheery.

"Strip off please and lie on the bed. All off, since you say you took a kick in the testiculars, we'd better make sure they're still there, eh? Let me see. Yes, one, two, a full-house."

He tut-tutted over my shin bone but decided on balance there was no break, and was confident enough to put an X-ray on hold… "until we see how it develops. If it gives you too much gyp then maybe we are having a closer look but it is being my opinion that if there is a hairline it will mend itself."

For the rest he gave me aspirin, and slopped some mercurichrome round my nose and mouth which made me look even more of a clown that the actual damage had done, and left me with some anti-inflammatory ointment in case the bruising elsewhere got to be a nuisance.

"But not your arsehole or your testiculars," he warned. "You'll need the services of the Nairobi Fire Brigade if you do. Actually, a good forty winks, make it fifty, will do more good than anything else. You are taking Lariam for the malaria? Once a week? Well, not for twenty-four hours, all right? Just keep the mozzies away from you if your dose is due."

Not Lariam actually – it doesn't go too well with a dodgy liver, and mine was still dodgy, the quack at home said, though it's five years since I had a drink.

He charged fifty quid, discounted from sixty for sterling cash, gave me a headed receipt. "Get it back from your insurance."

Insurance? Moi?

Chapter Four

I slept pretty fitfully until about half-four, came to with the sort of jerk that tells you, that's it, you might as well get up. I don't know that I felt any better, but it was different. Sharp, localised pains had become more general, some new ones had crept in, like a sore throat, I felt stiff the way one does on the second day after a sudden burst of ferocious and unaccustomed exercise. Psychologically I felt miserable, damaged, picked on: fucking bullies, I kept saying aloud. But I felt restless too, and wallowing in my misery was not going to help that so I dug out the trunks I'd brought, still a touch sandy and damp from the Indian Ocean, which I'd been in, good gracious, only the morning before. Then I pulled on some of the clothes Dr Ray of Sunshine had made me take off.

The pool was OK, ten metres with shallow steps at both ends, and a warm gusher which you could sit near using the steps, and get a jacuzzi effect. On two sides it was shielded by high thick hedges, on the other two there were changing rooms, a bar and a kiosk with the hotel behind. A guy at the entrance handed out nice big towels and there were recliners, tables, and parasols dotted about. The deck was almost hot enough to be uncomfortable to the soles of your feet, though the sun was now struggling with low cloud above a hill. There was something about where it was that snagged in my mind, but I was in no mood to work out what.

Eight or nine people were sharing the facilities with me. They all seemed to be English. There was the family I'd seen on Kenyatta at the beginning of my walkabout: Dad, Mum, lad of about twenty, girl about sixteen. They seemed all right. Then there were a couple of couples: a pair of ageing yuppies, well into their thirties, and an older pair of women, I took them to be teachers, spinsters but not that good friends since I could hear them bickering at each other. Or perhaps that meant they were good friends. But one of them anyway definitely seemed the sort who was going to find something to complain of wherever she was, whatever happened. Just then she was whining that the tea the waiter had brought her was less than very hot. The ageing yuppies had the gear: designer shades, she in a floppy felt hat, he in a baseball cap, yes, black, but a lot cooler than NYPD, class swimming-wear, their own towels, a big canvas carrier-bag with a splashy flower pattern, sun lotions, drinks with fruit and brollies. From their conversation I worked out that they had all arrived that morning and that next morning they would be off on a safari tour. It occurred to me that even at this late date I might be able to join them – I felt that while it might be said that I had not yet 'done' Nairobi, Nairobi had done me. Six days it seemed like the trip lasted. If I could get on board for, say, six hundred quid, well that would be fine. In a dozy sort of way I wondered how I might make contact with the tour rep.

And the ninth? She joined me just after I'd ordered a tropical fruit-juice cocktail, no brolly or straw, thank you, but lots of ice.

"Do you mind if I join you?"

Well, what can you say? Second time this had happened in twenty-four hours. Coincidence, or my approachable good looks?

I looked up, squinted since she was against the sun, but more because of the way I felt than because of it – it was already hazed. Five-foot-four, hundred and ten pounds, gingery blonde hair, longish, slightly coiffured into near ringlets, a hint of a peek-aboo curl to the side of her forehead which was pale, pale greenish eyes, a recollection of freckles. Small nose, nice mouth, lines, but the smiling sort, thin neck, short green cotton wrap, gold bangles and an amethyst ring, thin thighs, reddish knees, long, slender feet in thin-thong sandals, toe-nails as well as finger-nails painted cerise. About forty, or near it. She was carrying a book: Isac Dinesen short stories, *Anecdotes of Destiny*, not *Out of Africa*. Score five for not having the obvious book but one by the same author. Go forward three spaces.

"If it seems like I'm picking you up, well, there's some truth there. If I sit on my own I'll have to fend off the real creeps of which, I have to say, there are a few around."

"I'm not a real creep, then."

She frowned, made a show of passing judgement.

"I don't think so. We'll see." Very slight accent. East Coast American? Or even educated soft south-west Irish.

She put her book down, open, cover up, bent towards her bag, came up with a pack of Sportsman and a Hotels Serena box of wax matches. But a passing waiter got in first and lit her fag for her. She had the looks and manner that waiters go for. She breathed out smoke, glanced across at me.

"I am sorry. Did you want one?"

"No thanks. Gave up. What are they like?" I nodded down at the paper packet.

"Cheap and nasty. But not too nasty. I always smoke the local brands unless they're really disgusting. If they are I fall back on Gitanes."

My waiter brought my drink and hovered.

"That looks nice. What is it?"

"Just fruit juice."

"No booze?"

"I don't."

"Poor you." She looked up at the waiter who was young, not bad-looking, and ready to fall in love. "I'll have one of those but with a large vodka in it."

He went, on wings of desire, to do her bidding and she turned back to me, raised her hand in front of me.

"Danielle Newman," she said. "You can call me Danny."

Which somehow made Irish the more likely.

"Kit or Christopher Shovelin," I said. "You can call me what you like so long as it's not 'creep'."

And I took her hand, gave it a slight squeeze. She took it back, leant towards me.

"So," she asked. "What happened to you?"

I was just in the action of putting down my glass with one hand and trying to catch and stop the dribble that was coming out of the corner of my mouth with the other. My top lip still looked like an inflated condom: as a lip it was inoperative. Danny rose to the occasion, found a tissue in her bag.

"Stupid of me to turn down a straw," I managed at last.

"So?"

"Got mugged. On the pavement of Kenyatta. Lunchtime."

"You never! Are you all right?"

"I'm all right now."

"Did he take anything?"

"Twenty quid in shillings. Not a problem."

"Tell me about it."

I did. She listened… raptly, which was flattering, for about thirty seconds, then her attention wandered before I got on to the police bit, so I cut the tale short. When her drink arrived she took the straw from her glass and put it in mine, without saying a word, which was nice of her. The sun, red from the cloud, dipped below the hill. Lights came on round the pool, and under its sill. Squealing swifts racketed across the surface, nipping up insects, mosquitoes I hoped. We had a second drink each, while Danny continued to work through her pack of Sportsman. Most of the others went, leaving only the lad and his sister who were setting each other competitive tasks like "Can you swim right round the pool underwater?" Danny watched them for a moment then turned back to me.

"Best of a pretty dispiriting lot," she said. "Are you one of the party?"

"Not yet. I thought I might try to join them. They leave tomorrow morning, I gather."

She pursed her lips, expressing minor disapproval. Then she raised eyebrows and lifted her head to indicate the lady of a certain age on the table next to us who was now berating her companion in a high-pitched whine for not bringing the mosquito deterrent down from their room. There was not a mozzie in sight that I could see. "Supposing you have to share a mini-bus with *them*," she whispered.

She looked at her watch and stubbed out the current Sportsman. "Taxi ordered at eight. If I'm going to swim it had better be now."

She stripped off the green wrap, sleek black one-piece underneath, did a shallow dive though a notice told her not to. Less gracefully I felt my way down the steps, holding on to the side. I glanced down at my torso. Maybe it was the quality of the lights but the bruises really showed now, not quite blue and black yet but on the way. I tried swimming but it hurt, so I sat by the gusher, holding on to a sort of pillar thing, one of a row, that stood near it. Presently she joined me there, attached herself to the pillar next to mine.

"You look like a Turner sunset," she said.

"The Fighting Teméraire," I offered and made with my fists in front of my face before clutching back at the pillar as the current from the gusher caught me.

She laughed.

"Where are you going at eight?" I asked.

"The Carnivore," she replied. "Do you know of it?"

"It's in the guide book."

"You can come with me if you like."

"I would like."

"We'll go Dutch, right?"

"Fine."

On my way back to my room I had to cross the main foyer. The tour rep was behind a counter next to reception dealing with some enquiry or complaint from the whiny woman I'd sat near at the pool. I thought about it. On the one hand I'd had enough of Nairobi, didn't really trust the place not to hit me on the head again, or elsewhere. The idea of safari appealed, but not if I was going to spend it in a mini-bus with the likes of the lady at that moment making the rep's life a misery. Anyway... would there be vacancies? Would I not just look a prat even thinking I could get on board at the last moment? For a minute or two I dithered, like the poor cat i'the adage, then shrugged my shoulders, and, with my mind firmly made up to leave the whole thing to the morning, see how I felt, headed for the lift. Indecision, I'm almost sure.

* * *

An hour or so later I was sitting in the back of an elderly Merc, half facing Danny across the cracked leather, watching the light and shadow of the street lights floating across her face. She was made-up now, looked quite glam, hair more gold than I remembered from the pool-side, hint of greenish eye-shadow, lipstick enhancing the upward tilt at the corners of her mouth, drop earrings, emerald, could be real. She was wearing a silk stole and short-sleeved dress, eau-de-nil could be the right description, though the Nile I've seen was never that colour, lowish at the front, full skirt. She carried a small sparkly purse. In short, I wondered if my best casual chinos and linen jacket, navy Ralph Lauder polo shirt, all albeit clean and decently pressed, were up to the mark.

You know, I'm not bad at my job, but I was so taken with her that I forgot to ask myself: had she really been planning to do this outing on her own?

For about ten minutes the road was dual car-riageway in intention, though twice we were in con-tra-flow, and the verges were rubble. The housing beyond the street lights went steadily downmarket from apartment blocks that would not have looked out of place in a working class suburb of, say, Marseille, to shanty-town. We passed an airfield, not Jomo Kenyatta, then took a left down what was really no more than a track, concrete cratered with pot-holes, hardly any light.

"Have we been kidnapped?" I whispered, not wishing to upset the driver.

"What fun if we have," Danny replied, eyes gleaming.

But no. Shortly we pulled into a crowded parking lot in front of low buildings. A liveried attendant opened the door, white teeth flashed in what I was learning was the Kenyan greeting: effusive, warm, transparently sincere? Well, almost.

"*Jambo*," he shouted. "Welcome to Carnivore…" and a burst of Afro-Pop and the smell of burning meat billowed in on us from behind him. But on this occasion the welcome turned out to be less than entirely warm. At the entrance, in front of the cloak-room desk, were four Men in Black, tall, lean, tough. Very quickly, with a minimum of fuss they patted me down and got Danny to open her purse.

"What was that for?" I muttered.

"VIPs, I guess, dining out."

You must have heard of Carnivore. It is precisely what it says on the label: a restaurant where you eat meat. Split level carousels of tables beneath timbered and tented roofs surround a lit water-feature, and a second large circular counter enclosing a battery of grills where chefs cook meat in lumps and on huge skewers: beef, lamb, goat, pig, obviously, but also antelope, zebra, crocodile, buffalo, water-buck, ostrich… it looks like one of the jollier circles from Dante's hell. The devils are tall hatted chefs, the flames are real enough, the noise pandemonium, and the sinners? The meat of course, except here it's the guilty who barbecue the innocent.

You are sat at a table, you have a starter, you can go to the grills and choose, or they bring the skewers and platters to you, there are sauces and salads on the side and in the middle of it all is a paper flag. Eating was not a problem, once the food was past my still swollen lip.

But what I had failed to hear (I don't always hear too well) was that when I'd had enough meat I was meant to take down my flag. I had five helpings, all from different animals, before Danny rumbled what had gone wrong, and told me. Maybe if she had not been so interested in a group of our fellow customers she would have spotted the problem earlier.

There were eight of them, at a big table not far from ours and slightly above us, behind me but out on my right. Eventually, I half-turned, had a look to see what was grabbing her attention. It was the Masters of the Universe, the same ones, I was almost sure, that I had seen at breakfast, although they had shed their operational suits and were now relaxing in what the catalogues call leisure-wear. Five of them, and hosted by three Kenyans in Hawaiian-style shirts whose patterns reflected Africa as seen through the eyes of Parisian or Milanese designers. One was big, not Sumo-big but on the way, the second had white hair, the third looked younger and meaner.

I reckoned they might have been amongst those who had arrived that morning at the Serena in ministerial limos. And if that was the case that explained the presence of the Men in Black we had passed on the way in.

"The new imperialism," I suggested as I turned back to face Danny.

"You could say so. Interesting bunch. The oldest of the whites, no, don't turn round again, is a vice-president of AFI…"

"Agrob-Food International…"

"No. Lots of people call them that because they merged with Agrob. Actually it's Associated. Associated Foods International. Another heads up the African subsidiary of Hunt Madison. I'm not sure about the others. But if I'm right one of them is Pepe Boltana, CEO of the Banco de Corpus Cristi whose head office is on Grand Cayman. They handle Mob money. And if I am right then that implies some of the money movements they may be putting in place are dodgy. From what I remember of our database the Kenyans they are with are land development, trade and industry, and internal security. High powered bunch."

I was flabbergasted.

"Do you really know all this or are you making it up?"

"To impress you? Why should I want to impress you?"

I'd needled her. She went on.

"No, it's all real."

I waited. She relented, smiled a touch, very slightly raising the corners of her mouth.

"I'm a... newsperson, what you might call a journalist, but more a hunter-gatherer. East Africa is my stamping ground. I'm part of a three-person agency with an office in Jo'burg. Now, let's at least pretend we're not interested in them, at all, shall we? They do good sorbets here."

I chose mango which turned out to be a bit sweet for my taste. Over coffee, which was very good, best local, Kenya triple A, I asked her: "Since you know so much about those guys," I tilted my head backwards, "I suppose you're actually here on business."

"Oh dear me no, strictly on holiday." But it came with a knowing grin, as she tipped sugar into her cup. "Though I suppose it's fair to say that wherever I go in these parts for a break it's bound to be a bit of a busman's holiday. But my professional brief on this trip is simply to suss out how tourism is holding up under the stresses of the times."

"Which are?"

"Global slump in tourism, war and refugees on the northern borders, a corrupt government getting more and more overt in its readiness to sell the country cheap to the big corporations. But the really bad guys need tourism to launder the hard currency they want to ship out to Switzerland or wherever so they have a personal interest in keeping it going."

On the way back in the taxi she put her hand on my knee in a very companionable unsexy way and said, "You can't just hang about Nairobi for a day or two and then go back, just like that."

"So I'll go on safari. I'll speak to the rep first thing

tomorrow. I'm sure she'll be able to fix it up. It's worth a try anyway."

"Oh come on!"

"Well, what do you suggest?"

"I've got the figures, the statistics I want, or as much as I can get. My plan now is to drive around a bit, see what it feels like on the ground. I'm hiring a self-drive car for a week. I'm going to Mt Kenya, Samburu, then the Aberdares where I have friends I can call on. Maybe we'll stay with them. I'll be driving through game country. The Rift Valley. Maybe as far south as the Masai Mara. Now, the thing is I don't want to do this on my own. In fact to be frank I'd be an idiot to try to. One of my colleagues was meant to come along but he had a spot of bother, and I got an email this afternoon to say he couldn't make it. In short…" She turned full on me and gave me her most seductive grin. Not sexy seductive you understand, but the sort of total flattering charm very few males can resist. Certainly not me. "I'd like you to come with me."

I chewed a lip, glanced out at a passing filling station which had been torched and abandoned.

"I'll treat you. All expenses."

"No you won't. I can pay my way."

"The car-hire and petrol, anyway."

I shrugged.

"Does that mean you'll do it? It does. Doesn't it?"

I let the taxi rumble on until the street lights came back. She moved her hand away. Well, perhaps it had been just a touch sexy.

And then there was that moment of slightly awkward intimacy as we shared the hotel's small lift. I caught her eye in the mirror and cast around for something more to say.

"Do I need anything special in the way of clothes?" Stupid really, since what was I going to do if she told me to put on my David Attenboroughs?

"If you pitch up in a safari suit I won't even speak to you."

Even.

Chapter Five

Well, I wasn't in a safari suit, but Danny damn near was: pale tan waistcoat with zip-up and Velcro-secured pockets over a white shirt cut like a man's, cotton combat trousers, darker than the waistcoat. Slightly incongruously she had a pair of slip-on, flexible shoes on her feet. Later, I realised these were what she kept for driving. We met over breakfast which was, as they used to say about that eaten by a condemned man, once more hearty. Over it she said that if it was OK by me we'd head north towards Mt Kenya, have a look at that, and then may be go on towards the Samburu National Reserve and spend the night there.

The car was a red Polo, about three years old, in reasonable nick. Danny had a smart soft red leather suitcase, a smaller matching hold-all, a professional photography bag and a laptop in a zip-up. I had a black cloth hold-all that had been a 'free' gift with a stationery order and a floppy document case, ditto. With a bit of care we got it all into the boot except my document case with the bird book in it and Danny's hold-all, both of which we kept in the car on the floor in the back. She took the A2 north-east out of Nairobi signposted for Thika and Nyeri. Boulevards and avenues climbed through parks and gardens with ministry buildings and embassies, clearly the nob hill end of Nairobi. We passed a sign for Jomo Kenyatta University of Agriculture and Technology. She looked as if she were about to say something about it, but then shut up.

Soon the road became a wide dual carriageway with wide grass verges and narrower roads for local traffic running parallel to the main road. Beyond them a ribbon of shanty towns unwound with occasional patches of cultivation between. The shanties were built out of split timber with corrugated iron roofs and were often quite long. Did several families live in them?

Every kilometre or so there was a market, spilling across the local roads on to the verges. They were crowded, bustling: the men in their non-matching jackets and trousers, the women deep hipped with the grace of caryatids balancing their purchases on their heads, often in traditional dress or a pick and mix of European and African. Lots of goats, some sheep, flocks of chickens and turkeys, donkeys, occasional cows, huge dewlapped creamy oxen used as draft animals, pyramids of cabbages and potatoes, sacks of greens and fruit. Cattle driven slowly along the verges in quite large herds, headed for the shambles in Nairobi. The stalls sold simple wooden furniture, pots and pans, ironmongery and hardware, racks and racks of clothes, potted plants in plastic bags, basket-ware. Almost everywhere there were hoardings for Tusker beer, Sportsman cigarettes, Raid insect killer – 'Deadly Doom Protects, Cockroach Extermination in a Can', and signs hand-painted to a formula with the slogan 'Let's Talk Trust'.

"What are they about?" I asked Danny.

"Aids. Use a condom. Use several condoms. The government admits to twelve per cent of the population infected. It's probably a lot more."

"That's terrible."

"Yes."

The consolations of religion: a big Hindu temple on the left, painted in white and day-glo colours, caparisoned elephants and gods and goddesses in plaster. Churches too: African Independent Pentecostal, Jesus the Fountain of Life Centre, Full Gospels Church of Kenya, Holy Spirit Revival Centre – most of them neatly built and evenly stuccoed in whites and pale ochres: clearly any spare money you had went to the congregation you favoured. Schools, church schools and municipal, kids often very neat in uniforms that English children haven't worn for twenty years. Ten anyway.

"It looks poor," I said, "but not destitute, not hungry."

"There's plenty of destitution and hunger. But out here they're still in touch with rural life." She drove carefully, with the traffic, only swerving to avoid the worst potholes and carefully checking out the rear-view mirrors when she did. Her speech was punctuated by the more noteworthy hazards. "Food at least is cheap. But if you want real work you have to go into Nairobi and take your chance. But it is still a network society. Get in with a strong group, extended family, clan, tribe, church, whatever, and it'll be self-supporting, self-sufficient, look after its own. But fall into a crack, and that's what is happening more and more with this lousy government, and you end up dead under a tree with a bottle of crystal meth clutched in your hand." The areas under cultivation became more and more extended. A lot of it industrial in scale, like I'd seen on the coast, monoculture across the rolling hills, the AFI logo.

"That's another problem. The big food giants use intensive farming, chemical intensive, land intensive, machine intensive, but labour cut to the bare bone. Cash-crops for processing and export. Even cut-flowers for Christ's sake. Smaller farms bought up, or their tenancy taken away, tribal land expropriated, it's all mega-bucks for the few and starvation on the city edges for the many. Starvation, crime, social breakdown."

"Britain in the eighteen hundreds."

"Not to mention Ireland. But we at least had emigration. Canada, Australia, New Zealand, the US, even God forgive us, Africa. We repopulated whole continents with our masses, used genocide when the natives wouldn't move over, but now, of course, you pull up the draw-bridge."

I couldn't persuade myself that it was all as bad as all that. Presently the landscape broke up into steep valleys between volcanic cones, long since extinct, covered in greenery. It was threaded with rivers crossed by high bridges and, in the valleys and on the hillsides, mostly grown in what were clearly prosperous small or medium-sized hold-ings, coffee, kumquats, maize, avocado, peppers, with tomatoes and potatoes stacked by the road-side for collection, huge and red. And bananas. Is it possible to starve in a climate where bananas grow?

Presently, having overtaken a large pick-up truck filled with passengers clutching the ends of cloaks and improvised turbans over their mouths against the dust, and seeing the road clear in front of us for several hundred yards, she half-turned to me with a smile lifting the corner of her mouth.

"You must have an interesting life in your line of business."

"Not really. Adulteries, missing persons, add up to getting on for half."

"Credit-rating?"

"Not unless I'm hard-up."

"Why not?"

"Boring and intrusive. Often illegal. And if a guy is getting a loan he's not good for, then good luck to him, say I. I've been there too often myself."

"No murders then."

"Only the one."

Something in my voice must have reflected the sudden cold stab that always affected me when I remembered...

That sidelong glance again.

"And you'd rather not talk about it."

"It was in another country and the wench is dead."

I shuddered minutely, seeing again the curtain of flame that folded itself round her.

Danny glanced at me and drove on. And the thought crossed my mind – how did she know what my line of business was? Had I told her at the Carnivore, or before that by the swimming pool? Must have. But I couldn't remember that I had.

"And you're married?" Of course she'd noted the wedding ring I wore on my ring finger.

"No. Divorced. I wear the ring because my daughter, who expects me to patch things up with her mother, gets upset if I take it off."

"How old is she?"

God help me, I have to give that five seconds thought.

"Twelve. She has a brother a couple of years older."

"Why did you break up? Infidelity?"

"Hers not mine. But infidelity, like alcoholism, is an effect, not a cause."

"I wouldn't know. I've never married."

She said this with a hint of smugness.

"You're asking a lot of questions," I added.

"Only one sort of person more curious than a PI... an investigative journalist."

"I'm not curious. Just inquisitive."

She shifted a little in her seat, changed down as we neared the crest of a hill. As we crossed the crest the plain to our left spread to hills on a distant horizon. The landscape on that side was dusty with only occasional stunted acacias, flat-topped, cropped, etiolated. A dust-devil rose like a white ghost out of the pale ochre soil, swayed like a drunk, and collapsed.

"That looks like Africa," I said.

Her mouth hardened into a line, then the tip of her tongue caressed her top lip, putting me in mind of a cat.

"I wonder if you know what you're saying."

I waited. Her knuckles whitened again but not out of driver's stress.

"Fifteen years ago it was savannah. Still subject to drought but with the means of recovering from long periods, years even, without rain. The soil was kept compacted at the right levels by the cattle of the nomadic herdsmen and fertilised by their droppings. There were wild herds too of zebra, giraffe, antelopes. It didn't belong to anyone. The nomads, Samburu or related tribes, had their own system of sharing out the grazing and browsing, and they knew how to keep it in sustainable bounds. Then government agencies moved in. Gave land title to the elders and then made them offers they couldn't refuse or found other ways of getting the nomads off the land. Next step was Canadian advisers who prairie-farmed it with wheat. But the soil is shallow, they found no way of making a reliable irrigation system. They created an uninhabitable dust-bowl within a decade. Yes. That's Africa. You're right."

Food for thought. I let it digest for twenty minutes then cleared my throat.

"You never married, then."

"Partners, yes. Husbands, no."

"One on the go at the moment?"

"Curious or just inquisitive?"

I shrugged.

"Or are you…" she grinned, "testing the water?"

"More a matter of putting my foot on the first rung of a ladder and seeing if it holds."

"It's a long way up."

"I thought it might be."

"Men!" And the smile turned to a grimace.

After an hour or so we left Nyeri down on the edge of the plain while in front and over to the right the ground rose and broke up into forested foothills, climbing to a grand massif lost in the long grey cloud spread over it like a table-cloth: Mt Kenya itself. Lying between the road and the first substantial hills there were patches of wilderness, uncultivated land, forest and grassland, watered by the run off from the big mountain.

Presently we pulled off the roadside and dropped on to a sandy parking lot filled with safari minibuses and a couple of bigger coaches. Almost instantly we were surrounded by urchins, smiling, earnest, insistent, but not, one felt, desperate, appealing for small coins and pens. Behind them were sheds filled with stacks and stacks of tourist stuff, a couple of stalls selling refreshments, two or three rather more permanent buildings advertising themselves as hotels.

"Toilet stop?" I asked.

"If you need it. But no. There's another reason."

She glanced up and indicated with a nod a metal painted sign set on a pole in the sandy verge between the parking lot and the road we had left. It was rusty and flaking, but the design was clear enough. Yellow background with what at first I took to be a black head in silhouette but then realised was an outline of the continent, bisected below the ear, above the jaw, with a broad red line and on the line, painted in white, the one word: 'Equator'. There was a crowd round it, nearly all white. I got out and joined them. She'd seen it all before, lit a Sportsman and waited for me.

The centre of attraction was a young man with a red bucket lidded with a white bowl filled with water which trickled into the bucket through a hole in the bottom. Two matchsticks floated listlessly, without movement. He picked it all up, moved twenty metres north and the matches began to turn clockwise. He moved twenty metres south and they turned anti-clockwise. I looked at my watch. Just gone twelve midday. I looked up at the sun, shining through broken, moving cloud. It was dead over-head, near as I could tell. And it burned, my face and the retina at the back of my eye which ached for an hour afterwards. A line at the bottom of the sign read 'Altitude: 6389 Ft.'. The man with the bucket wanted three hundred shillings for a signed certificate saying I'd crossed the Line. Since I was crossing back, having entered the southern hemisphere on the plane out, I refused the certificate, gave him a fifty. He wasn't pleased.

"Why not?" I asked, when I was back in the Polo.

"He was selling, not begging," Danny said, drily. "If you've got a spare Bic or cheap ball-point give it to one of the kids. The school will buy it from him for five shillings. They're desperate, the schools. They get very little government money, and parents have to pay fees. But it's not enough, it never is. Pens, paper, every little helps."

"And the coins? The kids keep asking for pennies, English pennies."

She laughed. "It's a little scam they run. They know you'll part with English coppers, small change, it's just in the way while you're here. Then they take them to the next punter and say a tourist paid them in pennies by mistake, will you give me shillings for them they're no use to me. And of course she, or he does! Again, it's a step up from begging which is forbidden, and anyway they don't like to beg."

She chucked her cigarette, and started the engine. "I know a good place for lunch."

She drove to the next village, on the outskirts of Nanyuki. There were more people on the road now – always you can see people walking in Kenya, apparently for considerable distances, but more nearer the towns. At one point a bend at the bottom of a slope led us into a cutting. Danny applied the brakes, we slewed about in the dust and hit a pot-hole that reminded me I'd taken a nasty fall on my coccyx only twenty-four hours earlier. There was a lorry on its side blocking one half of the road and behind it a large dead cow. The accident was barely five minutes old. You could tell because you could see it had been a live cow very recently: men with machetes were already hacking it up and one, bigger than the rest, was walking away with a huge haunch on his shoulder.

Danny drove on into the village, took a right. Shanty town beneath trees, eucalyptus and palm, dusty mauve bougainvillea, then farm buildings. The tarmac gave out, but the road was metalled and well-kept. We climbed slowly, not really hair-pinning, into thicker deciduous forest, passed a fork with a track off to the left which we ignored. There was a sign but I didn't take it in. A buzzard had my attention, soaring above the trees. White from below with black wing tips but more striking than that, a bright russet wedge of a tail. Augur, it's called.

Another mile brought us to a gated entrance made out of dark timber with a vaguely oriental looking lintel. A khaki-ed but private guard responded to Danny's Swahili and let us through. I couldn't decide whether he recognised or expected her or not. A few more turns took us into a carpark beneath pines, with needles on the hard earth floor. Four safari mini-buses were there before us, and a medium sized 4x4 SUV, not a Land Rover but the sort that has a stencilled rhino on the spare wheel cover. Beyond, on the far side of a low fence with a wicket gate was a raised wooden bar, dining area and kitchens, surrounded in the open air by longer tables with benches at which the safari tourists were waiting for their lunch. Already they were feeding their bread ration to the black and white, long-haired colobus monkeys who knew the routine and posed for their cameras. We parked, Danny opened her door and twisted so her feet were out on the ground and changed her shoes. She changed the lightweight black slip-ons for a pair of Wrangler trainers with raised ankle protection and sturdy soles, practically walking boots. Then she went round to the boot and got out the photography bag. I supposed, because she didn't like leaving it behind.

As we approached the building two men stood from a table under the roof and came to the top of the steps to welcome Danny. Us, actually. I knew them. One short and stocky, the other tall and blonde. Ludwig Holly and his übermensch companion.

"Hullo there, Mr Shovelin. I hope Danny has been looking after you properly."

"He's been looking after me," she said. "You're a genius, Ludwig. He couldn't be better."

He grinned with self-satisfaction and she kissed him on the cheek. Then, while I was still on the step below him, and struggling with what was clearly not a series of coincidences, he gave me his strong hand to grasp.

"Mr Shovelin," he went on in his deep, slightly mesmeric voice, "Kit. I don't think you've met my good friend Leo Vincey. Leo, this is the Kit Shovelin I told you about. The private eye. But not wearing his wonderful hat today."

"It's in the car," I muttered.

Vincey came forward and I shook his offered hand. Firm, manly grip. You know the sort: it says – in a tight spot, you can rely on me. He looked down at me. I'm five ten so not many men can do that. His sunny face clouded with sympathy.

"Whatever happened to your face?" His accent was East Coast American, Ivy League, almost British but more marked than Danny's. The sort that eludes you if you move your upper lip.

"I wish it was only my face."

Tell the truth, after several hours sitting in a Polo driven over some of the worst road-surfaces I had ever experienced, my shin and arse were giving me a bit of gip. "Got mugged. Par for the course, Mr Holly warned me."

"Ludwig, please."

They had formed a little group around me, were ushering me up the couple of steps on to the verandah that circled the bar. Chairs were re-arranged, we sat.

"Drink?" Holly suggested.

"Diet Coke. If not, then a fizzy mineral water with a slice of lemon or lime would be fine."

"Ice?"

"Not if it's already cold."

He stammered away in Swahili at the hovering waiter.

"No Diet Coke, so it will be the mineral water. And Danny, don't bother to correct my Swahili."

"Considering the short time you've been here it's very good."

Danny, opposite me and on the edge of the area, smiled at him, leant back, her face in shade, watched us. Vincey sitting next to me at the round table, angled his body towards me.

"Tell us about this mugging," he asked. "It does rather look as if they did a thorough job on you."

"Nothing to tell, really. But you can tell me just what is going on. I mean, have I been set up or something? How come you all know each other? Have I been kidnapped, or what?" I tried to get an edge into my voice without being threatening or plaintive.

"Hardly," Holly cried. "Does it feel like a kidnap?" He shrugged, spread his hands.

"I'd be hard put to it to get up and go."

Danny chipped in at last, moving her head so a sun-flake or two, filtered past the eaves of the roof, caught her hair. She offered me that easy smile.

"Don't even think of it, Chris. It's all exactly as I said. I've been stood up, the guy who was going to accompany me can't. The only thing I didn't tell you was that yesterday morning, when I told Ludwig there might be a problem about my coming, he told me about the chat he'd had with you on the plane from Mombasa, that you were staying at the Serena and that you were at something of a loose end. I checked you out, liked what I saw."

The drink came. Nothing for them, just my mineral water which originated, so the label on the bottle read, on the slopes of Kilimanjaro. It was ice cold without ice. So that was all right. I squeezed the circle of lime, wiped my fingers with a tissue from a dispenser on the table. Classy joint. Over at the long tables waiters were serving grilled trout. I began after all to wish I was on safari too. The punters all looked cosy, sure of their situation, nothing bad was going to happen to them, nothing really unexpected even.

I waited. There were a lot of questions in my head, but I sensed, the way you sometimes do in my line of business, that I might get more if I left it to them to decide what to tell me. I was wrong.

Holly put his hairy hands on the table, pushed his chair back, looked at the others.

"Shall we?" he said.

They nodded, stood up, made we-are-about-to-go sort of movements. Danny looked down at me.

"We're going, um, for a walk. Actually," hurrying on to forestall the move I was about to make to join them, "it would be better for you if you stayed here. I mean... you know, you're still rather stiff and you even limp a little and the going is a touch rough in places. They do good lunches. We won't be more than an hour." She looked enquiringly at the others.

"Make that two. Not more than two hours," answered Holly, and he followed Vincey up the steps. I got the impression that Vincey knew better than the other two where they were going. I was building a mild dislike for him. Too confident, a touch over-assertive. Body language as much as what he actually said. Danny followed, then hesitated, turned, fumbling in her purse.

"Here's the car key," she said, talking quickly now, almost whispering, "in case you want anything from your bags. Um, if we're not back by... five, drive back to the Serena, leave the car with them, and get the next flight back to London."

Well that was reassuring. Reassuring as hell.

They made their way up a track, up into the mountain. A monkey chattered at them, a big bird clapped its wings in the canopy above and a leaf swung and circled, catching the sun, before it cruised to a perfect landing behind them. Then they were gone and I was looking at the one single key. VW and a tag with the name and telephone number of the hire-firm.

Chapter Six

I felt confused, left out of it, excluded. I tried to feel angry but I have a long fuse, and anyway the surroundings were attractive. The waiter brought a menu. I ordered trout, farmed not river trout, but from their own ponds it said, and very good it was, salad, ice-cream. I made the mineral water last, and had a coffee to finish up. Then another one. The coffee came with hard white mints. I told you, it was a class joint. The safari people wandered around, apparently looked at the trout pools and the gardens, then piled into their Toyota mini-buses and drove back off down the hill. The Polo and the off-the-road vehicle were now the only two vehicles left in the park. I felt bereft. I went to the Polo, and fished Anecdotes of Destiny out of Danny's bag. It was all of thirty years, no, damnit, more than that, since I'd read it. It got quieter and quieter, just the noises of washing up and so forth a little way off. The barman stayed standing behind his counter, as impassive as a rock, staring straight out in front of him, not moving. A monkey checked me out, found me wanting, moved on. There weren't even any insects to bother me. I glanced at my watch. Five past two. They'd been gone an hour. I promised myself I would not look at it for an hour. Two twenty-three. Shit.

And then the distant rumble and hum of a motor coming up the hill from the main road. Another jeep, but this time painted khaki and with a badge stencilled on the door. The driver parked it next to the Polo and stayed on board while his companion got down on the other side. He was tall, thin, in a khaki suit you could have taken for a safari suit but for the badge stitched on to his left breast pocket and brass buttons. On the tight black, very short curls of his head a khaki baseball cap with the same badge. It added up to a uniform. The short bamboo swagger-stick he had tucked under his arm and held in place by a hand sheathed in white kid leather completed the impression. He took a slow walk, then came up the steps on to the verandah, ignored me, went straight to the bar and sat on a stool. The barman opened a bottle of Tusker, poured from it into a glass and left both at his elbow without saying a word. The visitor drank, batted a fly away from his forehead, peeled off his gloves and drummed his long fingers on the counter. He said something to the barman, presumably in Swahili: it sounded like a question. The barman shrugged, muttered what I took to be a non-committal reply and resumed his fixed, unwavering examination of the lower branches of a forest giant on the edge of the clearing.

Presently the new arrival emptied his bottle into his glass, came off his stool and strolled over to me, carrying the glass with him. He put the glass on the table, took the chair Holly had sat in, twisted it, smiled down at me, gold in the yellow teeth, a thin shiny moustache above them, and sat down. He arranged swagger stick and gloves neatly alongside the glass.

"English?" he asked.

"English," I agreed.

"Safari?"

"Not exactly."

He picked up his stick, tapped it on the leg of his chair, leant back, the smile came again.

"Just touring?"

"Sort of."

"On your own?"

"With a friend."

Thin eyebrows raised, he looked around. I began to feel irritated. And very slightly disturbed. Clearly I was being interrogated.

"She's gone for a walk. In the forest," I grudgingly offered.

"And you stayed here."

"I was mugged yesterday. In Nairobi. Beaten up. I still find it difficult to walk."

"She should not be alone in the forest. On the mountain. A white woman... on her own."

I felt a touch miffed. No comment about my mugging. Were such incidents that common? Didn't merit any curiosity at all? And anyhow, how did he know she was white?

"Actually, she's not on her own. We met two other... friends? Here. They are with her."

"They have the Polo. And you the four by four?"

"The other way round."

He nodded as if I had said something seriously wise, drank his beer, stood up, looked down at me.

"Passport."

I reached for the inside pocket of my jacket, then with my finger and thumb on the top corner of it, my hand froze.

Who is this guy? I thought.

"You have the authority to ask?"

"Oh yes, mister. I have the authority."

And his index finger prodded the badge on his pocket.

Now, I'm long-sighted and I had put on my reading glasses. I took them off and the badge came into proper focus. Machine-stitched to suggest embroidery it was a shield with scroll work across the top and bottom. The scroll work carried the message: Security Warden. The shield was blue with A F I in gold, except the 'I' was a corncob, gold and green. Associated Foods International.

I could have argued, this guy was not a government officer, but why look for hassle? I handed up the passport, he riffled through it. Was it my imagination, my innate paranoia that suggested the back page, with its very basic information about me, gave him the satisfaction of finding what he expected? He handed it back.

"Have a good trip, Mr Shovelin," and he tapped the side of the peak of his hat with the swagger stick before sauntering back to his four by four. The driver started up the diesel and with a puff of black smoke and a little cloud of dust, drove back down the hill, the way they had come. One bend and the trees closed round it.

His beer remained half-finished.

Twenty minutes later and I heard them: feet scuttering on loose stones, and whistling – the *Magic Flute*, Papageno's opening aria: *Der Vogelfänger bin ich ja, stets lustig, heisa hopsasa*! I'm the bird-catcher, always merry, always gay! And round the corner they came, Holly in front, then Danny, and Vincey last. It was Vincey who was whistling. Cocky bastard. He was carrying Danny's photographer's bag for her, but gave it back to her as they came up the steps and collapsed with ostentatious weariness around me.

"Whoof! That was quite a climb, quite a walk," Holly expostulated. "I could do with a beer."

"Tea for me," cried Danny.

"You're right. Tea's the thing. Much better idea," and he bent over his knees to loosen the laces on his designer desert boots.

"I'll stay with beer," said Vincey.

"Mineral water again?" Holly asked, looking back over his shoulder at me as the waiter hovered.

I went for the tea.

They were red-faced, sweaty, still even a touch breathless. But there were oddities too, like green grass or leaf stains on Danny's waistcoat. If she'd fallen it must have been quite a tumble. And Holly had a small scratch on his cheek, a line breaking up into dots, as if he'd tangled with a bramble or thorn.

Clearly they had gone off the track, which, at least at its start was a good six feet wide with a surface of impacted stones.

"Did you have a good walk?" I asked, somewhat innanely.

"Wonderful, wonderful!" Vincey cried, and it dawned on me that they were all a touch high. Clearly not on drugs, but excitement, adrenalin even. "We saw many strange things, wonderful things."

"Such as?"

"Um… monkeys? Sunbirds. A tree filled with weaver birds and their nests. That sort of thing, you know?"

"You'll make Kit jealous," Danny remarked. "He's into birds."

She turned to me, but glanced at my visitor's beer.

"You told me you didn't drink."

"I had company…"

But before I could explain, or she question me about it, Vincey had taken over again.

"You didn't hear anything while we away?"

I wondered what he meant. Holly filled in.

"There were some shots. Not far from us but when we were about as far from here as we got. Illegal hunters, I suspect. Poachers. It's not just ivory they come for, but the colobus monkeys' tails, exotic plumage, animal skins, that sort of thing."

"I doubt if I'd have heard anything at that distance," I said. "Or they may have coincided with the noise of my visitor's four-by-four."

"The visitor who ordered a beer. But didn't stay to finish it?" Danny, but all three looked a touch concerned, indeed glanced at each other, suddenly serious.

"Some sort of warden. He had a badge. AFI Security Warden, it said. He left about half an hour ago."

"How long was he here? Did he speak to you?" The questions came, nonchalant in a studied way, it seemed to me, and I told them what had happened, exactly as I have set it down. All the time they tried to keep it casual, but there was no hiding their concern.

"But you didn't give him names, our names?" This from Holly.

"No."

Vincey looked across the table at him.

"Car registration numbers? He could have got our vehicle numbers."

"If he had the sense to take them."

"He didn't write anything down that I saw," I chipped in.

The tea came and Vincey's beer, and the waiter cleared away the Security Warden's glass. With it gone they dropped it, contrived an impression that it was a matter of only very minor interest, went on to talk of other things. Then they looked at watches, settled up with the waiter, and we moved back to our respective vehicles. The two men kissed Danny, warmly, but like good friends, not lovers or anything like that. Holly climbed into the driver's seat of the jeep, Vincey stood at the passenger door and waved a final salute while Danny stowed her photographic kit back in the boot of the Polo.

"Hopefully we'll see you in the Aberdares, day after tomorrow."

The Aberdares? Hadn't she said she had friends who lived in the area?

We followed them. Half-way to the main road we passed the junction again and I looked back at the sign. The AFI logo. AFI Research and Development Station. Entrance restricted at half a mile.

"I suppose that's where he came from," I said, nodding back as it receded in the rear-view wing mirror.

"Your visitor? I guess."

Chapter Seven

The four by four went left, south, back towards Nairobi. We turned right on to the main road and drove on with the huge mountain, which looked more like a range than a mountain, on our right, slowly receding behind us. And not all that high, but then the plain we were on was already halfway up it. From a distance we could see the higher slopes and cliffs, a dun green with outcrops of rock emerging above the forested foothills, though the summits were still hidden beneath that spread of grey cloud towards which the sun was beginning its descent. A large town, Nanyuki, was bypassed on our left and we took the sun with us, left the mountain behind. To begin with, the road was for the most part reasonably surfaced and for longish stretches dead straight, slicing through a flattish landscape, in better nick than the dust-bowl we had passed through earlier, lightly covered with the thorny acacias and yellowish grass that figure in the safari adverts and the sort of films you see on TV in the early evening on a Sunday. I'm remembering the days, some time ago now, when for me family viewing on a Sunday was a routine.

But there were stretches too where the road was being widened or rebuilt behind barriers which had been erected out of empty oil drums and planks, and we were forced to cruise along the verge trailing huge clouds of dust or battling through the fog created by a battered bus or lorry in front of us. Whatever else the lorries carried, they were almost always topped out with passengers reclining on plastic covered bales or leaning over the tail-gate, rocking from side to side and waving cheerily at us.

There were villages too, set back off the road in ribbons, always with the same features: three or four rival churches, a Coca-Cola kiosk, shacks that called themselves hotels and doubled as brothels, truck drivers for the use of, since the road we were on was, Danny told me, part of the Trans East African highway, a tributary of the Trans African artery for the distribution of commerce and HIV. And everywhere there were the usual hoardings for Sportsman, Tusker and Trust. The larger villages had blue and white liveried branches of Barclays Bank which struck me as both comfortingly familiar and blatantly neo-colonial, though I suppose to the inhabitants they were just banks. There were checkpoints too: large heavy planks placed across the road with sharpened spikes of freshly hewn wood pushed through them, angled towards the on-coming traffic, primitive but efficient. Small groups of armed police stood at the roadside, smoking, chatting up kids or girls from the village. They waved us through after we had slowed to get round the spikes.

"Who are they hoping to catch?"

"Cattle rustlers, maybe. Moving their booty in

lorries. Did you notice the shoulder flashes 'Stock Theft Police' on that last lot? But also refugees or insurgents from the civil war in Sudan to the north, or raiders from Somalia to the west."

We were, she said, heading for the Samburu National Reserve where we would stay, at her expense, in the Samburu Lodge, so she could continue her investigation into the collapse or otherwise of the tourist industry.

"Oh yes?" I asked, and I meant it to sting.

She glanced across the small space between us, pale green eyes suddenly wary, and her hands tightened momentarily on the steering-wheel.

"Something bugging you?" she asked.

"Oh come on."

"I don't know what you're getting at."

"Holly chatting me up at Mombasa airport and on the plane. You latching on to me at the Serena. Then we all meet up back at the trout restaurant. Something's going on, right? And it's not to do with tourism."

"How do you know that? How can you say that? It's all exactly as we said. The guy who was coming with me couldn't make it. I said I wouldn't come on my own. Holly, who's a good friend, left a message for me at the Serena, telling me about you..."

"Bullshit."

She drove on in silence for five minutes or so.

"OK," she said, at last. "When we get to the lodge there'll be a safari group there. There will be vacancies, they really are in trouble at the moment, and

they'll be glad to take you on, fill a space. Cost you a
ton a day for five days and worth every penny. I'll
manage on my own."

But I wasn't ready to be dumped. I smelt adventure, profit, and let's be honest about this, um,
romance. Fairly honest. I suppose what I mean is
sex.

"That's not what I meant."

"What do you mean?"

"You know what I mean."

Silence for another two minutes.

"I'm not sure I do."

"Look. All I want is to know what this is really
about. Once I do, the chances are I'll want to remain
part of it. But not without knowing what you three
are up to and how you think I can be useful to you.
Really know. And no bull-shitting."

More silence, except that for a mile the road was
corrugated, no doubt as part of the preliminaries to
putting a proper surface on it, and it was like riding
on the back of a machine gun. Her knuckles
whitened again on the juddering steering wheel. We
couldn't have talked even if we had wanted to. And
then there was a barrier at the end of the stretch and
we had to swing left down on to what had clearly
been the old road. The ramp was steep and we had
to slow down which gave a cloud of urchins a
chance to settle round us and bring us to a halt. We
could have cruised through them but Danny wasn't
like that. She bought a water melon for fifty shillings,
fifty p, and they were very pleased indeed. Three

women, two young and startlingly beautiful, sat by the roadside dressed in red robes with collars made up of hundreds of strands of beads round their necks. They had baskets with the melons and other produce. They gave us smiles of pure pleasure, welcome, and waved pale palms at us as we picked up speed again.

"Samburu," Danny said. "Like the Maasai but not quite so way out in their lifestyle."

We passed a small herd of humped, dew-lapped cattle watched over by a youth in a red cloak, holding a spear, with one foot raised so the sole rested against the haft. His hair, reddened and plaited in thin strands reached half way down his back. I felt a surge of euphoria: this was Africa, real Africa. The feeling went through the roof when I saw the neck and head of a giraffe cropping the shoots off the top of an acacia. Then the nagging worries came back.

"You know what really worried me?"

"I can't guess."

"When you went into that spiel about how I should drive back to Nairobi if you didn't get back in two hours. Not send for the police or the rangers or whatever, just get out."

"Yeah. That was silly of me. Didn't mean to frighten you."

"You must have had a reason."

She shrugged, pouted, said nothing.

"OK. How about this?" I suggested. "You thought something bad might happen to you on your walk and you suspected that if it did, it could happen to me too if I hung around. So you weren't thinking of getting lost, or falling over a precipice." I thought about it a bit more. "Those shots Vincey spoke of. They were aimed at you?"

She replied with a sudden vehemence that took me quite by surprise.

"You have a lively imagination and you ask too many questions."

That provoked a sort of febrile irritation with her which also surprised me. Thinking about it I realised I already cared, after twenty-four hours, no more than that really, what she thought about me, about us.

Towards evening, we came to an arched gateway, neatly if plainly stuccoed, with a block house and out-buildings. Samburu National Park. Uniforms came out, took a small fee, checked a reservation Danny had, waved us through. Sign-posts to a couple of lodges and camp-sites. The vegetation was thicker now, the grass taller and greener, shrubs and low trees followed narrow water-courses, steep hummocky hills closed round us. There were a lot more animals. Giraffe and zebra, apparently of different types, and antelope, big ones like oryx, pretty ones like Thompson's gazelles, tiny ones like dik-dik. Lot of oryx. Danny suddenly said: "Alas, more oryx, I know them well," which had me giggling for a minute or so and softened the rather prickly atmosphere that had grown up between us. She pulled up at one point and let me have a good look at one solitary elephant, big with big unevenly curving tusks.

"Maverick," she said. "Trouble-maker. Been known to have a go."

"Have a go?"

"Charge vehicles."

She moved us on before Jumbo got any ideas.

"You've been here before?"

"Twice. In the course of business. But it's a good spot. Lots of game. Look. Secretary Bird."

"Crumbs!"

White head and chest, black wings and belly and thighs, which looked as if they had been squeezed into Lycra cycling shorts, orange predatory beak, stalking and nodding through the grass on long yellow legs. Crest behind its head, red round its eye.

"Hunts snakes."

I wished I had my own photographic stuff, the gear I take when I go birding or looking for evidence of adultery or whatever.

The lodge was great. We were taken to our rooms and we arranged to meet in an hour at the bar.

"Give me time to shower and change," she said.

Fine, I thought, but wondered if I could come out grand enough for such a well-heeled looking place. Well, I'd got by at the Carnivore, the night before, so I supposed I'd be OK.

Beneath its roof the bar was open to the wild, overlooking a river with crocs, and we had a drink or two there before dinner. She was right: the place was less than half-full which was fine for the guests who had made it, some of whom had been at the

Nairobi Serena the night before, but was bad news for Kenya. She drank a couple of long vodkas with natural lemon juice, mineral water, crushed ice, sprig of fresh mint. I had the same but without the vodka.

"Don't you ever drink?"

"Nope."

"Why not? Did you ever, or have you always been TT?"

She looked across the low table, leaned forward and I could see the shadows between small breasts and the top hem of a scant bra beneath the peacock blue plain top she was wearing above a black silk skirt. She prodded a slice of lemon with a plastic cocktail stick, so the lemon bobbed beneath the ice then, borne up by bubbles, struggled back through.

I get asked this. If I don't like the person I'm with or feel I don't know them well enough, I keep as much to myself as I can and get off the subject. But Danny had a way with inhibitions... mine anyway.

"In forty years I did a life-time of boozing. One morning I woke up, felt poorly, sat on the loo, then had to grab the wash-basin. I brought up four pints of blood. Later the same day I passed almost as much again, the difference being that coming from the other end it looked like used coffee grounds. By then I was in hospital and on the critical list. Oesophageal varices burst because of pressure from a swollen liver."

"Why did you drink so much?"

"Don't know really. Family trait I think. I hardly

ever got falling down drunk, I was almost never completely sober. Dad was the same. But he fell off his moped and got run over."

She nodded, as if I'd said all that needed to be said on the subject. Perhaps I had. Across the slow river a nightjar chattered and then something else went 'oo-hooo, oo-hooo!' a bit like a pigeon.

"Owl?"

Head on one side she listened.

"Eagle owl," she said.

"Really?"

"Really! Look."

And a large, pale, buttery shape cruised low in lazy flight over the tree-tops on the far side, tilted huge wings in a smooth scimitar silhouette, and was gone.

"This really is rather good," I said.

"Glad you came, then."

"Oh yes. But I'd still like to know why."

"What's puzzling you? Why don't you accept what I've told you? What else do you want to know?"

She spoke quietly, no irritation in her voice. I felt there was a gap showing that I might get through, if I went about it carefully.

"Well, let's start with Holly and Vincey. What do they do?"

"Ludwig is a biologist, to be specific a micro-botanist, of some reputation. He is on a year's sabbatical from MIT, setting up a genetic modification department within the botany department at Jomo

Kenyatta University. Leo is… I'm not sure what he is. He turned up a few weeks ago, moved in with Ludwig. I guess they'd known each other before. Maybe they were old buddies."

"Are they an item? Is it a relationship?"

She pulled back, a line creasing the space between her discreetly pencilled eyebrows.

"You mean like gay? I don't think so. Maybe. I guess Leo's a sort of playboy, single, perpetually on tour, never stays in one place for long. I'd say he was loaded, wouldn't you?"

"And how did you get to know them, know of them?"

She shrugged.

"One meets people. It's part of my job. Shall we eat?"

And that was as far as I got, after all. Virtually nowhere.

No difficulty in finding a table clear of the other guests. The big dining room was built like a tribal hall, at least I suppose that was what it was meant to suggest. Wide wooden roof supported on beams and by two rows of pillars, tables dotted beneath. Two semi-wild spotted genets, a bit like silver spotted tabbies, haunted the eaves and took food left in their reach while a big white moth, or was it a bat?, big as your hand, fluttered like a wind-blown paper bag along one end.

We had a reasonable meal, then watched a leopard mauling a goat leg left out for it on the other side of the river in a pool of dim light. We were once more sitting in cane chairs on the terrace and when what passed for the action was over she reached out, put a warm palm on the back of my hand.

"I'm going to make a phone call from your room, if you don't mind."

Well, I was puzzled, naturally, but assumed that maybe she had already established there was a fault with the phone in her own room. I pulled my key from my pocket and handed it to her.

"Carry on," I said.

"It's OK. You can come with me."

The rooms were in two-storeyed blocks along the river front behind a screen of immature eucalyptus. I had one on the ground floor with a small verandah, she was in the one above me. She took my hand as we strolled along the river bank. Dry, warm, oddly familiar. I fumbled with the key.

"I'll be down in a mo," and she went round the back to climb the outside stairs to her own room.

Well, you know what men are like. Was this a come-on? Quick dash to make whatever preparations or precautions she normally took? Stab of doubt in my case: marriage went bust five years ago, Bournemouth clients not in the same league as Philip Marlowe's, no real social life at all, apart from weekends with the kids, all in all I felt it was quite likely I could turn out to be something of a disappointment. A fling I'd had, a one-off, actually in Marlowe territory in LA a year before, the murder case I'd mentioned, actually, had been... exciting, but, I had to admit I had not performed that brilliantly. And, right there in Samburu Lodge, with an attractive, worldly but basically decent woman possibly about to offer sex, important bits of my mugged body were still aching, indeed quite painful, and I was fucking tired which at my age means you sleep if you possibly can.

"Right then," and here she was again with her lap-top and photography bag. She pushed back the mosquito nets the management had thoughtfully provided, put her gear on one of the beds, unzipped zips.

Her computer was a Toshiba, the Tecra 9100 series, and the camera she took from the bag was a Fuji FinePix 4900. There was a more conventional though new Canon SLR with it, but she left that where it was. The phone was on a small bedside table, between the beds, the socket in the wall behind the table and shielded by it. It wasn't difficult to shift the table and unplug the phone. Working briskly, clearly knowing exactly what she was about, she connected the computer to the socket with a six-way modem lead. She then opened it, switched it on and waited a moment or two while it booted up.

I picked the FinePix up off the bed and hefted it in my hand. It was almost familiar. Fact is I'd been thinking of getting one, or one of its close rivals, for several weeks and had been hanging about Dixons and Jessops, getting the sales staff to let me handle the things, but the four hundred quid or so that I'd have had to shell out held me back. Nevertheless, your aspiring PI needs to keep up with the technology and my old Pentax SLR with zoom lenses a foot-long was a bit of a giveaway.

"Please?" She held out a hand.

"Nice bit of kit," I said. "Point and shoot on default, but fully manual too if you want it to be."

"Yeah, it's OK. Not really pro, but very good amateur." She used a USB lead to connect the camera to the computer.

Her fingers flickered over the keyboard. An image came up on the screen of a steep hillside covered with a crop of low green shrubs.

"Do you mind?"

I was leaning over her shoulder.

"Oh, come on!" I really was getting cheesed off with this unvarying closing down whenever I might be getting near to what was really happening. Nevertheless I moved back to the verandah door, and peered through the glass at the lamplight playing on the eucalyptus leaves, with a gleam coming off the rippling water of the river beyond. Passing croc?

"Better for you not to see any of it."

"Why not?"

"I'll tell you why not." Her voice hardened. What she was about to say was for real – that was the message I was getting. "You won't see enough to understand what is going on, but you will see enough to convince anyone you talk to about it that you know more than you are letting on. That way they'll have an excuse to beat the shit out of you to get out of you what you can't tell them. And they won't readily give up."

Well, that shut me up. One beating per trip is all I'm prepared to take without heading for the nearest international airport, and I kept my eyes very firmly away from the screen. Though it crossed my mind after a bit that if I did know what it was all about and what was on the pictures, then whoever was beating the shit out of me might stop to listen.

"High resolution, eight pictures, it'll take about fifteen minutes," she said.

"As long as that?"

"There's no land-line out here. It's all going by radio."

You can do a lot of thinking in fifteen minutes.

Why come all the way to Samburu and use a radio link when there must have been landlines available at any of the larger villages or small towns, each with its Barclays Bank, we had passed in the hour or so after leaving the restaurant? And the answer that occurred to me was that though the radio link was unreliable it had one big advantage. It was less likely to be scanned and monitored than a landline. To do so would certainly require a higher level of technology. I followed the train of thought. If it was scanned and traced it would be traced to my room not hers…

"Hey," I said, still not turning back, "this is going through my phone not yours."

"Which means that it's that bit less likely that anyone is bothering with it."

Of course. She was booked in in advance. Which room she was in, and therefore which phone she'd be using would be known, assuming she was under that sort of surveillance. Surveillance? High level surveillance? This was fantasy land. Could she really be involved in something so big it had people sweeping the phone lines and airways for the sound of her voice or a digitalised picture she had taken?

Was she serious? Was any of this serious? You know how it is when you're in a strange place at night, and the lights are too bright in some areas and too dim in others, add to that a more or less complete stranger saying unthinkable things full of hidden menace, plus pretty near extreme tiredness… you want to say: it's all a dream and I'll wake up in my own bed. In short I felt the whole situation was characterised by a marked reality deficit. I tried to get a grip.

"There was an AFI research station near that restaurant. Their security guard came and checked me out. Ludwig, you say, is a botanist. Nice word. Suggests a Victorian amateur bumbling about an exotic landscape, picking flowers and giving fancy names to the ones no one has named before. But that's not what botanists do any more, is it?"

I pushed my silly head on to the next step.

"Agricultural research station. That used to mean raising new hybrids of crop plants by selective breeding, testing them for the qualities you wanted to breed into them, higher yields, resistance to pests, that sort of thing. Long process. Not any more. Now it's genetic engineering."

She lit a Sportsman, blew smoke. Take off twenty years she'd have looked like Lauren Bacall in To Have and Have Not. No, that's ungallant. Ten years. And I look more like Boris Karloff than Bogie.

"You know," she said, and picked a shred of tobacco off her bottom lip, "you must be quite good as a PI. Go on."

"Genetic modification. AFI's already famous for it. Or infamous. So, Doctor Ludwig Holly of MIT gets to hear they're up to something that's fishy in some way and he gets in touch with an outfit of investigative journalists in South Africa, and invites them to send a team in to look at what he's found. But one of them falls ill, or whatever…"

"Actually, he was run over in a hit and run car accident. He's in intensive care and on a ventilator."

"Oh shit."

"Just so."

I pulled in a deep, unhappy breath, sat on the bed that didn't have her computer on it.

"It's big then," I said as I let it out.

"It's big." She took another drag, walked past me to the window. "Do you remember the guys at the Carnivore? The ministers? The crook banker from the Banco de Corpus Cristi? The vice-president of AFI? That's how big it is."

I remembered them, remembered how they'd started the day in the conference suite at the Serena. Had she known they'd be at the Carnivore? Was that why she needed a companion, so she wouldn't stand out as a single white female? Yes. And yes again.

Five minutes later she closed the system down, unplugging leads, zipping the kit back into its bags.

Her silk skirt rustled as she stood up. She stood by the verandah door, holding lap-top and photography bag. I opened the door for her. It was what I was meant to do.

"Breakfast at eight."

And then she was gone. Not even a goodnight kiss.

Chapter Eight

The night, though, was not over. At about three in the morning I was woken by thuds, crashes even, the sound of tearing vegetation, and cracking wood. I lay in the bed for a few moments considering. Whatever was happening sounded nasty, dangerous. At least, I told myself, you have to have a look – your survival might depend on it.

Without turning on my light I pushed myself out from under the mosquito net, pulled back the net window curtain covering the verandah door and pressed my face against the glass. I was looking at the giant testicles and up the arse of the biggest elephant I had ever seen. Jumbo the Maverick. If he takes a step back I'm done for. But it was OK. With an even bigger rending sound he pulled up a quite large eucalyptus sapling, waved it above his head in triumph, dropped it, trumpeted like a squealing rubber-bulbed horn magnificently amplified, and lumbered off down the path.

At eight o'clock, I sat down at the table we had used for dinner, and looked around. There was only one elderly couple there, all the rest seemed to have had breakfast and gone, waiters were clearing the tables. One of them asked if I wanted coffee or tea, I chose coffee. But he was back almost straight away, not with coffee but two envelopes and a small packet. I gave them a professional once-over. You know what I mean, held them up to the light, weighed them in my palm, sniffed them, the way a PI should. Watson, this one was sealed by someone who had just smoked a black Sobranie, a cigarette favoured more by women than men.

Well, actually, not. I looked at them the way anyone looks at unexpected mail before opening it. One envelope was unstamped and carried my name, Chris Shovelin, nothing else. I'm not too wild about being addressed as Chris, I prefer Kit. The other was directed to J. Skiros, 118 Garlenda Drive, Twickenham, UK, and was stamped with one hundred shillings worth of unfranked stamps and an airmail sticker. As well as a letter I reckoned it also contained a tiny plastic card, the sort that supports a micro-chip – the memory card from her digital camera? Seemed likely. The packet was one of those bags that comes with 35mm transparency film, carrying the Agfa or Fuji logos, whichever, and with a printed address to a processing plant, usually in the country where you bought the film. In this case Brentford, Middlesex. Inside, as well as the cassette of exposed film there would be a completed address slip to be stuck on the packet of processed transparencies. I wondered: could I get it open and find out what that address was? I tried lifting the corner of the stuck down flap with my thumb-nail but it wouldn't budge.

The envelope addressed to me had one sheet of closely written notepaper.

Dear Chris (I read), Forgive me for rushing off like this, but I think it will be better for both of us if I do. There are a couple of things you can do for me though. I've booked you onto the Cheetah Safari. Just as I said, they are glad to take an extra paying customer. Judy, the rep here at Samburu Lodge, will explain the schedule and itinerary, but after you've left here you'll be in the care of Sami, your mini-bus driver. If you get up at eight you will have missed the early morning game drive, but there is a bird walk in the afternoon, and another game drive in the evening. Tomorrow you'll be taken to the Outspan Hotel in the Aberdares for lunch and then up to Treetops for the night. Next day you do a couple of the lakes, another stop-over, and then the Masai Mara for two more nights before they take you back to the Nairobi Serena. I'm sure you will enjoy it all, and it will only cost you fifty thousand Kenyan shillings. You can pay with Visa or Mastercard. After all, it is what you were planning to do before I intruded on you.

What I want you to do for me is very simple. In the foyer of the Outspan Hotel there are two letter boxes, labelled Kenya and Abroad, or something like that. Just pop these into the abroad one. That's all. Don't post them anywhere else, and certainly not here in Samburu Lodge.

It's been great knowing you, and I wish we could have spent some more time together, but there you go. Needs must when the devil drives, and the devil's certainly in this one.

Take care

Danny

My first verbalised thought was: bloody bitch! My first feeling was one of relief, albeit stained with a hint of nostaglia for far off things and tales of might have been. But no, genuine relief. I'd been briefly made part of some deep, deep nastiness with implications and ramifications way out of my league. Exciting? Yes. But at my age? I should co-co. All I had to do now was join the normality of an organised safari trip, post those two packages as instructed, and forget about it all.

Judy was a big girl with bushy semi-straightened hair like black shiny wires, bright big eyes. Her well-rounded figure was contained in a green suit with yellow piping. She occupied a space behind a sectioned off part of the reception desk, as if she were a garrison. And she was of course entirely helpful, went through the itinerary, explained what was inclusive and what wasn't, checked my passport, swiped my Visa card, and briskly, like a croupier handing out selected chips, scooped up three or four handouts and a brochure from the rack behind her.

I went back to my room. The awareness that I had nothing to do until lunch at twelve, in more than three hours time, followed by the bird walk, became a presence that felt like the start of a headache. I sat in the one chair and leafed through the pamphlets Judy had given me. No surprises there. I cleaned my teeth. I pushed the packet and the envelope to the bottom of my hold-all. Then I thought… no, and pulled them out again, pushed them in the forward facing velcroed pocket of the cotton trousers I had dug out. No, not combat trousers, nor safari-type, just holiday trousers. Until I'd posted them the packets would stay with me, I decided… least I can do.

Time ticked on. Then I had a thought, prompted more by boredom than anything else, and I walked round to the side of the block, climbed the outside stairs on to the first-floor walkway, found the room Danny had had. The door was open. Cleaner inside. Well, if she'd left anything at all it was gone now, and anyway there wouldn't have been anything that could have told me anything I didn't know already. Which was zilch.

I put my elbows on the outward facing rail of the walkway and looked out, wished I hadn't given up smoking the very occasional cigarillo. An eagle owl, roosting in the branches of a big spreading tree, I wished I knew what sort of tree, batted an eyelid at me, it was that close. Down to my left there was a quite large enclosure round a swimming pool where a man in a red jacket with a long handled brush was doing the things staff do to swimming pools early in the morning. I wondered: was Danny all right, driving around the wilder parts of Kenya on her own? Something tightened in my chest at the thought. Anxiety? A sort of tenderness? I chucked the virtual cigarillo I wasn't smoking, made my way back to the bar, had another coffee, leafed through the Lonely Planet guide in a desultory sort of way, took a wander round the public rooms, went back outside and eyed a croc. Bet you blink before I do. He won, I took another wander.

I passed the elderly couple sitting at a table. He was doing a very competent water-colour. She was doing crochet, a circular lacy mat sort of thing. I passed the time of day with her. She had a hint of Devon in her voice overlaid with school teacher diction. She told me that when the mat thing was finished she'd soak it in a solution of sugar and, as it dried, shape it into a bowl which would be quite sturdy once it was dry.

"I give them to my friends at Christmas," she said. "They use them for pot-pourri or to serve bon-bons in."

"They don't eat them then?"

"I beg your pardon."

Shit. Overstepped the mark. Shows what a foul mood I was in.

"I just thought… soaked in sugar, you know."

"The sugar is to stiffen them."

"Of course. Silly of me."

Christ. Suppose I was detailed to share their mini-bus? I looked over her husband's shoulder. He was a small man, wearing an old-fashioned cotton sunhat, a linen jacket over a striped shirt, cotton trousers, sensible shoes. He had a portable easel which supported a board angled just slightly towards him, almost flat. His brushes and portable water-colour palette looked serious. He was working some detail into the river, carefully negotiating the spots where he had left the paper almost white to represent sunlight on ripples.

"Golly, you really have caught that, haven't you?" I muttered. "The light, you know? The movement?"

"Just a sketch. If I like it I'll work it up into something bigger when I get home. The information's there, you see. That's the main thing at this stage. Collect the information."

"He sells them," his wife supplied. "Five hundred usually, don't you darling?"

"Five hundred?" Five hundred paintings, I thought, the mind boggling.

"Guineas," he said, his voice as dry as dust.

Ah.

"That's out of my range."

The silence said it all. We expected as much, it seemed to say.

"So you gave the morning game drive a miss?" I hazarded, trying to retrieve something from the wreckage.

"Alfred can't paint on the drives. They never stop for long enough. And the tracks are too bumpy for me to crochet. Really, we only come for the scenery."

Not far away a diesel engine turned over, fired, ticked over, going nowhere. Raised voices from the direction of the reception area. Worth a look, better than staying where I was.

It seemed dark after the bright mid-morning sunlight. The wide, almost circular area was like a cave, a cave with ferns and so forth, palmettos, that sort of thing, one of which I was able to get behind. It seemed the best thing to do.

An argument was going on, in what I supposed was Swahili, between Judy, the tour-rep, and a big man in a black leather bomber and a black baseball cap. Feeling suddenly rather sick, I turned back out on to the verandah, but remained in earshot.

The man smacked the counter and gave a shout. Reprimand? Incredulity? A bit of both. Then he turned sharply and headed out to the main entrance. I let the swing door flap to behind him and then moved after him, reaching it in time to see him crossing the wide semicircle of tarmac in front of a bed of tropical flowers. He hoisted himself into the front passenger seat of a working, non-luxury Land Rover, painted black or dark grey. He slammed the door and I saw the crest and read the lettering: Kenya Police. The uniformed driver let out the clutch, span the wheel and it slewed round in front of me before heading up the slope away from the Lodge. I only got a brief glimpse of him... but enough I reckoned to suppress the thought that it was paranoia talking to me and not the evidence of my senses. I mean, when you've had your face only six inches from his and smelled his breath before he knees you in the balls and smashes your mouth and nose, his becomes a face you tend not to forget.

I turned back into reception. Judy looked battered but still in possession of her space. She smiled at me wanly, shrugged, showed pale palms. Her eyes glowed in the darkness, what light there was reflected from tears that did not fall.

"Not my fault," she said, and her voice trembled.

I smiled, sympathetically, I hoped.

"I gave the station a bell as soon as I knew she was leaving," she went on.

I shifted my smile from sympathy to polite enquiry.

But she pulled herself together, professional defences closing down again.

"It's no matter," she said, "no matter at all," and she pulled a ledger towards her, opened it, picked up a pen. The breach was repaired. She was back in charge but in the interim she had said more than she should have done. 'As soon as I knew she was leaving'. That had to be Danny, didn't it?

Chapter Nine

Ten o'clockish the four minibuses cruised round the flower beds and the toured tourists spilled out. Goodness, they were excited as they streamed into the bar and surrounding public spaces. Chatter, chatter, chatter. The things they had seen! Four immature lions playing in the bush, tiny dik-diks, big impala, African buffalo (the most dangerous animal in Africa!) and best of all a troop of elephants with a baby only six weeks old, and you should have seen the way they all looked after it, especially when they crossed the river and gave it a push to help it up the bank on the other side. And I never realised mummy elephants had their tits between their front legs, did you know that? I was jealous I suppose, I'd have liked to have seen it all. I blamed Danny. Breakfast at eight, to give her time to get clear. If I'd been up at seven I'd have gone with them.

Next on the agenda was the optional bird-walk, my initiation into the tour. It was no more than a short stroll through a copse, along the riverbank, but the guy who took us knew his stuff. Grey-headed kingfisher, pied hornbill, black-capped oriole, a flock of superb starlings which were just that, blue-collared, red breasted, green in the wings, and, best of all, a bateleur eagle, cruising beneath a perfectly

unblemished blue sky, not soaring, just moving
steadily forwards without, apparently, moving its
wings. Looking up at it I suddenly realised how hot
it had become, sensed the heat building over the
savannah, the steady winding down of movement,
activity, both human and animal. The heat also
brought up the not so subtle smells of Africa, the
stable smell of dust, straw and dung, cut with something sharper, menacing, the secretions of predators,
lions, cheetahs, leopards and hyenas. The walk
ended beneath the tree behind the residential building looking at the roosting eagle owls I'd seen hours
earlier, and two pearl-spotted owls I'd missed, tiny
ones, much like the little owl, *Athene noctua*, my
favourite, my private totem.

Then lunch. Again I sat on my own. A Samburu
warrior, a youth of about sixteen, stood at the maître
d's desk, inviting us to come to the enclosure behind
the swimming pool at three o'clock to see a display
of Samburu dancing. He was probably the most
beautiful human being I had ever seen, Adonis in the
flesh. Big eyes, small but perfect nose, mouth like an
angel's, wearing a red plaid robe round his waist like
a skirt, which gave him an oddly epicene look,
exposing a lot of torso and arms that were lean,
smooth, all proportions perfect. His reddened hair
reached halfway down his back and was plaited in
hundreds of thin strands. He had a bead collar, a
bead necklace, bracelets and anklets and he carried a
spear with a willow-leaf metal point. Magnificent.
And what was best about him was that he knew it.

A swim first? Why not. The evening game drive was scheduled for four in the afternoon, it would be getting dark by the time we got back. The pool was very decent, surrounded by dry grass beneath trees, sunbeds, the water, constantly replaced, cool but not cold, a bar and they did have Diet Coke. Being for the most part British, no one appeared to notice the now fading signifiers of the beating I'd had, though this may have been due to the way the very bright sun drained out some of the colour. But it was here that her absence hit me. After all it was by a pool that she had first picked me up, just forty-eight hours before. I felt uncomfortable about it all, irritated, bothered, resentful that I was being used as a postman without really being told a thing about what it was all about. Just her muted confirmation of my reasoned guesswork, that was all. But there was more than that. Clearly there was danger in what Danny, Holly and Vincey were up to, and I surprised myself by feeling, really feeling, not just saying it to myself as a matter of course, that I did not like the idea of her being in danger.

For an evening and a whole day I had been constantly in her company and now I missed her and feared for her. I missed her easy, unassertive good looks, her intelligence, her sensitivity, her humour. I feared the sense I had of her as someone driven, driven by concern, understanding, awareness of the things that are done in Africa that most of us would prefer not to know too much about, that we keep ourselves deliberately ignorant of. I feared it all

because this drivenness was what could bring her
into danger. And, damn it, with kids running around
splashing each other, married couples and unmar-
ried couples enjoying each other's company, in the
warm air and beneath the immaculate sky, I was
lonely. Presently I dried myself off, finished my
Coke, and got dressed.

Probably, I felt, she would not have enjoyed the
dancing, which began at three. It took place in a circular compound with wooden benches roofed with
thatch for the punters, a couple of dessiccated trees
shading trestle tables and covered with beads and
other hand-made-for-tourists stuff, a floor of beaten
earth. Eight or so men and youths, all almost as
handsome as the guy at lunch, who was one of
them, seemed happy enough, opening with voiced
bass and baritone chords beneath an ululating
extended cry and then moving off into a shuffling
dance broken by extraordinary leaps into the air.
But the five women, with massive collars of beads
round their necks which rose and fell and gave out
a sort of gasping rasping noise as they did so, the
beads I mean, looked distanced, bored, withdrawn,
and then the word came, humiliated. Once, how
long ago?, these dances and songs had been parts
of massive liturgies, marking the stages in the year
and in their lives, and had gone on for days and
nights, especially the ones when the tribes came
togther and the elders sorted out the grazing strate-
gies for the months ahead, and the shamans fore-
cast rain or drought. Now a handful did selected

snippets for twenty or so one-eyed whites. One-eyed, because the other eye was always hidden by a view-finder.

Well, I was still feeling sour, a spoilsport. A couple of us got up and joined in at the end. The lad with his family I'd seen on the street in Nairobi, he had punkish bleached hair and a pierced eyebrow, especially got into the mood of it, chucking himself about like nobody's business. And even the Samburu women cheered up when people bought bracelets and necklaces from the tables. I bought a bracelet, seeds and mock pearls, for Rosa, my daughter, three hundred shillings.

"You're meant to bargain."

At my elbow a plump lad with a mop of black hair, arse big in cut-for-comfort cotton shorts, hair above his knees, socks pulled up and sandals, not a pretty sight.

"No you're not."

"Why not?"

"Because if I knock her down to two pounds I rob her and her family of a meal."

As I walked away I was aware of him making screwing motions with his podgy finger in the side of his head.

So, I'm a nutter? So what.

"Let me take you to your driver, and your companions, for the next few days." Judy, that evening. She singled me out from the little crowd drifting through the reception area to the mini-buses outside. I

followed her. Although she was wearing the
international uniform of her kind, padded shoulders,
fitted waist, tight skirt, she walked with the upright
stance, chin in, shoulders back, that dignity and
grace of just about all Kenyan and most African
women, that comes from carrying loads on your
head from early childhood. Or maybe from uncon-
sciously imitating the walk of your mum and aunts
who really did.

"This is Sami. Sami, this is your new passenger,
Mr…," she glanced at her clip-board, "Shovelin."

A spatter of Swahili followed. She turned back to
me.

"You will be very happy with Sami. He is one of
our best drivers. Tip-top."

"The best," he said, and shook my hand.

Sami was immense, gross, obese, with arms that
filled the short sleeves of his red shirt so it was like a
second skin, and wodges of flesh above his buttocks, but he had a nice smile, and turned out to be
great as both driver, guide and source of information, though not wholly reliable at bird identification. Less promising was the presence of Alfred the
water-colourist and his crocheting wife, sitting in
the middle row of seats, exposed by the open sliding side-door. There were three seats in front of
them and three behind.

"Joining us, are you?" the woman asked.

You look pretty well joined up already, I thought,
but this time managed to keep it to myself.

I hesitated. Front or back.

"So far," she said, "Bianca and Peter have always had the front seats."

And that is set in stone, I thought, the way these things are. I took the back seats, sitting in the one furthest from the door.

"Not painting then, this afternoon," I said, as cheerily as I could.

"The light changes and fades too quickly," Alfred replied, turning to peer across the back of his seat so he could see me, "at this time of day."

"Well, that's the tropics for you," I offered, somewhat inanely.

Silence. The vehicle lurched a little beneath me as Sami got in the front and pulled his door to. He began to drum fingers on the steering wheel. The mini-bus behind pulled out, slid past, the driver leaning forward to grin across at Sami, who sighed and turned away.

"Bianca and Peter are always late," Mrs said with the sour satisfaction of someone who rejoices in the failings of others. "They've been late every time so far. I am afraid that annoys Sami who likes to be first away."

"Except the first time," Alfred chipped in. "When we left the Serena."

Which is how they got the front seat. Clever Bianca and Peter.

"Best to get acquainted properly," he went on, "I'm Alfred Cobleigh and this is my wife Doris." This time he thrust a brownish, thin-fingered hand over the back.

"Shovelin," I said. "Chris. You can call me Kit."

But no, for the short time I knew them, they both called me Christopher.

Bianca and Peter arrived. They turned out to be the aging yuppies, that is they were I would guess in their late thirties, I had seen by the pool at the Serena. She was blonde, attractive, pleasantly chatty. He was dark, quiet. Both wore designer baseball caps, designer shades, tops with short sleeves and collars, whose designer labels were so small you'd have to be into such things to be able to recognise them, full-cut shorts, woollen socks turned down over walking-boots which looked serviceable without being clunky. She had her straw bag and he had an Olympus SLR, not the latest slimmed-down version with built-in zoom, but not an old one either. Sami was off before they were properly settled, which meant the intros had to be called out across the Cobleighs and were managed without the handshaking routine.

We followed the other buses over a bridge and into a bleaker landscape, dryer, stonier, with less vegetation, just scattered thorn-bushes for the most part, dotted across low but steep and irregular hills. The sky was overcast above us now, but on the rises we could see across the plain for maybe twenty miles to black mountains beneath banks of dark cloud that hid the sun.

There was not much to see. A small group of antelope glided away from us, and then there were three black-masked dog-like creatures who looked up at us from ten yards with cat-like curiosity. Sami stopped, Peter snapped away, his automatic reload whirring on after each click .

"Jackals," Doris announced, with heavy certainty.

"Bat-eared foxes," Sami grunted.

His radio suddenly gave a low pitched scream, a voice came through, Sami answered, and suddenly we were off again, much faster, slewing away off the track, the bus, which had no four-wheel drive and I should imagine only standard suspension, clanging and jolting.

Doris fastened her fingers on the grab-rail on the back of Peter's seat.

"I would have thought foxes are shyer than those animals," she muttered, and then more plaintively, "he's not meant to leave the approved tracks, you know."

Within two or three minutes we reached the curving spine of a ridge looking over a long gulley that narrowed as it climbed towards us. There were four mini-buses parked on the ridge on the other side, their roofs raised, one eyed punters leaning out. Sami pointed down the slope to his right.

"Cheetah," he said.

We were far nearer than any of the others. Well done, Sami.

She was… She? Yes. Bianca asked Sami, and Sami said female… she was washing. Spread out in a scree-filled hollow beneath bushes, head up, front paw sweeping down over her ear and cheek, quick lick and back it went again.

"Going to rain," said Doris, with knowing satisfaction. "Cats always do that when it's going to rain."

On the far side two more mini-buses arrived and a pair of four by fours from some other lodge, not ours.

"We're lucky to see a cheetah," said Peter.

"Really?" asked Doris. "After all, we are on the Cheetah Safari."

I was beginning to feel I could get really irritated by Doris.

"There are so few left, the gene pool has shrunk. They're inbreeding. Can't last much longer." He snapped on, for posterity one presumed.

Cheetah got up, stretched a bit, cat aerobics, and walked slowly up the hill, found another hollow, slumped into it but this time remained on the qui vive, head up, slowly taking us all in, tail lashing the air behind her in slow motion. She stayed like that for five minutes, during which I got bored and then my attention was caught by a large hawk or small eagle that landed, claws spread, in the top of the acacia about ten yards in front of us. Bianca noticed my attention had shifted.

"The bird, is it?" she asked.

"Yes."

She reached over Doris's head and handed me a pair of slim light-weight modern 'nocs.

"Come up the front."

I did. Doris's bag was on the floor. To avoid it I had to step over the well in front of the side door.

"What is it?"

"Harrier," said Sami.

Well, I didn't think so. Granted it was basically a very pale grey, almost white and had black primaries, OK, but also it had bright red on the back of its beak, and black round its eyes. Very handsome. I fumbled for *Birds of East Africa*. At the same time Cheetah made a decisive move up the slopes behind us, going at a steady loping trot now. Sami fired the motor to follow her and the bird took off with a sharp descending call – 'whioooh'. I sat down quite sharply as we lurched forward, and then into reverse as Sami did a sort of racing two point turn.

"Oops, sorry."

Bianca took the middle seat, Peter stayed by the window,

"Stay here," she said. "Much better view. So? The bird?"

I fumbled a bit more and came up with the answer.

"Dark Chanting Goshawk," I said. And later marked it with a tick, the place, and the date.

We followed the cheetah back up the ridge and watched it as it trotted off down the long broken slope on the other side. The plain stretched out in front of us, near desert, to the west and heavy black clouds above the Laikipia Escarpment. Livid sunlight lit patches here and there, and elsewhere columns of dark grey drifted between clouds and parched earth, but many miles away.

"I said it would rain," said Doris.

We trundled about the hillsides for another half hour or so but saw only some distant zebras shadowing a pair of giraffes and a few antelope of one sort or another. Amazing how quickly one accepts and dismisses all but the rarer and more dramatic sights, how quickly one begins to resent it if they don't turn up.

I had dinner on my own and went to bed early.

Chapter Ten

Bianca cheery, fresh, morning-scrubbed and fragrant, patted the seat beside her as I climbed in after her. I looked round. Doris and Alfred looked slightly peeved, perhaps because my place in front of them now seemed established, fixed. I slammed the side door, sat beside Bianca, and grinned at Peter as he smiled a welcome across her. Another bang as Sami slammed the rear hatch on our baggage and then the lurch as he hoisted his eighteen stone or so into the driver's seat.

"So, Sami, where are you taking us today?" Bianca chirruped, making conversation really, since we all knew darn well where we were going.

"First to Nyeri in the Aberdares," he replied, adjusting his rear-view mirror, "for lunch at the Outspan Hotel. There your main luggage will be placed in a safe room. Leaving at four in the afternoon you will be bussed up to Tree-Tops. You will take only one small night bag each." Sami, I had begun to realise, rarely used two words where one would do.

He fired the engine, let out the clutch.

For the first hour or so, once we had left the national reserve, we kept to the main roads Danny had come up two days earlier – the same strung-out villages, the same parched landscape, the same stretches where the surface was being reconstructed and we dropped behind the other vehicles to let their dust settle in front of us. Occasionally the radio gave its screech, and above the purr of the engine and the rumble of the wheels, Sami chatted to the other drivers. I told Bianca and Peter how I had come out to do a job in Mombasa and found myself with time on my hands and money to spend, when it was done. I did not explain how I had got to Samburu Lodge. It came out though that I was a PI and that provoked the usual interest and curiosity. I don't mind this. I've been told, most often by my wife, that I lack most of the social graces, and certainly I don't chat easily, so it gives me something to rattle on about.

Mt Kenya lay like a giant sleeping tawny lion on our right but then we headed off south-west and it slowly sank away again. Presently the road climbed, the landscape became greener, richer, plantations and crops re-appeared., the hills and valleys became sharper, deeper. Clouds collected in the mountains above us and there was even a spatter or two of rain. We skirted a big straggly, unkempt town in a basin in the hills, climbed above it, swung between gateposts guarded by paramilitaries with automatic weapons, and entered another world of shrubberies well-tended, flower-beds and immaculate lawns. Views across terraces opened up to blue and green hills, and beyond them, Mt Kenya again, a low hump beyond the horizon, now nearly a hundred miles away. A final turn took us to a long building stretched across the slope – it looked like a colonial but modernised mansion. Which is what, I suppose, it originally was.

"Welcome to Outspan Hotel," said Sami, standing up and facing us. "Lunch. Then buses to Treetops. Before that there is time to visit the Baden-Powell museum in the bungalow you see down there or witness a display of Kikuyu dancing. Tomorrow you will be brought back here, and I shall resume being your driver."

"Rest of the day off for you then, Sami," crowed Bianca. "Have a nice time!"

He flashed us a white grin, and let himself out.

"I bet he will," Peter grunted. "He probably has a wife in every lodge."

But all through this my mouth had dried and my pulse was up. Supposing the letter boxes were not in the foyer as Danny had written they should be? What would I do then?

The rest of the tour were already gathering on the gravel in front of the big doors set in the side of the building. Inside it reminded me of the neo-gothic pile that housed the small private school I was sent to in my teens. The tour was a mixed lot in age and background, but with one thing in common – money. Not hugely wealthy, not rich, but solid middle-class citizens, professionals, academics, solicitors, with wives and often enough children, teenagers. A couple of families were looking disconcerted – wearing shorts, unpressed t-shirts, sandals, they were faced with the embarrassment of entering the sort of establishment they would normally have suited up for, or at least worn their best casual. With the air of those entering a stately home with awareness of the heritage they are tres-passing on, we all filtered into a baronial reception area while our drivers humped our cases into a side-room. An elaborately laid out dining room, I believe it even had chandeliers, stretched in front of us, but we were ushered towards an oaklined room on the corner of the building where drinks were served in a parody of colonial ceremony: weak buck's fizz, is what I remember, or straight orange juice for the non-alcoholics, before being shunted into a less formal dining room with the usual buffet. I ducked about, turned and twisted my way back, accosted a black-suited white-gloved functionary.

"Letterboxes?" I gasped. "I have mail to post."

He waved a casual hand across the vestibule.

I had of course been looking for… letterboxes. These were oak cabinets, labelled in dark carved gothic lettering, 'Abroad' and 'Local'. Stooping I ripped back Velcro from the pocket above my knee, extracted the envelope and the packet from where they rested against my lower thigh, and with a last glance at the addresses, slipped them into the slits near the tops of the boxes. And that, I thought, is that. Goodbye Danny, and, for the matter of that, Holly and Vincey too.

Well, I don't want to make this My Holiday Diary, so I'll skip the Kikuyu dancing, the trip up to Treetops, the night spent watching the waterhole through gusting cloud whose droplets looked like tiny flakes of snow, and seeing two hyenas drive a waterbuck into the shallows of the pool before the cloud closed over them. The carcass, or some of it, was still there when the mist rose and the dawn came up. Back to the Outspan, and reunited with Sami we set off through the Aberdares for Lake Nakuru.

The country we went through was amazing – rich, fertile, well-watered by the run off from the Aberdares, with tea and coffee plantations and rolling grassland that looked like well-kept golf-courses. No wonder, when the British first saw it a hundred years ago, they said – 'we'll have that!' White mischief, replaced now by a newer, less inno-cent sort of nastiness. Many of the plantations car-ried billboards with the AFI logo and others, and there was even another AFI plant research station, a small complex of gleaming glass and chrome that looked as if it would be more at home on the Bath Road out of London than in the middle of Africa. It was set at the foot of a long, wide, ordered slope of green, but different shades of green, planted in squares and oblongs, divided by roads and breaks, climbing to a crest maybe as much as two miles above us. I wondered: was it to photograph this that Danny had headed for this area the day before? It would not have been easy: the outer perimeter was punctuated with small watch towers and a small helicopter in the livery of yellow and green cruised above it.

We crossed the equator, twice, again without a stop, but we did stop at Thompson's Falls where hucksters charged us to hold chameleon lizards tied to sticks so we could see them change colour against our clothes, and where Bianca bought postcards with batik pictures of savannah fauna stuck to the card. Doris wouldn't let Alfred buy an ebony statuette with pointy breasts. The falls themselves were OK too.

And although much of the town of Nakuru looked as haphazardly put together as the other towns, had that frontier feel that comes with inadequate resources, we motored briefly through a suburb where the streets were lined with palms, jacaranda, and oleander, and the porticoed bungalows gleamed with fresh white paint. On the edge a pine wood and wired and guarded gates opened into the Lake Nakuru Reserve, and through the screen of trees and bush we could see the brilliant blue of the lake and the shocking pink of the flamingos which, in colonies hundreds of thousands in size, ringed its edge. On the other side of the road grass alternated with managed forest, grass patrolled by falstaffian rhinos, who marked their territory with clouds of secretions expelled, pumped even, from their rear ends. Presently we left the main track and followed the convoy onto dried and cracked mudflats to within a couple of hundred yards of the flamingos and the soupy water, a solution of centuries of bird shit which fed the small crustacea the stilted birds fed off... talk about nature's economies. For once we were let out of the vans – no big cats here or poisonous snakes. It all pen and inked a bit, very like the artificial fertiliser smell you get where intensive mono-culture of, say, tomatoes, is carried on. The birds themselves were amazing, especially in flight. I seem to remember there were plovers too, but I must confess it's all a bit vague, the memories smudged by what came next.

After twenty minutes or so we got back in the mini-bus and Sami drove us back to the lake shore and the main track. We rounded a gentle bend that followed the distant edge of the lake, with reeds and bush on the lake side and acacia forest on the other, and there it was.

"Stop, Sami, please stop," I shouted.

He did so, perhaps thinking I'd been summoned by a sudden call of nature, or seen an animal or bird he'd missed – he had by now gathered I was into birds.

But it was the ruin of a burnt out car that appeared to have run off the road-side and into a tree that had grabbed me, a red VW Polo.

It was as if I had been plucked from an almost paradisial world and dropped into an alternative universe where much was the same, but everything was tinged by horror and nightmare.

I hauled back the sliding door and ran across. The front of the car was crushed up against the young tree it had smashed into, partially uprooting it. A bough had cracked and like a broken limb hung askew across the bonnet. Its slimmest twigs poked into the space where the windscreen had been and were singed. The rear of the car had burnt furiously, perhaps explosively for a time. The trunk lid was twisted, warped, and sprung open, the rear window had fallen in, the paint-work was blistered and in places burnt down to a raw brownish colour. The upholstery was blackened and covered with tesserae of glass.

Sami was pulling at my elbow.

"Please to come back immediately. It is not allowed, not allowed to leave the vehicle at any time without I say so, and especially not in a game park. If I report you you will be excluded from the rest of the trip…"

He was really very agitated, and glancing back the way we had come. Later I worked out that he was scared we might be seen by a following minibus, in which case he would have to report the incident and possibly be blamed for letting me out. But they were all in front of us – thanks to Peter and Bianca's usual reluctance to get back in after we had done watching the flamingos.

But Bianca had joined us, and Sami, confronted now with two bolshie clients, smacked his shiny black forehead in frustration.

"Is it your girlfriend's car?" she asked, her voice full of… anxiety, I suppose.

I walked round to the back. The registration

number, like that of almost all the vehicles I had seen began with two letters, the first a K. I'm good at remembering numbers, but it's an acquired skill I manage in my own way. I can retrieve them only if I have made a conscious act of filing them.

"I don't know." I looked up at Bianca, quite sharply. "She wasn't really my girlfriend."

Bianca shrugged, eyebrows pulled together in a sudden frown. I suppose I had sounded gruff. I walked slowly round the back of the wreck and up the other side, the driver's side. There was churned up dust, footprints, quite large boots for the most part, at least three different people, men probably. Well there would be. Police, Park Rangers, whatever. There was dust inside the car, and some seeds, a dry leaf or two, rain-drop marks in the dust on the roof. I reckoned it had been there, in the condition it was in, for at least twenty-four hours.

"Please to get back in. Both of you. I am instructed to report any non-compliance." Poor Sami.

I began a more careful examination of the interior but without touching anything, and it was clean, almost as if it had been cleaned out. Not even a sweet-paper, apple-core, or pocket tissue. But there was blood. Not much, and dried hard, a deep brownish maroon colour, smeared thinly as if someone had tried to wipe it up. Again, at least twenty-four hours old, a patch of it on the edge of the driving seat as though it had bled from a face or head wound, and dropped between her knees. Her? I remembered she had worn trousers when driving.

I straightened, looked at Sami and Bianca, and Peter too had come out and was standing behind Bianca, face even more serious than usual, a hand on her shoulder.

"Best do as he says," he muttered. He meant Sami. Alfred peered at us from inside the minibus, Doris beyond him, leaning forward so she could see too. They looked as angry as Sami, sensing a serious threat to the success of their holiday. In his other hand Peter was still holding his Olympus SLR.

"Sure," I said. "But first, do me a small favour. Take photographs of the wreck, just three or four, don't fuss about getting it all in, but include the license plate."

He glanced at me very soberly for a second or so, and I thought he was going to refuse. But there must have been something pretty determined in my face. He nodded, pushed back the peak of his cap, and very quickly fired off six or seven frames.

"You'll have to wait until we get home for the results," he said. "There's stuff I took at Treetops I don't want to lose."

And at last I let Sami almost push us back towards the van, me and Peter that is. Bianca was behind him. I didn't see her stoop and pick something up. And the reason why I didn't was that something had caught my eye too, a gleam of yellow metal about ten yards down the track, in the dried grass and thorns on the verge. The sun must just have flashed off it at that moment and then the leaves shifted above and it was gone. I walked over to where I had seen it, poked with my foot in the secondary growth and it chinked against a stone. One spent cartridge case. I picked it up, put it in my pocket. Sami was now looking very angry indeed, so I only gave the area a quick look more, trying to see signs that a gun had been fired, possibly at the Polo as it approached. I couldn't see any.

"Well!" said Doris, as we got back in.

"Was all that really necessary?" asked Alfred.

Sami slammed the side-door behind me, and slammed his own door too. He'd copped a moody all right.

As we pulled out from the verge where he'd stopped, Bianca placed what she had just picked up on my knee and I took it in my hand.

It was a shoe. Black, soft-leather, slip-on. Inside a label – Next.

"Is that hers? It was under a bush."

I remembered how Danny had taken off shoes like this and put on boots on Mt Kenya, how she kept a pair like this one for driving.

"Could be," I said, and then a wave of awful inse-curity and longing broke over me. "I think so."

Chapter Eleven

Peter leaned forward.

"Sami," he said, "How do you think it happened?"

"Driving too fast. Rhino came out of the trees. Better to hit a tree than a rhino." And he shut up.

More quietly, looking down at the shoe in my hand, Bianca asked: "What's her name?"

I blessed her silently for making that present tense.

"Danny," I said. "Danielle Newman. And she isn't my girlfriend. I've only known her a couple of days."

"We all thought she was your girlfriend, and that you'd had a major row and she'd driven off because of it."

Suddenly I had a sense that I had not had before of the group as just that... after three or four days together they knew each other well enough to gossip about each other behind each other's backs. Especially about a late arrival, an interloper.

"No. Like I said to you earlier, I was at the Serena with time and money on my hands, thinking of joining the safari, but she offered to take me instead. She wanted company."

I explained how Danny was a journalist, how she was planning an article about the collapse of tourism in places like Kenya, and so on, and her proposed companion had been unable to make it... It all sounded even more hollow than it had before. Bianca gave my hand a squeeze and left me holding the shoe.

It took another twenty minutes for us to reach the lodge where we were to have lunch, time for me to get my feelings under some sort of control and work out something of a plan. Clearly I must do something – if nothing more than check out whether or not the Polo and the slipper were or were not Danny's, and if they were try to find out what had happened to her.

We broke away from the lake and the trees and climbed a long curving road up a gently undulating grassy slope for a mile or so. The lodge was a long low complex of buildings, modern but well designed to sit in the hillside, with terraces, a ha-ha and low walls to keep the larger fauna at a distance, with artfully disposed boulders rising hump-backed from the ground. Sami said we had an hour for lunch but he himself stayed in the van, at least until we were out of the car-park and out of sight.

The view from the terraces was magnificent, the lake with its ring of pink, dark mountains beyond, forested but riven with deep valleys, a huge sky with shifting cloudscapes sending fitful patches of sunlight cruising across the lake and the land. But I was not prepared to bother with it. I looked around for a uniform, for authority or officialdom, but saw none, so I picked on a maître d' type, a short man in black with a black tie, holding a big menu.

"Table d'hôte? This way, sir."

There was buffet on one side, which the party were heading for, but a step up the split level there was also an area where the tables were dressed with linen and silver.

"No thank you. But I would like to see the manager."

He fed a look of solicitude and concern into his eyes.

"About what matter sir? If you have a complaint to make I am the person to whom it may be addressed."

"No complaint. Just an enquiry."

He pulled his brows together, pursed his lips.

"The manager is very busy, perhaps I –?"

"The manager, please."

"Very well. Come this way."

He minced off giving the menu a flap as if to fan his face, and I followed him, back towards the car-park, then through a timber back-door and into a functional corridor. Another door, labelled 'manager'.

"Wait here, sir, if you please. If I could have your name?"

"Shovelin. Christopher Shovelin."

He knocked, went in, closed the door behind him. And kept me waiting for four minutes which seemed like forty. Then out he came.

"Mr Tuku will see you now." That's what it sounded like, and he stood aside.

Mr Tuku was sitting in a dark, plain room behind

a modern desk, with the usual contemporary office furniture on it – telephones, computer, fax machine and so on. There was a large photograph of President Moi on the wall to my right and one, taken in the air, of flamingos cruising above the lake to my left. The light behind him was blinding, framed by a square window from the car-park. Tuku was also wearing a black suit but sharper than his maître d's – when he stood I saw it was full-cut and double-vented. A grey shirt and a silver-grey tie. The corners of a matching silk handkerchief stuck up out of the pocket. His hair was cut short and grizzled at the temples, his face long and thin, and, apart from a certain wariness in his eyes and a sour mouth, quite handsome.

"Mr Shovelin, what can I do for you?"

He gave my hand a perfunctory squeeze across his desk, and sat down again. He didn't suggest I should. He leant back in his self-adjusting leather-covered throne, fingers together beneath his chin. Gold flashed in the smile he stitched on to his face.

"It's a simple enough matter," I began, and at least I had had time to prepare what I was going to say, "on our way up here we passed a car that had crashed into a tree by the road-side, a VW Polo, red. It is possible that it was being driven by a friend of mine when it crashed, I know she was driving a car very like it, and I would like to be sure that it was not hers."

"When you say 'on the way here' do you mean actually within the reserve?"

You know bloody well I do, I thought.

"Yes."

"On the main road between the gate and here?"

"That's right. And I would guess it's been there for at least twenty-four hours, may be more."

"I should have been told." He frowned, leaned forward over his desk, examined a pad of buttons by the answer-phone, selected one and dabbed it. "Sergeant Nkeli to the Manager's Office immediately…" and then he added something in Swahili which included the word 'Polo'.

Bugger this, I thought, if I'm going to have to wait… and I sat down in the only other chair in the room, black leather slung from a chrome frame. He raised his eyebrow at that, picked up a matt stainless steel Parker, and tapped the desk with it. We waited. No flies this time, but a distant clash of plates and so forth, kitchen sounds. Thirty seconds and then a knock on the door and in came the sergeant. Whether or not his dark green uniform and black beret were official army or that of a private security force I would not know, but he was the genuine article. Six feet tall at least, robustly built, neatly trimmed moustache beneath a pale scar on his very black cheek-bone above it, carrying a swagger stick. Again a quick, sharp exchange I could not understand, then in English…

"Sergeant, Mr Shovelin here has complained that there is a car wreck in the preserve, close to the road."

"I am not complaining," I butted in, "my concern is that the driver may–"

Manager Tuku bore me down.

"Why was I not told about this?"

"Sah! It was a trivial matter. The occupants were not hurt. I gave orders the car should be removed. I do not know why it has not been dealt with. It will be seen to immediately."

Suddenly Tuku's voice was hard, cutting, saw-like. For the first time I felt he was speaking from the heart, not putting on an act.

"Sergeant, get it done. Now."

The soldier, whatever, saluted, turned smartly, stamping his feet the way they do, swagger stick in his armpit, the other arm and hand dead straight aligned with the seam in his trousers, and was gone. Tuku leant back again, tapped the steel pen casing on his teeth and smiled, then came forward briskly.

"You can find your way back to the dining area, Mr Shovelin?"

"I don't think you understand," I said, "I want to know what happened to the driver."

Tuku shrugged. "You heard what the Sergeant said. Unharmed. I imagine they went back to Nakuru, hired another car, and went on with their trip."

For a moment I wanted to continue the fight, say that the crash was not the sort that you could easily walk out of, that as far as I knew there had only been the one driver, and so on. Had there really been two people in the car? Or were Tuku and the sergeant attempting to put me off the track by asserting there were? But I sensed Tuku had had enough of me, and would continue to stonewall until he threw me out. I also realised that any further pursuit of the matter with him would reveal I had got out of the mini-bus and examined the Polo, and that this might well get Sami into trouble. But mainly I just felt the uselessness of it all.

I went back to the terrace, stood away from the tables, looked out across the wonderful huge bowl of the lake. Nearby a troop of baboons messed about with each other, jabbered a bit, and moved on. Lower down the slopes a couple of giraffes with a young one sauntered across the grass towards a clump of trees, their movement like that of high-masted square-rigged sailing boats. I once saw a very similar sight, doing the Sunday visit with my kids, at Marwell Zoological Park near Winchester. I felt a sort of loss, as if wonder had leaked out of me. What I was looking at was not wild, unspoilt Africa. It was a bloody park.

I fetched the spent cartridge case out of my pocket, turned it over in my palm. I'm no sort of expert in this sort of thing, what gun-crime does occur in Bournemouth is always a police matter, but I could see it was 9mm parabellum, which meant it had almost certainly been fired by and ejected from some sort of automatic or semi-automatic pistol or machine pistol. It was odd therefore that I had found only one. No, it wasn't. Whoever fired it had picked the others up afterwards, but missed this one that had fetched up in the plants on the verge. Anyway, one thing was for sure. This was not a gun a ranger would use or even carry as a protection against the larger fauna. It could, let's face it, have been fired as part of a short burst at the approaching car, causing it to leave the road and crash into a tree. But there had been no bullet holes in the car. Still, both the windscreen and the rear window had been thoroughly smashed – perhaps to remove evidence of shooting.

So who are the users of Brownings, HKMPs, Uzis and the rest? Anyone who wants a weapon that can be carried easily, brought into use instantly and at short-range: police, security, body-guards, and criminals.

I turned back to the dining area. Bianca and Peter were nearby with an empty chair at their table.

"Come and join us," Bianca called out. "It's help yourself, but very good. Especially the curry."

"Sort of fruity," Peter added. "Anglo-Indian, I'd say."

Once I was settled in front of her with a plate of curried chicken stew with mango in it, plain rice and a couple of poppadoms, she looked to left and right as if checking for eavesdroppers and leant forward over her nearly empty plate.

"So? What did you find out?"

"Nothing. I saw the manager and the head of security. Could have been regular army. They said whoever was in the Polo had walked away and disappeared."

Peter shook his head and waved his fork from side to side.

"Not possible," he commented. "Not from a shunt like that. Well, not likely anyway."

"So what are you going to do?" Bianca took it up.

"I don't know, I really don't know."

"You're quite sure it was, what was her name? Danny's car?"

"The shoe you found was hers. I'm just about as sure as I can be of that. She kept the pair in the car for driving." I let out a sigh which was a poor expression of the emptiness I was feeling. "I've got to do something."

The curry was good but suddenly I didn't want it any more. I pushed it away.

"Of course you have. Of course you must. But what?"

"Embassy?" Peter sugggested. " 'Her Britannic Majesty's Ambassador requires and expects...' however it goes. You know what I mean. 'Afford such assistance and protection as may be needed'. Something like that. They might be able to tell you if they've had news of her. They might be able to make enquiries after her."

"It's an idea..." But a doubt nagged at the back of my mind.

"No harm in trying."

The doubt coalesced.

"Problem is..." I couldn't hold back a silly, apologetic laugh, "I'm not even sure she was English, British. She had a slight accent, you know? Could have been Irish. Or East Coast American."

Then, at last, a flash of rational thought or memory blessed me and my fingers flew to the breast pocket of my linen jacket. What I was looking for was so small I thought for a moment it had gone, but it was still there. The card Ludwig had given me when we parted at luggage retrieval at Jomo Kenyatta Airport.

"But I do have the telephone number of a mutual acquaintance who lives in Nairobi."

I pushed back my chair and headed back into the reception area. Again I was intercepted by the maître d'.

"Telephone," I said. "I need to use a telephone."

"I am most sorry to inform you that in the restaurant area there is no telephone for the use of guests."

"Where then?"

"Perhaps at residential reception, but that is five minutes walk away." He waved his hand at another group of buildings further across the hillside.

"The manager has a telephone." I made it sound as peremptory as I could.

And I headed off down the short corridor, knocked on his door and went in, with maître d' bleating at my heels. Mr Tuku was surprised and angry.

"I have a call to make to Nairobi," I said. "Please let me use your phone."

Instant refusal was on his lips, any fool could have seen that. But what this fool, I mean yours truly, did not take in sufficiently well was how quickly it changed to almost obsequious acceptance, promoted by the gold-filled grin.

"Of course, Mr Shovelin. Please use the phone at your convenience. And in case your call is of a confidential nature, I shall be pleased to wait next door while you make it. Get out!"

The last two words were directed at the maître d' who scuttled out ahead of him.

"Please to press nine for an outside line. The code for Nairobi is 02."

On the sixth ring the answerphone cut in. "I cannot take your call at this moment. Please leave a message after the tone or call back later." Yes, it sounded like Holly's voice. The bleep came. Then the slightest, tiniest of small coughs.

"Mr Holly, are you there? I think I can hear you. Chris Shovelin speaking…"

Then a came a click, but the line remained open.

"Oh fuck," I said. "Oh SHIT!

I was professionally mortified, apart from anything else. A Member of the Association of Private Enquiry Agents caught so easily: I'd have to keep quiet about it. They wouldn't drum me out if it got to be known at the next annual conference, but by god I'd be the laughing stock… But that mattered nothing in comparison with what I might have done to Ludwig Holly.

On the way out of the park, just as we were approaching the gate we passed a yellow towing vehicle, a pick-up with a small crane on the back.

Behind it was the VW Polo, nose in the air, trundling along on its rear wheels. The lid of the boot had sprung up and was banging up and down like the mouth of a ventriloquist's dummy. What do you think of it so far? Ruddish.

Chapter Twelve

I made an effort to set my mind to it all as we continued to rumble along the sides and occasionally the bottom of the Rift Valley. The traffic was fairly heavy – we were now on the Trans Africa Highway, Mombasa and Nairobi to where... Kampala, Lagos? Green volcanic cones rose out of green pastures, fat kine drifted across it. Sami told us an English lord owned most of it.

"Just fancy," said Doris. "An English lord!"

She looked around with more interest than she had yet shown, as if trying to seek out someone she could curtsey to.

Mountain ranges floated beneath the sky ten, twenty miles away on both sides of what was soon a very flat plain. We passed another saline lake also ringed with flamingos and presently acacia forest took over from grasslands. On the verges women hawked oranges and others stood hopefully by big plastic bags recycled to hold what looked like green fodder. Big lorries with ZA number plates – Zambia, Zaire? – were parked beneath eucalyptus on the edge of the town of Navaisha, together with a double-decker red Route-Master. Was it serving as a bus or a hotel? A railway ran with us like a narrower thread than the road for most of the way, but we saw no trains or rolling stock.

And I tried to get my head round what was happening, what had happened. Go back to the beginning. Holly at Mombasa airport, Holly on the plane, Holly giving me his card, met by Vincey at Jomo Kenyatta. And what did I know about him then? Nothing, really. Next, leave out the mugging and all that, that was surely irrelevant, next was meeting, being picked up by, yes, surely that was right, she had picked me up not I her, Danny, Danielle Newman by the Serena Pool. No, that was not next. Rewind. Next was the morning, the corporate bosses and the ministers arriving at the Serena and what made them next was the way Danny had seemed to know all, well, a lot, about them when we saw them again at the Carnivore. Agri-business in the shape of AFI, government, and finance, some of the latter at any rate decidedly dodgy. Grand Cayman and a bank with a Spanish name, tied into the Mafia. Really the mafia, I wondered, or was that just shorthand for organised crime, like it could be the cocaine cartels? The Spanish name suggested cartels.

Then I'm persuaded to go with her as she goes round the tourists spots checking out how they're making out after Nine-Eleven. Accompany her because the guy, the colleague who was to have gone with her dropped out. Or, possibly, was taken out in a hit and run. Could all be true, or partly true. Certainly Holly had backed up the friend-who-had-dropped-out scenario. But then, since they were all in cahoots, whatever cahoots are, he would, wouldn't he? And then off they go on a private walkabout on the slopes of Mt Kenya, leaving me on my tod. And I'm interrogated by a ranger working for AFI. And it could well be their walkabout took them close to or even into an AFI research station. And a local boss of AFI was at the Carnivore. Yep. Here was a link, a thread that poked up more than once out of life's rich tapestry: Associated Foods International.

Now, it may not have come across all that blatantly in what you've read so far but back in the good old pre-marital bliss days I was a bit of a leftie. Trot, even, in the late sixties. Paris, Grosvenor Square, flogging the Socialist Worker on the unemployment marches in the early eighties. Then, you know how it is, marriage, kids, you need a job, a three bedroomed house, one car, two cars. But I knew that whatever happened I had to be my own boss. Of course you never are to begin with, but this is how it went. Her dad, Charlie, had been a Bournemouth bookmaker. Bought out by William Hill in the late seventies, he was well-to-do, nearly wealthy. "Chris," he said, once we'd made it clear that he'd be a grandfather in a furlong less than the full mile, "I'll set you up in your own business. Once, mind you. I'll only do it once. What's it to be?"

"Private Eye," I said.

"That tatty magazine?" he exclaimed.

"No," I said. "Like a Private Enquiry Agent."

Bookmakers know about private eyes, they have recourse to them. Charlie always used Tommy Pilger who had the traditional two room office above a jewellers in Westover Road, just below the Royal Bath Hotel, next to the first casino, and opposite the Pavilion. If you stood on a chair in his office you could see the sea – until, that is, they built the Imax. He was thin, was Tommy, with the emaciated look of a forty a day man, and he was having big trouble getting up the steep stairs to those two rooms. I was his legs for four years, learnt the trade, then he topped himself the day they delivered him his own oxygen mask and cylinder, and it was mine, all mine.

But I was still a leftie, though of course I'd dropped all my old connections, let my memberships lapse and so on. What did it mean then? It meant I undercharged widows and orphans, soaked the rich, like the Margeons (remember them, where we came in?) and read enough magazines and samizdat stuff, and nowadays the websites, to keep up to date with the big corporations, client states, neo-colonialism and the rest, and what they get up to. So, I reckoned I knew where I was, in the broadest sense, you understand, with AFI. Certainly, and you'll forgive me if I reveal whodunit right now, when we're barely halfway through, I was ready to believe that if there were villains behind what was going on, then AFI were behind them.

Sorry, back to my resumé.

Holly. I knew a bit more about him now, thanks to what Danny had told me. Micro-biologist on a sabbatical from Massachusett's Institute of Technology

– but I was pretty sure he wasn't American, certainly not from birth. He had neither the accent nor the attitudes, you know, the sincerity, the concern they all cloak themselves with, until you find out what their agenda are. Let's do a bit of guessing, see how he might tie in with Danny. Suppose he finds out something he wants to know more about, or perhaps make public, that AFI are up to in Kenya. He calls in Danny who belongs to a South African-based news collecting agency, possibly 'investigative'. He is, in effect, whistle-blowing. She doesn't want to travel on her own, and Holly doesn't want to be seen too much in her company, so she plans to bring along a colleague. Colleague is removed violently from the scene. They recruit me to take his place. Pause for thought. That's a bit wild, isn't it? An odd, not to say unlikely thing for them to do?

But… think about it. Did Holly have this in mind when he sat down next to me at Mombasa airport, while he chatted with me on the plane? Probably not. Not necessarily. The idea came later. Perhaps at that time he didn't even know Danny's friend had been hospitalised. Perhaps when he got home there was a message from her, from the Serena, saying she was on the next plane out because she was on her own and he said, hang on, there's this bloke at the Serena, I met him on the plane, he's at a loose end, why not see if he can't be recruited as a substitute? Or… hang on. What was it he had said when we parted? *I know where you are so if I need a private eye, and I might, I'll get in touch*. Something like that.

All that I could believe. Just.

Naivasha, the town of. The road took a by-pass, but we could see it spread out in the plain to our left. Palms, eucalyptus, jacaranda above shanties, bungalows, even some taller buildings further off. An abattoir, which you might expect on the main road outside the town, but one of those branches of Barclays as well – presumably there was a main office in town. Some cattle, and oxen pulling carts. Overloaded bicycles, men pedalling with those sacks of fodder on their cross-bars. The usual checkpoint, wooden dragon's teeth, sour uniformed men with machine pistols (9mm? Almost certainly), Sami took us through the two ninety degree corners the barriers made, his face as dour as those of the police.

Go back to thinking, speculating, resumating. The trout café on the flanks of Mt Kenya. The AFI research station. The three of them go off for over two hours. I don't hear distant shooting but they seem to think I should have done, certainly they return on adrenalin highs. And by then I've been questioned by the AFI Ranger.

Samburu Lodge. I'm getting to know her, like her. What's that sudden surge of feeling in my diaphragm, that comes as I remember her? Sense of loss. I think 'like' might not be the right word. Anyway, we go through wiring, or radioing the digitalised photos she's taken of the Mt Kenya AFI Research Station and I see one on the screen of her lap-top. Low green shrubs on a hill side. Did they look faintly familiar? Have I seen pics of similar crops? Maybe, but I can't place it. Coffee? Tea? We'd seen both between Tree-Tops and Naivasha, up in the Aberdares, the tea densely grown, the tops of the bushes flat where the leaf-tips had been picked, the rest glossy evergreen camellias just like we grow in our Bournemouth Winter Gardens. Not tea then. And not as tall as coffee or as straggly. Unless they were GM versions, prepared to rock the tea or coffee markets and economies of the Third World. How's that for a scenario?

What was next? Night, and Jumbo tearing the riverside apart. Presumably not part of the plot. Then breakfast, her note and the packets to post. Undeveloped film and probably the card from her digital camera. What was all that about? Not difficult to guess. She'd taken pictures which people unknown would not like her to have taken. Which they might try to get off her before she'd had them printed. And suspecting they'd be after her, she dumped them on me and asked me to put them in the post, even though she'd sent the digital ones by radio. Fail-safe. It was that important. And that was it. Except she had been right. They'd ambushed the Polo and presumably either killed her or at best kidnapped her. They'd have looked for the film, the card. Did she have substitutes she could pass off on them? Or would they... persuade... her to tell them what she had done with them?

Meanwhile I'd had two days being a safari tourist until, bang, the red Polo, and her slipper, shoe. Oh fuck. When things are bad I'm as ready as the next man to clutch at any straw that let's you say maybe they're not *that* bad. But the shoe did for that.

We were slowing down. We were slowing down quite quickly. We were approaching what looked like a small village characteristically strung out along the road, and yet another police check point, with the overlapping dragon's teeth in front of it. Except they weren't overlapping they were strung right across the road so we had to stop. A policeman, dark blue uniform, peaked cap, carbine in his left hand, was waving us down. There were five more like him, backing him up, as if he needed it. Personally, show me just one man with a gun and I'll do what he tells me. Sami's point of view too. He swore audibly and pulled us into the road-side.

The policeman hardly waited for the mini-bus to come to a halt before yanking back the sliding side door.

"Out," he barked. "Everybody out!"

Doris was first, bundling her crochet-work into her knitted bag. She put out a hand, as she always did for Sami to take, but this guy ignored it. Her knee gave as she set her first foot on the ground, but he still wasn't going to help her – mind you, she probably put on the lurch sideways to get sympathy or make him feel awful. Fat chance of either. We all followed her out of the mini-bus, one by one, and huddled up into a little group the way threatened sheep do. They snapped at us like so many

sheep-dogs, hustled us down a low dusty bank,
across the track pedestrians and cyclists used and
into a dark doorway beneath a corrugated tin roof
with a Kenyan flag above it. We blinked in the darkness, saw whitewashed walls, a counter with a fan
and a half-empty Coca-Cola bottle on it. Behind it a
photograph of Moi. There were some stackable
chairs against the back wall, but they pushed us on
into one of two side rooms. It had a small unglazed
but barred square hole for a window, four chairs for
the five of us and nothing else, no fan. And there we
were penned.

"What's all this about, then?" growled Peter.
And sat down on one of the chairs next to Bianca,
with his photographic case on his knees. Alfred
and Doris took the other two. I thought about it
for a moment, then pushed back through the door
thinking I'd get one of the chairs from the front
room. What I got was a nasty push in the chest,
but not before I had caught a glimpse of Sami sitting in one of the chairs I had been heading for,
looking up into the face of one of the policemen.
Already Sami had a red welt across his black
round face and in the second I was looking at him
before they moved in on me and pushed me back,
he took another back-handed swipe from the
swagger stick his interrogator, who had his back
to me, was wielding. He wasn't wearing a peaked
policeman's hat. He was wearing a black baseball
cap.

"What the fuck is going on?" Peter repeated,

and then as he got up and peered through the bars of the window: "Oh, shit. They can't bloody do that."

"Do what?" Bianca cried.

"They've only spilt my hold-all out on the ground. Jesus! Hey, they really cannot do that!"

He, in turn, made for the door.

We heard him shout: "Hey, leave those alone," then the door was kicked shut behind him.

I heard the blows that thudded into him.

Bianca didn't. She was now at the window.

"What are they doing?" Doris cried.

"They're stringing the film out of the cassettes of his exposed films. Now they're undoing Alfred's portfolio."

"No!"

And Alfred was up, trying to see past her, but she broke away then as the door slammed open again and Peter came through, crashing on to his knees, hands over his face, blood streaming between his knuckles. Two of the thugs followed him in, one of them grabbed me, twisted my arm up. Pain streaked through it as he forced my fist up between my shoulder blades. Bent double and howling as I was they had me across the central room and through the other door and into a sparsely furnished office on the other side, where they dropped me on to a stool in front of a scuffed and seedy deal and hardboard desk. Nursing my arm, I looked up through streaming tears at the man behind it and caught my breath, cutting off the noise I was making, almost as if they had also managed to thump me in the solar plexus.

The man behind the desk was wearing a taupe suit, had short grey hair above a bony, sculpted sort of a face – Commander Tom Komen.

You know, one thing I've learnt since I started in that office in Westover Road, is that coincidences do not happen. If I was going to end up in front of Komen's desk every time I took a beating, there had to be a reason.

Chapter Thirteen

Problem was Commander Komen, who was, let's face it, in a similar line of business, didn't believe in coincidences either.

"Mr Shovelin," he began, "I have some questions for you. You will answer them truthfully and fully, because the security of the state demands that you should. Lies, prevarication, and omissions will be punished most severely. Do you understand?"

Nursing my upper left arm in my right hand I managed a nod.

"You do understand?"

"Yes. Yes, I suppose so."

He looked at me hard as if he might be about to question that 'suppose', then gave his head a slight shake, pursed his lips, made a church out of his fingers beneath his chin.

"The day after you were mugged you travelled to Samburu Lodge with a Miss Danielle Newman. Correct?"

"Yes."

"On the way you stopped at a restaurant on Mt Kenya where you met a Mr Ludwig Holly. Was this your first meeting with Mr Holly?"

Well, by then I had my wits about me, more or less, and I spotted the trap. He had not asked me if I had ever met Danny before, so why ask me if I had ever met Holly? Because he knew the answer.

"No. I met him in the departure lounge at Mombasa airport, two days earlier, on my way to Nairobi. I sat with him on the plane."

"That meeting was prearranged?"

"No. Indeed not."

"Nor that with Miss Newman?"

"No."

"You were not acquainted with them before you came to Kenya?"

"No."

He leant back, folded his fingers and gave the slightest of nods directed above my head. A crack like thunder, flashes of light and pain. One of the heavies behind me, I'd even forgotten they were there, had given me a hell of a belt over my right ear.

I felt sobs welling up and I tried to control them.

"You don't believe me, do you?" I burbled.

"No, Mr Shovelin. You say you are a private enquiry agent. You have some knowledge of inter-rogation techniques. Ask yourself, would you believe your story?"

See what I mean? A cynical attitude to coinci-dence.

I stumbled on, trying to give him Holly's account of how he knew I was at the Serena, that Danny was there but thinking of aborting her trip because she'd been let down by a colleague... blah, blah. I was hav-ing serious doubts about it all myself so I could hard-ly fault Komen's scepticism. Which, fortunately, he expressed not by signalling another thump or two, but by yawning a little and drumming his fingers on the desk.

He interrupted me.

"With or without your connivance, these people were using you."

A long pause during which I said nothing. He took my silence for assent.

"So-o-o…" he drew out the word with a sort of relish, "in what ways did they use you, Mr Shovelin?"

I didn't take my eyes off his, which was just as well, for I caught the way they glanced across my head. I flinched, pulled up shoulders, made as much like a scared tortoise as a man can, and waited for the blow.

"Well?"

I calculated, rather quickly. Surely the mail boxes at the Outspan Hotel would have been emptied by now, the packets well down the line and presumably jumbled in with all the other mail leaving Kenya. Take a chance, I thought. Why not? What did I owe Danny or Holly, anyway?

"Miss Newman left a note and two packets for me at the Samburu Lodge. In the note she asked me to post the packets in the Outspan mail boxes when we got there. I did as she asked."

"What were the addresses on the packets?"

"I don't remember."

The answer was too pat. Before I could duck, the brute's knuckles came from behind again and smashed my left ear in a back-hand swipe. This time

I went with it and it didn't hurt quite so much. Or at any rate it wasn't quite so cataclysmically shocking. Indeed I felt a tremor of anger as well as pain and humiliation.

But I made a scene of it, gasped, spluttered, whimpered... and collected my thoughts.

"One," I mumbled, "was a pro-forma packet containing a film cassette. It was addressed to a film processing laboratory in England. There are hundreds of such places. I did not record the address or try to remember it. The second looked like an ordinary letter with, I would guess, not more than one sheet of paper in it. It was directed to an address in Twickenham, a small town on the Thames to the west of London. I don't remember the name or the rest of the address."

But, I decided not to add, if you go on beating the shit out of me I might be persuaded to.

"I know Twickenham. It is not far from the Police College at Hendon where I attended a six month course in 1985. Interrogation techniques were on the curriculum." Komen offered the smile of a cop who has decided to play Good Cop after a spell as Bad Cop. "What did you do with Miss Newman's note?"

"It's in my hold-all."

Again he raised his gaze but this time he rattled away in Swahili or whatever, then glanced back at me.

"George will take you outside. You find that note and bring it back, right?"

George, a big lanky character in a cotton suit that left his wrists and big hands exposed, hoicked me out of the chair, and pushed me through the door, across the front room, and out on to the wide strip of dried up ground that separated the main carriageway from the police post. I blinked in the bright sunlight. Our mini-bus was where we had left it, but with all the doors open. Sami was back in his seat, his arms across the wheel, his head resting on them. All our luggage had been taken out, forced open where it had been locked, and tipped into the low creeping thistles that poked through the stones and dust, and then turned over, picked through, and probably kicked about a bit. Alfred and Doris were on their knees trying to shake their stuff out and fold it back into their cases. I noticed the remnants of one of his sketch pads, the sheets torn into twos, drifting about in the hot, gusty breeze. Alfred looked up at me, his eyes filled with the purest hate I think I've ever seen.

Peter and Bianca had already repacked their stuff and she was sitting on one of the cases, like Kathleen Turner in *Romancing the Stone*. If you have a daughter who was at the right age when the film became available on video, you'll know what I mean. Mine watched it at least fifty times. Peter who was hunkered beside Bianca and drawing patterns in the dust beween his knees with a piece of dried grass, looked up at me, squinting against the glare. His face was bruised and there was blood on his shirt.

"They smashed my camera in there," he said, jerking his head back towards the hut. "It's going to look fucking funny on my insurance claim when I say the police did it."

I pushed the few things I had about a bit, found Danny's letter. I desperately wanted to see if it contained anything that might harm her, assuming the car crash had not left her beyond any further possible harm, or compromise me, but I sensed George would not take to me holding things up while I gave it a read through.

We went back inside. I handed it across the top of the cheap, scuffed desk and Komen took it. He actually pulled out a pair of glasses to read it. The frames NHS, circa mid-eighties? Could be. He read it, placed it on the desk top and smoothed it out, head on one side, as if it were a prized possession. Then he looked up.

"You can go now," he said.

"Can I have the letter back?"

"No." He grinned, and there was a hint of sarcastic cruelty in it. "The value... sentimental?"

That really pissed me off, partly I suppose because there was truth in it, and I suppose I must have let it show because he was laughing as I went through the door.

Baseball cap was there, leaning against the counter, talking to the local sergeant. He half-turned as I went through and I saw him clearly for the first time. Yes, it was him. NYPD machine-stitched above the peak which was bent into the short tunnel wearers of these hats affect these days. Leather jacket, pocked skin, yellow teeth, but he'd changed his t-shirt – no longer GAP, it now claimed to be Calvin Klein, the big cK tight across a well built chest, pecs and six pack, but I bet his breath still stank.

We hoisted ourselves back into the mini-bus. Alfred and Doris remained totally silent for the half hour it still took us to get to the Lake Navaisha Country Club, staring stonily in front of them. They were in shock, frightened, and, in Alfred's case, angry. Bianca and Peter gave me blank, almost expressionless glances, which, at least in her case at any rate, seemed to carry a hint of sympathy mixed with the bewilderment that was clearly their main response to what had happened. Sami was the worst. I caught his eyes, bloodshot above bruised and cut cheek-bones, in the rear-view mirror. They were sullen, pained. What did I do? they seemed to say. But it was the silence that was the worst. Not a word for half an hour. Clearly they all blamed me, the interloper, the johnny-come-lately, the guy who hadn't made a proper booking and had been dragged off for personal questioning, for what had happened.

We took a right turn, sign-posted to Hell's Gate National Park. Perhaps the name prompted Pete to speak.

"Well, you know," he said at last, and leaned in front of Bianca so he could speak to me across her, "you hear stories like ours. But you never think

they're going to happen to you," and he smiled
wanly at me. "Not your fault, I'm sure."

"They said my sketches showed I was a spy,"
Alfred said. "Damned bloody fools."

"Language, Alfred, language," muttered Doris
and then she began to weep, silently. It was as if
Alfred's lapse was the last crumb of a world that
had turned into a crumbled cookie.

Which capped the train of thought my still
singing, buzzing, dancing head had been trying to
follow.

In Nairobi I'd been mugged. By the police. Unless
there were two identical guys in the story, both with
NYPD caps. Not, if the guide-books and popular
wisdom were right, an entirely noteworthy thing to
happen to one. And then I'd been rescued by them
and taken to be 'interviewed' by Commander
Komen. Who had been more interested in who I
was and what I was doing in Kenya than in tracking
down my muggers. So why had I been mugged?
Simply so he could have the opportunity of asking
me these questions while I was in a fragile state?
Possibly. But why had he been interested in me in
the first place? Well, I could think of only one reason. Because I had been seen talking to Holly,
Ludwig Holly, in the departure lounge at Mombasa,
and had sat with him on the plane. Which meant
they were very interested in Holly, and very interested in any contact he made, had had him under
surveillance, even then. And that was as far as I got.
Big deal. For here was the Country Club, by the

lakeside, with the usual polished reception area, immaculate lawns beyond, established shrubberies, water sprinklers going, tropical flowers everywhere, muzak of a particularly soothing nature, hot towels like you get club class on a plane and drinks – five star civilisation. Doris burst into noisy tears again, and I wasn't far off myself.

The rooms were in cabins, chalets, whatever the right term is, set in a wide semicircle round a marvellously green and manicured lawn with trees and shrubs. On one side there was the main building, public rooms, bar, restaurant, even a billiard room with a full-size table, on the other, three or four minutes walk away across the lawn, the lake itself, a big expanse of calm pewter coloured water fringed with rocks, trees, and the distant hills. It was quite big, the furthest shore ten miles away, and, this time, fresh water.

I sat in my chalet for half an hour or so, feeling bruised, hurt, lonely. I wished I'd never come. I wished I'd never met Danny. I wished I knew what to do about her. Then I heard voices, looked out and saw the family with the youth and younger girl heading towards the lake, and four or five others as well. Quickly I checked the itinerary Judy had given me at the Samburu Lodge and found what I'd half remembered, that an optional and recommended extra here was an evening boat-trip on the lake. What the hell, I thought, pulled on a sweater since I'd taken off my jacket, and followed them.

Well, the family were OK, gave me sympathetic sort of half grins, budged up, made a place for me on what I think must be called a thwart, though I couldn't be sure about that: although I've lived on the south coast of England for most of my life I never joined the yellow-welly brigade. No, I'm wrong. A thwart of course goes athwart the boat and this was a seat on the side. My reception from the rest was not so cordial. A lean grey tall sort of a bloke, with a halo of white fluffy hair round his bald dome and glasses – there with his wife, who looked like an ostrich, and a couple of teenage daughters whose accents suggested the snobbier north London fee-paying day schools – made a joke, except he wasn't joking.

"Abandon ship while we can," he said. "Here comes Jonah."

So, in the forty minutes or so since we'd got there the story had got round the group of our adventure on the way. How much more? Did they know that the crashed car at Lake Nakuru was my 'girl-friend's'? Whatever, they certainly suspected or feared I was trouble.

Couldn't fault the boat-trip. The first excitement was a group of lithe naked men a hundred yards or so away, casting nets, and I mean naked. The young girl, from what I have called the family, I suppose she was about sixteen, picked them out with binoculars, went bright red, and handed them to her brother.

"They've got nothing on," she said.

The north London girls went into paroxysms of the 'Hey let me have a look,' and 'Can you really see their dongers?' variety.

We rounded a headland and there in a pine tree was the nest of a pair of African fish-eagles, white heads and breasts, red scapulars and tummies. There were plovers and pelicans too, moorhens and kingfishers. And what of course excited everyone most, apart from the fishermen's dongers, were the hippos, families of them, a colony, huge double-bar-relled snouts and ears above the water, backs like rounded mudbanks, puffing and snorting if we got too near. Well, you know, it all took my mind off things.

Not for long. I walked back from the tiny jetty across the lawn, dodged the swinging sprinkled water, rainbowing in the last shafts of sunlight against the dark spreading cedars, heading for my chalet, thinking to change back into my jacket for supper, when I realised there was a light on inside, a table-lamp, that I was pretty sure I had not turned on at all before. The window was curtained with lacy cotton, and the circle of light was all I could make out until I crossed the small verandah and pushed the sliding door open.

He was sitting in the armchair. At his elbow, on the glass-topped table a tumbler, and a half bottle of The Macallan. Leo Vincey.

"Hi," he said.

Chapter Fourteen

"Snifter? I think there's a second glass. But of course you don't, do you? Oesophageal varices. Nasty. Very." And he took a slurp.

I looked down at him. I was conscious that my blood pressure had gone up, blood thumping in my ears.

"Would you mind telling me what you're doing here? And how you got in?"

"I wouldn't mind at all. Why don't you pull up the other chair, and I'll tell you? Do you mind if I smoke? I don't often, but it's been a stressful day, what with one thing and another. The answer to your second question is that you didn't lock your door properly. I imagine you're pretty stressed too."

I fetched the ashtray off the dressing table, pulled in the other chair, sat on it. He clicked open a slim gold case and offered it across. I could see the Dunhill crest above the filters, all neatly laid out in a line like soldiers, facing the right way. I hesitated but turned it down. Even when I did smoke, I kept off Virginian. Instant sore throat as far as I was concerned. Slim rectangular gold lighter, old-fashioned, liquid fuel. The smell of both lighter and, to me, harsh tobacco, made me feel sick.

"First," he said, blowing out a thin stream of blueish smoke, "you know about Danny, don't you?"

A cold fist gripped my innards.

"What about her?"

"After she left you she drove into the Aberdares where she photographed the third of the research stations AFI has in Kenya. She then headed for Nairobi, stopping to phone us, Ludwig and me, on the way. But by then she suspected that she had been spotted and was being followed, so she headed in the opposite direction, heading for Nakuru. When she got there she phoned us again. She hoped to hole up in one of the lodges near the lake. By now it was almost night. She was ambushed, her car was shot up, crashed, we're not sure what happened to her, but we think she's dead. You're not taking this well. But I thought you knew it all already. You saw the car…"

"But not her body. I hoped…"

"I'm sorry." He leant forward, flicked ash. "I thought you knew. If it helps, we don't know where her body is. Until we do…" he shrugged, "there's hope."

"I really am sorry," he repeated. He ran his fingers through the golden curls above his forehead, reached for his glass again. He was wearing a linen jacket, just creased enough to make you feel at home with him, over an open white shirt revealing quite a lot of hairless but ruddily bronzed chest. God, but he looked fit… and rich. A combination that usually gets up my snout and did this time. Call it the politics of envy if you like, but you don't get like that without grinding the faces of a few at least of the poor.

"Now it's you we have to think of."

"What do you mean?"

"The police have been giving you a hard time, haven't they? Well, believe me, it could get worse."

I got up from the chair and stood with my back to the window.

"I do think," I said, "I really do think it's about time you filled me in, gave me the whole picture."

And then damn it, something in what he'd said, something about my whole situation, whatever it was, got to me and I realised I didn't like standing with my back to a window, not one that looked out onto a lawn and shrubberies that were now dark apart from pools of light from the globe lamps that were dotted about the place and had been turned on. I moved so I was against the wall by the dressing table. And, damn it again, he smirked ever so slightly as if he knew exactly what had gone through my head.

"Of course. You're very right. It is about time."

He re-angled himself, leant forward, wrists on his knees, looked up at me, took a pull on his Dunhill, let smoke out through his nostrils as well as his mouth, cleared his throat, and began.

"Ludwig is a scientist, specialising in genetic modification of mycota, not a thing he necessarily approves of, indeed much of his recent work has been devoted to studying the possible bad effects. As of now he is on a sabbatical from MIT, where he normally works, to Jomo Kenyatta University. A couple of months ago the department he is working with, indeed setting up, was approached by a landowner down on the coast who grows hemp for fibre, canvas, oil and so on and whose crop, more than a thousand acres worth, had withered and died for no apparent reason. Ludwig flew down there and found the plants had been attacked by a mycoherbicide which was both extremely virulant and appeared to be hemp-specific –"

"Mycoherbicide?"

"A fungus that kills plants. He returned to Nairobi, examined the genetic structure of the spores and concluded that not only had they been genetically engineered to be pathogenic to hemp, they were the same as those already being produced by laboratories in America, to be used by drug agencies, the DEA and others, to eradicate hemp crops grown for cannabis. The hemp-farmer's land borders an AFI research station. There was a small plantation of hemp on it which was healthy…"

"But…" I could see what was coming, "but this is not what he expected. He would expect their plantation to be filled with dead or dying plants."

He nodded, appreciating I was up to speed. More or less.

"You'd think so. But he approached AFI and they told him that what they were actually doing was creating a strain of hemp, with low cannabis content and high in fibre, which would resist the anti-cannabis fusarium. The seed will be patented thus ensuring AFI a good profit on the whole shennanigans, but the genuine hemp growers will benefit too. All well and good. But at this point, and I am talking about eight weeks ago, a bit more, he, we, were approached by Danielle's firm. They had heard, on whatever grapevines they plug in to, that AFI was conducting secret experiments with genetically modified or engineered plants and fungi, including fusarium and not just on hemp. They are also developing mycota strains that will attack tea and coffee plantations, while at the same time developing teas and coffees that will resist them. By indiscriminate use of the former and patenting the latter, they plan to get a hold on the whole global tea and coffee market. Did you know more money changes hands buying and selling coffee than any other commodity? And of course, one of the global leaders in coffee wholesale and retail is bidding for a slice of the action. That's by the way. Knowing Ludwig's reputation in this area, Danny's lot were wondering if he could help them. Ludwig was interested all right. Danny flew up here a couple of times and we arranged that she should come with us on a tour of AFI research stations in Kenya, and see for herself what we had so far found. It was at this point that things took a more sinister turn."

Vincey stubbed out his Dunhill, stood up, moved across to the window and looked out over the darkened lawns.

"They say the hippos come up at night and crop the grass," he said, and then turned back to me. "She had planned to come with a colleague, a man. Two nights before they were due to leave he was mugged. He took a knife between his ribs which put him in hospital…"

"Danny told me…"

Vincey looked up very sharply, eyes grey like year-old ice.

I left it in the air, what Danny had told me. That this colleague had been the victim of a hit and run accident.

"Never mind," I ended up. "Go on."

He held the look for a moment then leaned across his body to pick up his glass. That exposed his wrist. Yes, he was wearing a heavy gold chain. You'd expect that, wouldn't you? He downed what was left and refilled with a couple of fingers or so.

"Sure you'd rather not? OK. Where were we? Yes. Danny's chum in intensive care. She rang us and asked to postpone the trip. I took the call. Meanwhile Ludwig was returning from his latest jaunt to the coast and he ran into you at Mombasa airport. We told Danny. You know the rest."

"I was a lousy minder."

"But a damn good courier, and that's what she really wanted."

I thought about it. Got up, went to the bathroom, poured myself a glass of Kilimanjaro water the management had left there, came back, sat down again facing him.

"There's still a hell of a lot I don't know, a hell of a lot I don't understand."

He raised an eyebrow.

"Well, for a start, what are you doing here?" I

blundered on. "Why have you come here? Indeed, who are you?"

"That is indeed the nub. The fact of the matter is we have put you, largely unwittingly, in very serious danger and we think we have a responsibility to get you out in one piece. You are a private investigator…"

"Enquiry agent." I like people to get this right, otherwise they take me for some sort of sleazy gumshoe. I hardly noticed that he was ignoring my questions.

"Enquiry agent," he conceded. "You have been seen in the company of people, us, who are investigating experimental plantations where genetically modified mycoherbicides are being tested possibly with illegal intent, certainly controversially. They probably think you know a hell of a lot more about it than you do. Certainly they believe you were instrumental in getting the photographs Danny took out of the country. Add all this up and you must see that you are in danger. In danger, not to put too fine a point on it, of being rubbed out. Wasted. Killed. Clipped. Like Danny."

I struggled to appear unfazed.

"And you too," I chipped in, "and Holly."

"Not to the same extent. Ludwig is a well-known figure, much respected, a possible Nobel laureate. He is an alumnus and prominent teacher in the most noted academic establishment in the world. No doubt they think they have ways of coping with him, but murder is not one of them. As for me, well, I can look after myself. But you..."

"I am a sleazy gumshoe from a town no one outside Britain has heard of, and no one would bother much if a hippo or an elephant trod on me."

"Precisely."

He was reaching for the cigarette case again.

"I think perhaps I will try one."

"Be my guest."

The lighter flared beneath my nostrils. I gagged, stubbed the thing out, after one throat-rasping drag.

"Sorry," I mumbled. "OK. So what are you proposing?"

He straightened his back, leant forward again so his face was close to mine and I got almost as much of his cancer stick smoke as if I had after all kept the one he had given me. He dropped the drawl, became brisk.

"We have to get you out. And not by any normal route. Stick with the safari and they'll know where you'll be all the way. They'll be able to pick you off at will."

His voice dropped. Almost as if he were afraid of being overheard.

"Tomorrow the safari you are on goes into the Masai Mara National Reserve. You'll arrive at the Keekorok Lodge shortly after noon and you'll be taken on a game drive in the evening. Between the two there will be time to book yourself on to the advertised balloon flight which takes place at dawn the next day. The balloon, which holds about twelve passengers, takes off ten minutes or so before sunrise. The flight lasts about forty minutes. The balloon then lands. You have breakfast, during which your normal safari vehicles arrive to take you back to the lodge. While everything is being loaded up you will hide in a nearby thicket, possibly, if necessary, announcing a peremptory call of nature as your reason for going there. However, if anyone does ask you why you are not boarding a vehicle you say you have arranged to be taken back on a different one that hasn't arrived yet. The balloon will have taken you at least three miles or so in the right direction. That's the way the wind always blows at dawn at this time of year."

He peered through the lazy spiral of smoke, searching my eyes out. I noticed his were a little bloodshot and the skin around them more lined than I had thought. That air of youthfulness was something he was holding on to. He was older than I had thought.

"The lodge is just ten kilometres, less than six miles, from the Tanzanian border. The balloon will drop you anything between two and four miles nearer. When all the vehicles have gone we want you to slip away and head south until you come to the Mara river. You follow the north bank going east until you reach an ancient crossing point where there are still big boulders that serve as easily negotiated stepping stones. Continuing in the same direction you will eventually come to the road. The border is now less than a mile further south and there is a small Tanzanian post. The Kenyan post is further back at the road bridge, which is in Kenya. We have arranged that the Tanzanian officer in charge will take immediate care of you and see you on your way by bus to Mwanza on the southern coast of Lake Victoria. You get a plane from there to Dar-es-Salaam, and so back to Blightie."

"A four mile walk. An hour at least. I'm bound to be seen. Isn't it illegal to wander about without a guide? And dangerous?"

"Certainly not illegal. Camping is allowed in the reserve, people, admittedly for the most part back-packers and the like, do far crazier things. There is so much game the predators hardly ever attack humans. Elephant or water buffalo with young are the most likely to go for you, but only if they take it into their heads you're a threat."

"Snakes?"

"Most species are very shy and will avoid you before you see them."

I leant back, fidgeted. I can't say I was at all ready at that point even to contemplate going walkabout in safari land.

"And you?"

"I'll hang about until tomorrow morning and then I'll be off."

"Why don't you take me over the border?"

"In my little Cessna? I don't think so. If I flew across, the Tanzanians would probably scramble their Migs and knock me out of the sky."

He flicked a switch on voice control and turned grumpy.

"Look," he went on, "we, Ludwig and I, put all this together as soon as we heard your message on his answer-phone. At two o'clock this afternoon. We thought it was urgent enough to warrant my flying here. We've gone to a hell of a lot of trouble organising this, so don't come coy about it, right? If you do, you'll end up like poor Danny. That's the bottom line."

You're lying, I thought. But I felt sick with worry, no, fear and indecision. Vincey got up and took a stroll round the room, pausing to peer out at the lawns and the moths that were fluttering over a nearby white hibiscus. I'd decided I'd had enough way back when Tomen was supervising the brute who thumped me. Like I said, two beatings and I'm out of it.

"OK," I said at last. "I'll give it a shot. But the moment any of the fauna show signs of hostility, I'm going back."

"Good chap. Your best interests at heart. Believe me. Right." He stood up, patted his pockets the way you do when you think money or a credit card might be needed. "Let's have a bite together, then there's a reasonable billiard table here, the real thing. Do you play?"

"Snooker."

"We'll have a couple of frames. Best of three? What do you say? Take your mind off poor Danny, eh?"

* * *

We were very closely matched, and were one all after two games with both going to the last black. In the third I notched up a break of thirty odd which left me fifty ahead before an error let him back to the table with three reds left. He cleared the lot taking the three blacks after the reds, then the twenty-six points for clearing the colours in the right order.

"Game, set and match. Close run thing, eh?" he said, racking his cue. "That's... what did we say? Five hundred shillings you owe me."

Now the reason why I play a fair game of snooker is that my dad was, for a time, paid secretary of a posh social club, and I spent a lot of the afternoons of my misspent youth pushing the porcelain around with him between the lunchtime swill and evening opening. But I also learnt, from watching him play with the customers when they couldn't find anyone else to play with, that you don't argue with the punters. Not over a fiver anyway. For you see, I knew, and Vincey damn sure knew too, that his final break actually netted him fifty points, not the fifty-one he was apparently claiming.

After that the two north London girls moved in on the table and began to fool about with the podgy son of a lawyer who lived in Wimbledon, the one who told me off for not haggling with the Samburu. He seemed to think the girls ought to rate him in spite of the long floppy shorts he wore over very hairy legs. I shook hands with Vincey, whose hand was hot and damp now, and went to bed.

I lay on my back and thought about Danny. I couldn't believe, didn't want to believe, she'd walked into my life and then been snatched from it.

Blood, the 9mm cartridge case, her slipper. I felt alternately horribly upset and frightened.

It's only the funk I was in that can explain why I agreed to go along with this barmy plan for getting me out of Kenya. OK, I know, guys who walk the mean streets in fairy stories don't get spooked that easily, but this was no fairy story and I had been beaten up twice, apparently been close to some shooting on the slopes of Mt Kenya, and had seen the wrecked car. All in all it did seem a good idea to take the opportunity to dip out.

Chapter Fifteen

There was no sign of Vincey in the morning. I assumed he had been up with the lark and a little later soaring with it, flying back to Nairobi in his 'little Cessna'. However, I was not alone at breakfast. First the Wimbledon lawyer, carrying his own coffee cup from his family's table came over and, with a "May I?" parked himself in the empty chair on the other side of my small table.

"I gather you were questioned by the police yesterday."

"That's right."

"And they roughed you up and the others in your mini-bus, including the driver."

"Yes." I pushed a piece of tomato and cheese omelette the chef at the buffet had cooked for me round the plate and on to my fork. Sort of nonchalant, you know? An occasional run-in with the local fuzz all par for the course.

"Well the others, Doris, Alfred especially, and Peter with his photographic equipment, are looking for some sort of compensation."

"Not from me, I hope?"

"Noo-o!" With a not quite committed shrug, he slurped coffee, pushed his body sort of sideways on, and put his elbow on the table. He was wearing a white shirt with long buttoned sleeves, navy voluminous shorts like his son's. He had a round darkish face and very black thick eyebrows, pepper and salt hair with a wave in it. He took off half moon gold framed specs, gave them a polish on the unused napkin, put them back on.

"But it would help," he added, "any claim they choose to make if they know just why the police wanted to speak to you."

"I think that's my business, really, don't you?"

"Of course. Up to a point. But their insurance companies will want to–"

"And it's certainly not yours."

"My business?" He turned back to me, glasses flashing. "The Cobleighs know what I do for a living and they have asked me for advice."

"What are you charging them? Hundred quid an hour? That would be about right wouldn't it?"

He gave me a long, slow, burning, God-forgive-you sort of a look, picked up his cup and trundled back to his brood.

Next in the queue was Peter. His face was still puffy with the beginnings of a moderate shiner. He came over to me on his way back from the buffet, with a glass of freshly squeezed in his hand, as if it had just occurred to him that a chat with the jail-bird might be fun.

"Everything all right, Chris?" was his opening shot as he took the chair the lawyer had vacated .

"Of course, Pete. Why should it not be?"

"Everything sorted then?" And since I didn't answer, he went on: "Like with the local old Bill."

"Look, I'm sorry about your camera, film and stuff –"

"Yes, well, I was pissed off about it for a bit, but the tour rep says he'll sort out a document for the insurance and meanwhile the others have agreed to send us prints of the best of their lot when they're processed, and Jack Mayer is lending me a spare SLR he has, so it's no big deal. I must say everyone's been most sympathetic."

Not to me, they haven't, I thought.

"But anyway, that's not really why I dropped by."

I waited.

"I'll not beat about the bush. The Cobleighs, you know, Alf and Doris… well, they've actually asked me, and I wouldn't have worn it, but Bianca said I should, they've…"

It dawned.

"They don't want me in the mini-bus".

"That's about it." He grinned, now the worst was over. "In case there's a repetition. Can't blame them really. In fact Doris wanted the tour operator to ship them back to Nairobi right away. She was in shock. Understandable. And I can see you you understand, so that's all right."

And he was off, back to Bianca, before I could ask him which mini-bus I would be in.

As I walked back through reception the tour rep or whatever, not Judie, they didn't travel with us but at each lodge there was a new one, buttonholed me and explained that a second group had caught up with us the evening before and there was an all male bus I could travel with for the three days that were left. An hour later I was in it, rolling down the Rift Valley on the last outward leg of the tour.

They were as weird a bunch as you could meet. Four blokes. All from Stoke on Trent as far as I could gather. They consisted of an oldish man in his sixties, with his nephew and two of his nephew's friends, all in their late teens. The older man, Uncle George, had come into some money, possibly, from the way he talked about it, a lump-sum payout from life insurance, that sort of thing, and was treating the rest. He was pale, overweight, got out of breath far too easily. I put him down as a retired youth leader, scout-master, or maybe a Sally Army colonel or whatever, a working-class do-gooder. At least two of the young ones had done time, or anyway had been held on remand for some months, but they seemed simple, even retarded, rather than naughty.

They tried to talk to me but their minds seemed to wander after a sentence or two. They plied me with peppermints and Werther's Originals. They had a bottomless bag or two filled with stuff they'd bought from England: baked beans they ate cold from the tins, crisps, Cheddars, Hula-Hoops. They drank bright green or crimson sodas from small plastic bottles with screw-caps. And they sang. A mixture of Robbie Williams ("We know his Mam, y'know? She used to live oop our street!") like 'Rock DJ', and 'Let Me Entertain You', and, worst of all, 'Angels', football anthems, and – led by Uncle George

– old camp-fire chants with nonsense choruses of the "Wally, wally, boom, boom, bonk" sort, even 'We're Sailing Along on the Crest of a Wave', for Christ's sake. It was like a travelling Ralph Reader Gang Show. George touched them a lot: a hand on a bare thigh here, a pat on the cheek there, so you began to wonder…

"Lodda niggers in this part of the world, eh, Uncle George?"

"Where they come from, innit, Uncle George."

"Get stuffed, wanker. Niggers come from what's that island called? Jamaicy."

"And Brum."

"Yeah. Lodda niggers come from Brum. Pakis too."

Uncle George looked at me with a sad twinkle in his eye and murmured: "They're like good lads, really. Wouldn't hurt an 'air on yer 'ed."

Well, I do try not to be a snob, I really do, but honestly, I preferred their company to that of the lawyers and professors, let alone Doris and Alf, though I have to admit I missed Bianca.

It was a magnificent drive, especially early on when we crossed the western wall of the Rift Valley with truly wonderful views, then dropped slowly through hills to the Masai Mara. A lot of wheat grown up on the high ground, being harvested by combines but with lines of women bent double over the stubble, gleaning what the machines had left. Danny would have had something to say about that, I reckoned.

Danny... Oh, shit! As we dropped to the plain there were signs of drought too, the acacia forest, more parkland than what you or I would call forest, with trees dotted about quite sparsely, looked dried up with almost leafless branches above dusty, yellow grass. After a time it petered out in vast featureless spaces that shimmered with mirages. Occasionally men in red wrap-arounds, clutching spears like the Samburu, herded white and skewbald cattle across the flats, stirring up white dust devils in the hot wind. The animals looked listless, their ribs deeply corrugated, and they moved as if they'd given up hope of ever finding more than a scant mouthful every twenty yards or so. Yet the most extraordinary sight on the way were two huge dishes on an east-west axis, one facing north the other south, so they covered the heavens above them, reducing space to two quarters of an orange. Satellite tracking? The Evil Empire watching its frontiers? Although they were set a mile back on the west side of the road they dominated the landscape.

We by-passed the town of Narok, no more trees now, just tussocky grass and ochre dust, a flock of goats which might explain why the trees had gone, and a couple of ostriches. But we were still heading down into the plains and the land greened up a little, especially close to water-courses marked by snaking lines of bush and greener grass. There were gazelles too, Thompson's and Grant's, and small villages of round huts made from mud and branches, behind impenetrable thorn hedges, and many more herds of cattle with their red-clad herders. Jimmy, our driver, much like Sami but not quite so substantial, announced that we could pay about a fiver each to see a Maasai village. They'll dance for you, he said, show you inside their huts, you can take photographs, they don't mind.

He pulled off the road and parked in a wide flat space in front of a thick wall of chopped down thorn bushes. We were welcomed by a tall character in full regalia, wearing a high hat made of tawny fur. He clutched a spear as tall as himself, hung with the tails of various beasts.

"He is allowed to wear the hat because he has single-handed killed a lion. The hat is made from its skin."

This drew cries of admiration from most of the lads, who clicked away with their instamatics.

Uncle George clasped his hand.

"Respect, man!" he cried.

We were shown inside an impenetrably dark hut made from a cow-dung loam over wattle. There were cots made from hurdles to sleep in, and a low fire: it stank of smoke and dried cow-shit. The eyes of one of the lads adapted to the dark quicker than others and he claimed the floor was crawling with cockroaches. I got out. I can't stand the buggers.

Outside about thirty people, mostly women and children, did a dance for us, much like the one I had seen at Samburu, and two of the men demonstrated with dextrous efficiency how they lit fires by spinning a stick in a socket, and that was about it. Apart from the opportunity to buy necklaces and bracelets made from beads and twisted copper and wire stripped from old car engines.

The lads declared themselves well impressed but Uncle George took a more cynical view.

"Rip-off," he announced. "It's treating them like animals in a zoo."

But his charges were already moving on and thinking of the next item on the agenda.

"I want my dinner," his nephew cried.

"You could have had it there," one of his friends suggested. "You know what they do? They puncture their cows' necks wiv an arrer, bleed'm off into a jug, smack some mud on the hole in the poor bleeder's neck, mix the blood with some milk, and then when it's thickened up a bit, they eat it."

"That is disgusting."

Minutes later we went through another gateway. Guards checked us in, in a routine, bored sort of way and we were in the Masai Mara National Reserve, the high-spot of the trip, at last. But in spite of the name Maasai warriors no longer herd their cattle over these plains, as they had for centuries – they belong now to the animals, the birds and the tourists. The Maasai, apart from those who work in the lodges, are excluded.

The lads were not that happy about the game drive out of Keekorok Lodge that evening. It started all right when a zebra crossed the track in front of us to a chorus of "Zebra crossing, geddit?"; they were amused by a couple of secretary birds strutting their stuff in the long grasses; they sang 'We Are Your Friends to the Bitter End' from the *Jungle Book*, when they saw three vultures and a nest in the flat top of one of those trees, and they duly gasped when we skirted an enormous herd of wildebeest which was yet just a fraction of the migration that had just started. It began to go wrong for them though when a couple of male lions padded across the track in front of us and one of them squatted and let loose a huge viscous puddle of black shit.

"Too much blood," Jimmy grunted, "he's drunk too much blood."

It got worse when we came upon a lionness literally eviscerating the carcase of a wildebeest whose torn guts revealed a dung-like mixture of the grass or whatever it had been cropping. Then she went for an eyeball, which she seemed particularly to enjoy. But it didn't get really bad until Jimmy's radio screamed, whistled and gabbled and with the one word "Cheetahs!" on his lips he took the van – remember: no four wheel drive or improved suspension – off the track, up over hillocks, across dried river courses and up a rise to the top of a down.

There were at least ten mini-buses there before us, parked untidily in a loose semi-circle across the top of the hill which was like an inverted saucer with a couple of shrubby trees crowning it. More vehicles arrived behind us. There were four cheetahs under the trees, magnificently nonchalant, holding court, accepting our homage. Occasionally one would give another a lick, occasionally they yawned. Cameras clicked and whirred, a susurration of whispered talk hung like a miasma over the raised roofs of the vans. From the mini-bus parked next door I heard Bianca's voice, saw her leaning forward under the raised roof, blonde hair held back in a pony tail by the back of her baseball cap.

"Their faces, they're so strange! Like a clown's make-up with black tears running down their cheeks."

Then up came her 'nocs. No sign of Alf or Doris, she and Pete now seemed to be sharing Sami's van with the family with late adolescent children. The girl was one-eyed with a camcorder, dad and mum also had their 'nocs up, so they looked like insects with protuberant black chitinous eyes.

Then it happened. One of the cheetahs, as it rolled on to its front and stood, slowly lowered its long low-slung belly close to the ground, and with neck stretched out, ears flattened, pointed, began to edge forward.

"She's seen something, she's hunting." This was the mother of the family. "Just like Winny when she's seen a bird on the lawn."

It was not difficult to guess that Winny was the pet cat they had left at home. Here her distant cousins slowly, almost languidly, pulled themselves on to their feet or haunches. They turned towards the very young kid, a Thompson's gazelle that had wandered into the arena formed by the safari vehicles. Like all Tommies she was chestnut above, white underneath with a broad black brush-stroke along her lower flank separating the chestnut from the white, and a black tail. I doubt she was more than eighteen inches at her shoulder but with her neck and elegantly curved black horns adding another foot. She tripped on ebony hooves further into the circle we had made, looked around for a moment, clearly puzzled, a touch lost, and uttered a short high double noted bleat.

"Mum-mee?"

The cheetahs edged closer, their bellies stretched oh-so-closely to the ground, their necks thrust forward, their ears flattened, the strength of their concentration making a force field around them. This, I thought, could be *Bambi* with an H for horror-rated unhappy ending.

And so it turned out.

The cheetahs were a team. One drew a semicircle behind the kid, padding noiselessly on the soft leather of its paws, head angled across the line it made, eyes now focused like lasers; the second completed the circle in front of her, but more slowly, long belly slipping over the grass almost like a python, thighs coiled ready to strike or launch her into a fifty mile an hour dash. The third inched forward towards the centre of the trap their movements had made. The fourth kept her distance, patrolling the outer perimeter: either to cut off a final break for safety should the kid get past the others, or, more probably, keeping a look out for other predators, hyenas or lions, that might dare to take their prey off them. The whispering died away. Engines were turned off. Even most of the cameras fell silent. Then suddenly gazelle was off, like an arrow from a bow, obliquely away from the cheetah in front of her.

Almost she broke the circle but the one behind leapt forward to cut her off, one swung paw smacked her on the rump and sent her tumbling awkwardly across the slope. Twisting and turning she got her rear hooves under her, was up and off again, but straight into the leader who slapped her across the neck and sent her rolling again. This time as she came up she bleated again, higher, more frantic: "MA-MA!".

They made her the centre of a three pointed star with each of them at the extremities, five yards off, and there they waited, rib cages inflating, deflating, long tails, each bobbed with a white powder puff behind the last black ring, swaying briskly behind them.

It went on for five, nearly ten minutes. Each time she ran they biffed her and she lay on the ground till they nosed or prodded her up again and coaxed her into another rush. The lads around me were shocked, angry.

"Christ, they're fucking playing with her!"

"Bastard sadists!"

"Hey, Jimmy, start your motor up and get at them, stop it, fucking cruel it is!"

She made a dash for it, almost got through and

this time the blow she took across the joint in her right back leg broke it. She twisted away, trailing the useless limb, dragging herself forward on her front legs and, up against a four by four luxury Land Rover from another tour, not ours, seemed to fall forward. This was it, I thought, but no, she'd seen the space, it was just big enough, neck stretched, horns lying along it, nose questing into the darkness beneath, she dragged herself under.

"Jesus, she's got away with it!"

"Not with a broken leg she hasn't."

"Well, drive'm off, get her to a vet or sumfin."

From the mini-bus next door I heard the lad comment to his mother: "If that was Winny you'd have got out by now and given her a good slap."

The cheetahs circled the Rover, heads down, tails thrashing, momentarily frustrated, then one of them, hugging the floor, squeezed most of her long lithe body into the darkness under, got a set of claws into the buttock of the trailing leg and awkwardly, bum and tail in the air, backed out. A quick scuffle between the four of them with snarling wicked teeth exposed, before the three waiting let her wrench off the leg and carry it five yards off. Then they fell to butchering the rest.

Uncle George's nephew was quietly sick over the side of our mini-bus. On the other side the professor, or whatever, the guy who had called me a Jonah the day before, was launching into an aesthetic appreciation of the event.

"That was worth the whole trip," he was saying

to his mute family, the North London Collegiate. "What immortal hand or eye could frame thy fearful symmetry? What art could twist the sinews of thy heart? But did you see the teamwork, how they worked together? Wonderful! Wonderful! What I'm sure you all noticed, what made the deepest impression on me…"

But we never learnt what it was, for his high braying voice was drowned in the surging rumble and rasp of motors starting up, while the black exhaust fumes drifted across the four cats as they munched their way through their supper.

Chapter Sixteen

I should have bought my ticket for the balloon ride before the game drive and, as we motored back to the lodge, I was more glad than sorry that I hadn't. What I had seen of the Masai Mara had done nothing to encourage me to think I could go walkabout without ending up as lunch for some monstrous cat. The place was seething with animals, preyed on and predators, nature red in tooth and claw, every cliché you can think of, including the Rector of Stiffkey. But when we got back into reception he was still there: Mr Balloon Man taking bookings behind his desk.

"Mr Shovelin?" he asked, as I approached, and that he knew my name should have told me something. "I've got just the two places left, and I guess you'll want one of them."

He was American, possibly Canadian, had a nose like a hawk's beak, sandy hair, skin freckled and red with exposure to the sun, and possibly the bottle, wore a cowboy hat, checked shirt, jeans and calf-high boots.

"I want you on the site by six, we leave you behind if you're not there, turn left as you leave the lodge, climb the hill past the trees, you can get a coffee down here at a quarter before. Make sure you go wee-wee, and don't have the runs. Once you're on board you stay on board unless you got wings. One hundred and seventy of your pounds, Visa's fine."

Shit, I thought. Somehow I'm just going to have to get this trip allowable as expenses and get some of it back. And how do I get up at that hour without an alarm-clock – this time there was no telephone in the room. But the concierge or whatever said he routinely sent a boy around for the ballooners at five o'clock, he'd put me on the list.

It went off OK. Five o'clock in the morning in the Masai Mara was as black and even as chilly as it is anywhere. I got up, wondered what I should take. I could hardly take my hold-all on a forty minute balloon ride. In the end I found a an ASDA shopping bag I'd used for my swimming things, emptied them out, and put in instead a small Keekorok Lodge towel, my shaving things, the Lodge freebie toiletries, spare reading specs, the guide book, the bird book, my second complete change of clothing, and Danny's slipper. Don't ask me why the last – I couldn't begin to explain. All in all it just about emptied my freebie hold-all, which I wasn't sorry to leave behind. Stupidly I did not include water or anything to eat. Too heavy I told myself but probably because in my heart of hearts I was pretty sure that I was not going to go through with it.

Nevertheless, one side of me was pretty determined. The one feather that tipped the scales was the feeling that I did not think I could stand the company of the wankers I was sharing the trip with for yet another twenty-four hours. On the one side, the Stoke on Trent side as it were, there was affect but almost total ignorance; on the other, the very well-heeled side, knowledge but no affect. Oh yes, they knew a lot about the corrupt government, the appalling poverty, the onslaught of AIDS, the internationals' organised brigandage, and, rather seriously nodding their heads, they would argue, and indeed I had heard them do so, that perhaps the best way they could help the Kenyans was by going on holidays like this one. But did they *care*? Fuck, no. I pulled my hat on, at least I was not so stupid as to think of going walkies in the sun without it, and pulled my door to. Shit. I've locked the key inside. OK. That's it. I'm really going for it.

Blearily we had coffee and went wee-wee, three couples I didn't know, the English family and me, and followed each other, as if someone amongst us knew where we were going, up the hill as instructed. We were soon guided by the roar of a gas-fired flame thrower, the incandescent orange of the flames, headlights from a lorry and a couple of four by fours, and the sight of the slowly filling red and yellow striped envelope they call a balloon. At first it was like a giant condom in festive colours, flopping about, then, as tumescence swelled. it rose and rocked and finally took on the shape of a mango standing proud above the basket. Somewhat to my consternation this was exactly what the label said: a big wicker cube divided into compartments, the walls about three and a half feet high. No doors.

"Why no doors?" asked the English lady,

hoicking herself in with minimal aid from the Captain.

"At five hundred feet you'll know," he said. "Doors can open. You'll be glad there are no doors."

He directed us to different compartments, like eggs in an egg-box, carefully putting the heaviest of us on the corners, and introduced us to his wife.

"Spare place this morning so the little lady has come along too."

Not that little, and wearing a folksy scarf over dark hair with wisps of silver in it, an embroidered waistcoat over a black shirt and a folksy skirt. Large hoop earrings. You only had to look at her to guess she could be bad news.

A smaller flame thrower in the middle of the basket took over from the big one; ropes were cast off, sand bags dropped; and to a variety of screams of delight, panic, and cheers we got lift off. Almost immediately, as we cleared the crowns of the nearby trees, we all fell silent. There was no noise except for a quiet sighing in the rigging as the great plain slowly spread its vastness beneath us. Its rolling downs flattened, the big hills in the distance stood out bold and black, behind them the sky shifted from a deep aquamarine to a blush to a moment of gold and then here he came, the Sun-God himself, a sliver, a half disc, a blinding light and day flooded across everything, not like a tide but more a sudden spill, giving form and substance to what had been indistinct, throwing purple shadows that seemed to shorten even as we watched. The few wraiths of mist that had snaked through gullies evaporated, and a heap of cumuli nimbus above the distant escarpment that formed the horizon opposite the sun went from stony grey to eye-piercing white in moments. And it all began to seethe, like a turned over ant-hill, with wildebeest, antelope, giraffes, elephants and quite close beneath us a pair of loping hyena.

"Oh boy, Mrs Antelope had better keep an eye on her kiddies if she doesn't want them to end up as breakfast to that pair of meanies..." Yes, it was Mrs Balloon Man. Well, Mr had her measure, but the cure was almost as bad as the disease, for he cut her off by giving the flame thrower a blast. This not only lifted us up and away but made a noise like the steam engines of my childhood when they let off steam. Still, though it didn't stop the inane chatter of Mrs, it did render her inaudible. In short between them they did not do a lot for the magical near silence that had been wrapped round our first moments in the air. And so it went on.

"So many beasties, you'd think Noah's Ark was just round the corner..." Whooooosh!

"How do all the gnus know where to go? Because Old Mr Wildebeest has done it lots of times already and they do what he says..." Whooooosh!

I heard the English Dad mutter: "If she doesn't shut up, I'll want my money back." Fair enough. Presumably he'd paid out for four... nearly seven hundred quid!

Landing was one aspect of the whole experience

that Mr Balloon Man had not gone into. When it happened you realised why not. Nobody would buy a ticket if they knew. He had us dropping towards a slight incline facing us. The bottom of the basket bumped, then acted as a break as the balloon, pulled by the slight breeze, rushed on up the slope, so of course the basket tipped on to its side and we were dragged for many bone-shaking yards while the actual ground came nearer and nearer our heads until finally the basket was grounded on its beam ends and we were all stacked as if in pigeonholes above it. Getting out was not easy – indeed, if you were in the mood for it, it was a laugh. For a terrible moment I thought my hat was under the basket, but no, Mr Balloon Man found it, dusted it off and smacked it down on my head. And over the crest of the hill came the four by fours with trailers for the balloon, a trestle table, and breakfast: coffee from flasks, croissants and rolls, fruit, and… champagne.

And there was a thicket nearby, filling a shallow gully, which Mr Balloon Man announced would do if we couldn't wait until our buses arrived to take us back. Did he give me a look as he said this? Did he even half bat one eyelid as he said it? I don't know.

Three mini-buses turned up. The English family's was the last. By then I was deep in the bushes, with my trousers authentically round my ankles as a sort of alibi should they come looking for me, and defi- nitely letting I dare not wait upon I would. Like the poor cat i' the adage. You're being a bloody fool. Just stick with these people and nothing will happen to you. No? What about being mugged in Nairobi? Hauled out of the safari vehicle and given a good thumping by Commander Komen's henchman? And maybe others will get hurt, as they were before, when they come for you. Remember Sami getting a crack across his face with a riot stick. Pete smashed in the stomach. Poor Alf chasing his torn up sketches through the dust. Remember the gazelle kid crying for its mum as the cheetahs circled. Take the chance. Get away, get out of it while you can. You're nothing but trouble.

"That man Mr Shovelin, where is he?" the girl asked.

"I'm pretty sure he went in the first bus," said her dad.

The sliding door clanged shut and they were gone. I pulled up my trousers.

I set off, walking towards the sun, over the rise through savannah grasses with occasional bushes. Crickets rose around me, looking like the bi-planes that bother King Kong in the old movie. There were big conical ant-hills dotted about, and, at that time of day lots of birds: a violet-chested roller with its swallow tail, some green sunbirds, and a small group of guinea fowl scuttling away from me. A pair of large buzzards or small eagles – without my 'nocs I couldn't decide which – soared at a great height against the blue of the sky. The air was still and hot. Near to you could hear and then forget you were hearing the rustle, chirp and buzz of insects,

and from far away, very far away, the sound of a
vehicle and the hum of a generator. I crossed the
visual ridge. Ahead the ground undulated towards
higher hills a few miles off, behind and much further away, hardly more than a line on the horizon, a
much bigger escarpment marked out in violet and
blue the limit of the rolling plain. The heavy clouds
we had seen from the balloon were gathering above
the nearer hills. About five miles off a huge herd of
wildebeest was scattered like a winding trail of
grains of black dust across a long wide slope, there
must have been a thousand of them at least, and no
doubt the lions and cheetahs were scouting for the
calves and weaker ones on the peripheries, but I
couldn't see them at that distance. A bit nearer, in a
winding shallow valley, I could just make out three
giraffe heads, poking about in the green foliage that
marked a water-course. I felt not only alone, but
alien, an interloper. And worse than that when I
tripped on the oyster grey, friable skull of a wildebeest.

I also felt insecure and when I came on a track
made by the repeated passing of safari vehicles I
decided to follow it. Perhaps I still hoped one would
come along and pick me up. Left or right? South,
anyway.

South. Where was south? I glanced at my watch.
Seven minutes to eight. I stood up straight, turned
slowly round on my heels. My shadow was not
long, even as early as this, but clearly fell to one side
and not the other. At midday the sun shines from

the south. Every boy-scout knows that and at that dreadful prep school I had been a scout. When it's not midday you point the twelve on your watch at the sun and bisect the angle between it and the hour hand, and that's south. The track ran more or less on a north-south line. I did the coarse geometry and set off, more confidently than before.

Fine dust rose in puffs around my feet and an occasional stone skittered away. The track I was on bifurcated, and I quickly saw that both prongs joined another, which made the base of the triangle on whose apex I was standing. About three hundred yards away there was a simple telegraph pole with maybe two wires on it, and then I became aware of a moving cloud of dust half a mile away. I stood and watched as a lorry came out of it and sped by with a rattling roar. Clearly the track I was about to join ran parallel to a road. The great clouds over the hills were nearer now and shedding sweeping curtains of rain, but the sun still shone where I was. Once again I checked south.

Chapter Seventeen

I walked. Four miles to the frontier, Vincey had said, and then a bus. Four miles, two hours, tops. All right. I had no food or water – so what: after all this was not the Gobi desert or even the Kalahari. But it was hot, flies became a nuisance. Was I in tsetse fly country? Malarial mosquitos? Remember, as a guy who had had liver disease I was not taking Lariam. The prophylactic I had been on dealt with the coastal variety but not those inland and upland. And what about the botfly which lodges itself in the wildebeest's brain and drives it mad? Talking of wildebeest, a couple of thousand snuck up on me from behind and surged by, a quarter of a mile away I admit, but in such numbers they felt a lot nearer than that, a huge irregular column mooing or bellowing in their creepy melancholic fashion, heads twice the size they should be for their bodies, lumbering hooves they seemed ready to trip over stirring up a low cloud of dust. Suddenly the rearguard took off in an attempt at a stampede which concertinaed against the main body and the bellowing rose in volume.

Why? A couple of spotted tawny brutes with wedge-shaped heads and shoulders too large and too high, were scouting round the peripheries in a fast loping stride. Hyenas. Maybe the pair we had seen from the balloon. Ugh! OK, that's specism. Speciesism. Are hyenas really any more horrible than lions or cheetahs? Yes. They have ugly faces, a dirty laugh, and they scavenge. But when they kill they often, apparently, give up on eating the prey once it is dead, preferring the living flesh. And at a very impressionable age, at the Odeon, Bournemouth, I saw *The Snows of Kilimanjaro* with that hyena snuffling round the tent in which Gregory Peck's leg is going gangrenous. It had such an effect I can hardly remember Susan Hayward and Ava Gardner in it at all. Whatever. This pair cut out a valetudinarian gnu, or at any rate one that was, for whatever reason, slower on its pins than the others, and after yapping around its heels for a moment or so, went for its haunches and brought it down. The herd, having paid its dues, settled down and continued to file past the munching crunching predators, and ten minutes later were winding across the slope, round a bend, and, apart from their dust, out of sight. No gnus are good gnus.

Now things began to go wrong. I'll rephrase that. Now I began to realise, but only slowly, how things had gone wrong from the start. First of all those clouds came over me like a blanket pulled over my head and the first warm heavy drops on a gust of hot wind splashed about me. I sighted the sun just before it disappeared, found it disconcertingly less on my right than I had expected, took a bearing from it on a distant conical hill with an acacia on the top, and put my head down, and the collar of my cotton jacket up and headed for it even though it meant leaving my track. The dusty ground was pockmarked, then reduced to a splashy sticky skin. Tiny rivulets formed and tumbled past stones and hummocks of grass. Puddles formed and, of course, in moments I was soaked. The brim of my hat flopped over my eyes and ears. Lightning forked and thunder rumbled after, but, thankfully, several seconds away. I kept that hillock in front of me and plodded on. That slightly acrid but not unpleasant smell that comes with such storms filled the air. I used to think it comes from dust suddenly laid by the rain, but no – actually it comes from the nitrogen fixed as nitrates in the water by lightning, and without it no plants would grow. Anywhere. Not many people know that.

You see, after less than an hour, I was already almost exhausted, very wet, miserable, lonely, my plastic bag felt heavier than it should, and my mind was wandering randomly.

I laboured up the slope, which close up was a lot steeper than it had looked from a distance, to the tree on top, and looked down and across the vast, broken, hilly, rainswept plain in front of me. And then caught the eye of one of the three young male lions that were sheltering amongst an outcrop of rocks just below the summit.

Oh Christ, I thought, I do hope you've had your breakfast.

"Don't turn away," a voice murmured in my ear. "Above all don't run. Keep your eyes on his eyes. Out-stare him if you can. No, don't look at me."

Oh shit, I thought, this is the hallucination lost exhausted travellers crossing deserts or Antarctica get when they're reaching the end. Some say it's Jesus come to give a helping hand across that bourn from which no traveller returns. Odd, though, that His breath should smell of fried onions. Meanwhile young lion waved his tawny tube of a tail with its black paint-brush end above his back like a panache and growled. I thought. Then he put his bearded chin on his paws, so his eyes now appeared to look up at me, and blinked.

"He's purring," said the voice. "He's saying that for the time being we're the boss."

"Could have fooled me," I replied.

"No, really."

The rain eased. A pool of sunlight drifted across the plain towards us. I looked up. Again the sun was a touch less to my right than I expected. Lion 2, behind Lion 1, heaved himself up on to his feet and gave himself a shake. Tiny drops of water made a momentary rainbow nimbus round his outflung mane. Then he yawned. Lion 3 did likewise, then Lions 2 and 3 turned and lolloped off down the slope. After a pause Lion 1 did likewise but paused after five yards or so, and gave me, us, the last lingering look over his shoulder an overindulged diner might give the pudding trolley before calling for his bill.

Us.

"Hi. Europeans find it virtually impossible to get their tongues round my real name but at Guy's they call me Golly."

Golly. Golliwog. Guy's? Must be Guy's Hospital. Medical students are such wags. I turned round and faced him.

I don't know what I expected: not, I presumed, a white-coated intern with a stethoscope round his neck. What I got was a naked *moran* or Maasai warrior. Naked? You can't call a guy whose long hair is finely braided in hundreds of strands and covered in grease coloured with red ochre, who has tattoos and paint on his body and face, is wearing earrings, collars and bracelets of twisted metal and beads, naked. But he wasn't actually *wearing* anything. His skin was the colour of pale teak and his face and body were those of a youthful Greek god except that he was circumcised. He was carrying a spear in one hand and a small bundle of red cloth in the other.

"And you are…?"

"Christopher," I said, "but I prefer to be called Kit."

"As indeed did the poet and playwright Marlowe." His accent was demotic – not posh but careful. "You were heading north, I think. So am I. Well, north by north-west. Shall we?"

And he gestured with his spear down the slope, the way the lions had gone.

North!?!

Still, I fell in with him. We could argue the toss about north and south later.

"Or perhaps you should return to the Lodge. You really should not have gone so far out into the wild without a guide."

"But now I have you," I replied.

"Yes, but," and he glanced critically at me and at my feet, "I'm heading for my village outside the national park. It's thirty miles away and I expect to be there by nightfall."

Already he had adopted a long loping stride, which even on the wet ground was noiseless. No wonder I hadn't heard his bare feet coming up behind me through the storm. Although it was a sort of walking, I could hardly match the speed with which he covered the ground without running, or at least jogging. With wet clothes and that damned bag. I gave the sun another glance. Still too far to the left, or was that my imagination?

"Your village must be well into the Serengeti," I panted. "In Tanzania. If I can keep up with you, or you slow down enough, we should be at the border quite soon and that's as far as I mean to walk."

He stopped and faced me, head on one side. He was no taller than me. His lean, smooth, youthful body belied the strength he obviously had. He frowned.

"You know," he said, "you're not going in quite the right direction if you want to get to the border."

"I'm not?"

He pointed ahead with his spear.

"That's north." He and his spear swung round

through one hundred and eighty degrees. "And that is south. Tanzania is south of Kenya."

"I know where Tanzania is," I riposted, somewhat testily, and batted away the flies that were homing in now we had stopped moving. "And the sun—"

"The equator. We are in the southern hemisphere."

I gave that some thought.

"Fuck!" I said.

He let out a crow of laughter, saw my irritation, suppressed his mirth, contrived to look concerned.

"Trust a Western European not to take note of the consequences of crossing the equator."

And off he went in that confounded speed walk.

"Please," I called out at his twinkling receding buttocks, "could you go a shade slower?"

He waited for me, then forced himself to go at a more reasonable speed, first handing me the red cloth he was carrying and taking my bag from me. There was a label on one corner of the cloth, which was light-weight woven wool and had a simple sort of tartan pattern. It read Spinners and Weavers Coop, Kenya.

"Actually," I said, "I've crossed the line so many times in the last fortnight I'd forgotten which side I'm on."

Not strictly true, but mildly face-saving. I looked up at the sun again, thought about it: no wonder it kept moving to my left when I was going north. The bastard was going from east to west as usual, of course, but anti-clockwise. I remembered the matches slowly turning in the bucket between Nairobi and Mt Kenya. I remembered Danny.

Presently we saw three mini-buses in convoy rolling along in what I now knew was a southerly direction beneath the line of well-spaced telephone poles. They were still, I would guess, even at their nearest to us, a good eight hundred yards off, with rolling hummocky savannah spotted with bushes and ant-hills between us and them. The sun was out again and it was hot. I could see my clothes steaming if I stood still. Golly stopped, handed me my bag, and held out his hand. I passed over the red cloth. With neat practised movements he wrapped it round his waist, leaving a length which came up over one shoulder. There was a lot of it, eight feet by six.

"Your government started this nonsense," he said, as he went through the process. "Stupid fetishising of nudity. And our own government, once we had one, took it even further. Afraid we'd frighten the tourists if they saw us as nature intended. Or seem uncivilised. Of course we refused to buy clothes but they got round that by handing these out for free, and fining us or sending us to prison if we forget to put them on."

And we all, safari tourists that is, thought the fetching red cloaks or wrap-rounds the Maasai and Samburu wear were part of their tribal gear.

A final tuck, and then he looked at the still damp, steaming earth in front of us.

"Here. Have a look at this."

A squirming but neat runnel across the track.

"Puff adder. Bitis arietans. Must be close by since he was here after the rain."

Suddenly the road seemed a good place to be. The road and a vehicle on wheels. First lions, then snakes. But that's not how it turned out.

Meanwhile...

"Always something new out of Africa," I offered, as we trudged on at a more reasonable pace, "but you are even more of a surprise than most of what I've seen or come across."

"*Ex Africa, semper aliquid novi.* The older Pliny. Again, you are guilty of that so British insularity. I am Maasai. I will shortly qualify as a doctor. Is that so strange?"

"It can't be that usual. I suppose you got some sort of scholarship."

"Not at all. The Maasai lands were held communally until quite recent times. Your lot, who are so hung up on property and ownership of land, did not approve such an anarchic arrangement. Private ownership was handed to the elders of each tribe and clan. My grandfather was one such. He exploited the situation in ways I do not approve and became quite wealthy. Wealthy enough to ensure that I and some of my siblings received good educations in Nairobi. Good enough to get me into Guy's."

"But in the holidays you come back and dress up, or rather down, and pretend to be a Maasai warrior."

He flashed a very angry look at me.

"Certainly not. At the age of fifteen, three years before I went to England, I went through the full initiation ceremony and became a *moran*, a warrior, a herdsman and owner of cattle. Which is what I shall be until I reach my thirties."

"Why?"

"Why not? It is what male Maasai of my age do."

"And, at the same time you will become a doctor and come back to look after your people?"

"Would you, in my situation? No. I shall become a specialist in some branch of consumerist diseases, bowel cancer, say, and either set up in Harley Street or go to America where I will make even more money than I could in Britain."

That crow of a laugh came again, so I remained uncertain as to whether or not he was serious.

"What are you doing so far from your village?" I asked. "You don't seem to be herding your cattle."

"You must surely know that we are not allowed to herd within the confines of the National Park. No. I came to be by the pool at Keekorok. It is a holy place for us. Even though it has been suburbanised by silly walkways. Every time I come back I make a pilgrimage and talk to my ancestors."

"Are they buried there?"

"Only those who died after the Occupation. Before that it was our custom to leave bodies out in the savannah or by a watering pool like the one at Keekorok for the scavengers. The hyenas even dealt with the bones. But I'm afraid your lot could not countenance the exposure of corpses and we were forced to bury them. I am not at all sure that the buried are as fully with us as those that inhabit the animals and birds."

"But they still speak to you?"

He flashed me a coy sort of a smile.

"In a manner of speaking. But mostly they say what I want to hear."

He said all this in a very matter-of-fact sort of a way: there was little or no anger or regret in his voice, that I could detect, that ancient customs had or were disappearing.

A little later we reached the road which was surfaced at this point with ragged edged bitumen. There were shallow broad ditches along each side.

"Something will come along before long. You really do want to go south, to the border? Is that right? In that case we should stand on the other side. I think. Let me see. Let me take a bearing from the sun…"

He was sending me up, taking the piss. We crossed the road and took up our position. We must have looked an odd couple – he elegantly posed against his spear, part of the landscape really in spite of his red covering and privileged education, me bedraggled, damp, grubby, with my bulging ASDA bag and my misshapen hat.

A truck went by but the front bench was filled not just with the driver but three fetching looking girls as well, while the back was crammed with at least six cattle.

As it belted away towards Tanzania, Golly cleared his throat of the fumes it shed behind it.

"And you," he asked. "Your situation is far more strange than mine. I take it you are a tourist. Tourists are not often found trekking across the savannah, albeit in the direction opposite to that which they intend, seeking to walk out of Kenya and into Tanzania. I should like to be assured that I am not assisting you in some criminal or treasonable endeavour."

An even bigger lorry, its deck piled to twelve or fifteen feet at least with crates of Tusker beer, roared towards us. It swayed, no, it waltzed from side to side across the road and I was glad really that it didn't stop. I got the impression that it might not have been able to, even if the driver had wanted it to.

"It is a very long story," I began, "but no, I have not, as far as I know, and certainly not intentionally, been guilty of anything criminal."

His formal, careful way of saying what he wanted to say was infectious.

"I am, however," I continued, "on the run from people whom I take to be criminals. A… person who claims to have my best interests at heart, suggested that I could escape them by crossing the border, where he would arrange for me to be put on a bus to a commercial airfield, from which I could begin my flight back to England."

"Your story, without the corroborative detail I am sure you can supply, has the feel of a cock and a bull about it. However –" he gave an apologetic sort of grunt or cough. "I think it's time I came clean with you. Our meeting was not a coincidence. It was contrived."

But where this was leading remained unrealised, for a four by four, one of the big, luxury sort, was now approaching us but from the south. The windscreen was tinted of course, so it wasn't until it was quite close that I realised who was in it. The driver was in uniform, a uniform like that of the AFI Ranger who had interviewed me on Mt Kenya. The passenger was wearing shades, and a black baseball cap, with, yes, NYPD emblazoned above the peak.

Chapter Eighteen

I turned, picked up my bag, and set off at a brisk canter away from the road and into the savannah. About a mile away two hills, covered with quite thick vegetation, folded themselves in towards a declivity or maybe a valley between them. They appeared to be the nearest cover where a chap might get lost. After a moment's hesitation, Golly followed me. The Jeep, for that is what it was, the new luxury vehicle, not the WW2 maid of all work, pulled in. I did not look back.

"Mr Shovelin! Please come back." The shout was punctuated with the sound of the Jeep door slammed. I didn't look back.

We pounded on. I was aware of Golly behind me but all my attention was on my feet, dodging out-crops of rock, bushes, the larger loose stones.

"You must stop. We will shoot if you do not." Already they seemed more distant, as if they were not actually following us.

Golly's black hand brushed againt my forearm. He was holding his red robe, already partially bundled again. I got the message and took it while he once again grabbed the ASDA bag from me. A pistol cracked some way behind us, but I had no idea where the bullet went. It banged away three more times, and six yards ahead of me and two to the right, something clanged off a lump of rock, chipping it, and whining away ahead of us. You've no idea unless you have experienced it what such a moment can do for your physical prowess. I would imagine I damn near doubled the speed I was running at.

Golly pulled at my arm again and slewed me off to the left down a brief but steep slope, I slipped on the cakey, wet earth and did the last four yards on my backside. I was at the bottom of a shallow, winding water-course, filled with greenish but well-cropped bushes, and occasional small trees. I looked around for Golly and for a moment felt a desperate spasm of fear: I couldn't see him, had he been hit? And then there he was, body twisted away from me, above me, looking out round another rock. I started to scramble up towards him, but, without looking, he flapped a palm at me, clearly waving me back. I sat down a yard or so below the soles of his feet.

"They've stopped following us," he said, speaking softly. "They've gone back to their vehicle. The one in the black cap has lit a cigarette but is still looking in our direction. The other one is speaking into what I presume is a radio microphone. Now, he has joined the one who is smoking and both are leaning against the vehicle, looking out in this direction."

I got my breathing under some sort of control and managed to ask: "How far off?"

At last he looked round, and said, as if to an idiot: "As far as we ran."

"How far was that?"

"Three hundred yards or so. Well beyond effectively accurate range of his pistol. I take it you don't want to reconsider and give yourself up?"

"No."

"Then we had better get a move on."

He slid more gracefully than I had down the short slope to the bottom of the river-course, picked up ASDA which had preceded him, and we set off, moving more or less west from the road, though the riverbed twisted and looped. Its floor shifted from smooth boulders rolling up out of patches of coarse grass and dried up rushes to patches of gravel, and was overhung by a variety of trees, not just the flat-topped acacias and thorn bushes of the savannah above us, but bottle-shaped baobobs and lower shrubs I lacked the knowledge to identify. As we progressed we came across small pools and even places where a tiny rivulet had formed, trickling down a crevice in the high banks before disappearing in a patch of dark sand. There were insects of course, even a dragon-fly or two and butterflies, and small birds that flitted and darted from bush to bush ahead of us. The only animals we saw in the first half hour or so were a family of warthogs nosing up roots until we got near enough to frighten them: they scurried off into the undergrowth with their tails up like pennons. Golly said the larger fauna were resting up in the shadier places and most would stay like that until late afternoon. Which was a relief. There was no sign of any more rain: a disappointment for Golly. The 'long' rains, he told me, should have set in, brief storms like the one that had overtaken us were not enough.

And of course as we walked, I wanted to know just why he had been saying that our meeting had been 'contrived'.

"We have mutual friends," he began. "They felt you were in danger. They asked me to find you at Keekorok and take you to a safe area where your enemies would not find you. I suppose I was just in time." He pulled a switch of green leaves from a bush and used it as a fly-whisk as he went on. "That tale about getting you across the border seemed to me, right from when you described it, a ruse to get you into a situation where you could be killed with impunity. They only had to wait until you were in a suitable place to knock you on the head and leave you for the hyenas. Or push you in the river for the crocs. Or –"

"Never mind. I get the picture." I was dying to ask who these mutual friends could be.

"But their plan was foiled by your solar mistake –"

"Heading north instead of south."

"And when you didn't show they came looking for you." He stopped, looked up at the already almost cloudless sky, cocked his ear. The beat of a helicopter's rotor. He pulled me down and into the shade of a baobab tree growing between two boulders. The chopper soon came into view, apparently following the river bed. Small, a blister right at the front and a long boom at the back, much like the dragon-flies we had seen earlier. I'd like to show off and say it was a Sikorsky or something, but really I have no idea what make it was. It was brightly painted though, in a vivid green and a gold sort of a yellow like the one I had seen hovering over the Aberdare AFI research station. Golly shaded his eyes as it flew over our heads. He waited until its clatter had receded somewhat.

"If it's you he's looking for us, then you really are in serious doo-doo," he murmured. "It's as well I found you."

Since it was only forty minutes or so since we had been shot at with intent to kill, I wondered what could possibly be worse.

"They must have radioed for it," he went on. "I imagine, to have got here so quickly, it came from Narok. Or maybe even from Keekorok. There's a strip a couple of miles from the lodge. Look out. He's coming back."

Much lower this time, low enough for the rotors to stir the tops of the taller trees.

"Can they see us?"

"Not if we stay in the shade. Problem is they know we can't have got much further than this, and they can be pretty sure they'd see us if we were up on the veldt. So they know we're down here some-where. Hide your face. It shows up more than mine."

He was right. And not just because he was black. The painted slashes and whorls on his face had the

effect, in the dappled shade, of disruptive pattern
camouflage. Indeed the damn thing was creeping
along above the riverbed towards us so slowly I had
time to wonder just how far the face-painting might
be functional rather than ceremonial. Nevertheless
either their vision was very good or assisted, for see
us they did, or anyway enough to make them think
that that was where we were. The brute, no longer
looking that small, slowly circled the top of our
small tree. The racket was now deafening and had
we wanted to talk we would have had to shout.
Dust and leaves thrashed around us as if we were in
the centre of a whirlwind. Even though it was only
the one undersized chopper it felt like *Apocalypse
Now* with Dolby Surround. And of course my fucking hat, almost dry again, blew off, whirled away
like the one in Jeff Wall's *Sudden Gust of Wind*, and
maybe they saw it. Anyway they now saw enough
of something to know that was where we were,
under the baobab tree.

The fuckers opened a hatch or something and
dropped a hand grenade. It plummeted down so
fast we hardly had time to think what it was: it hit
the lip of the river bank above us, bounced, and in
mid-air blew up. Some casing whistled over us but
none hit.

"All mouth and no trousers," said Golly, and
stood up. Bullets shredded the air and the leaves
above him. He dropped his spear and sat down
again, right hand gripping his upper left arm. Dark
blood oozed quite quickly through his fingers. I

wanted to shout at him: Go, piss off, get out of here, this is nothing to do with you. The chopper took another slow turn round the tree and this time a canister, about eighteen inches long, a baton slowly turning on its centre, dropped about twenty yards away and immediately began to spew purple smoke, smoke and noxious gas: instant sore eyes, and nausea. It filled the little valley around us, and in the still heat lay close to the ground. We had to get out of it. But up river, down river, back up on to the plain? Spluttering and with Golly still clutching his bleeding arm, we were already, almost without thinking, three-quarters of the way up the bank.

He gestured upwards with his head, then cocked it on one side. I caught his drift. There was silence, apart from the hiss of the gas canister below us. Then I caught the much quieter and changed note of the helicopter's motor. It was turning over more slowly, ticking over, and was some way off. It had landed.

Golly clambered a bit higher, then slipped and landed on his side. He swore, at least I think he did. It wasn't English this time. He'd slipped because he couldn't use his hands to climb with.

"You've got to bind that up," I said. And without waiting unravelled the red robe I was still clutching, put one end on the ground, stood on it, selected a point on the edge and made a huge effort to rip off a length. I really had to put a lot of concentrated effort into it, but it went in the end, leaving me a bandage in my hand, a full six feet long. I looked round. He'd

gone again. No, he was lying along the lip amongst
stones and with a bush or two near his head. He
looked down, over his shoulder.

"They've landed about four hundred paces away.
Down river. On the edge of that patch of forest on
the hill-side above the valley. Three are getting out.
That's as many as it'll hold. They're not your
friends. They are in some sort of uniform. Yellowish.
Could be AFI Rangers, their own private army."

By then I was up with him. Both of us were still
spluttering and retching from the fumes we had left
behind us.

"Here. Let me bind your arm."

"OK. If you know what you're doing."

He took his right hand away revealing a furrow
a couple of inches long, running across the outer
side of his upper left arm. It was filled with dark
blood that now spilled out of it as the pressure he
had been applying was removed, although it was
already thickening where it had run down his
arm.

I bunched up a section of the strip of light-weight
wool over the wound and began to wind the rest
round it.

"There's far too much," he muttered, and put
the edge between his teeth and yanked with his
good hand. The tear ran the wrong way, and it was
a moment or two before we managed to do what
he wanted. He took the end out of my hand and
began to complete the binding. But I remembered
some Boy Scout First Aid, and took it back from

him, shredded the end into two, knotted it to prevent it spreading further down, took one end against the direction we had been winding and knotted the two strands together on the other side. With a reef knot of course. And then tucked the ends in.

"Oh, very professional! Now I think we had better see what they're up to."

The three had fanned out so there was a good ten metres between them and were moving away from the chopper towards us. They were carrying what looked like light-weight carbines across their chests. They were not being particularly cautious; why should they be? All we had between us was a spear. And that was still on the floor of the little valley below us. But they didn't seem in any great hurry either.

"What do we do now?" I asked.

"I'm really not sure. Wait until they get within range and throw stones at them? If they were coming from the other side we could get into the woodland. They'd never find us then. Not without dogs."

"They knew what they were doing then when they landed where they did."

"Maybe."

The heat bent the moisture-laden air they were walking through and for a moment they seemed blurred, darker, and looked as if they were walking on water. I wondered about that 'maybe', then saw what Golly had probably been aware of well before I was. Beyond the helicopter, coming down the hill, picking their way through the forest perimeter of scattered trees, two very large, enormously tusked elephants. Their ears slowly wafted like sails trimmed by master mariners to catch a fitful breeze, their huge jointed legs plodded lightly through the grass and undergrowth. They came out onto the plain and their stride quickened. The rangers, if that is what they were, still had not heard them and were now barely two hundred paces from us. They stopped, called to each other, the middle one shaded his eyes, pointed not at us but at a point some fifty yards to our right. His companion on that side raised his carbine and firing from somewhere between his hip and chest, loosed off a short burst in that direction. An ostrich that had been keeping a low profile, with its head down if not actually in the sand, unfolded its long legs, loped out of the grass and rocks and was instantly shredded in a cloud of blood and black plumy feathers. We could hear their laughter.

Behind them the elephants broke into a swaying, lumbering trot. The leader went past the parked chopper, and stood facing us and the backs of the rangers, whose ears were no doubt ringing with the shots they had just fired, so the first thing they actually heard was the slow rending crash as the second elephant, with its huge anvil shaped forehead against the side of the helicopter's cabin, with its back legs bent to give it a better purchase, slowly tipped the whole thing over. For a second it was poised halfway on one of the rotor's blades, then that buckled and the grinding became a drawn out splintering crunch.

They heard that all right.

Chapter Nineteen

"Why did the elephants attack the helicopter?"

"Poachers. They used choppers to herd the elephants to where the guns were. Elephants have long memories. More than that. Some say they can pass on acquired knowledge from generation to generation." He sensed my scepticism. "OK, I know. But there have been some pretty strange occurrences, not easily explained any other way."

We were stumbling on, along the same watercourse, and had been for what seemed like several hours. It had gone through a deep, narrow stage, almost a gorge if not a canyon, then as the forested hills parted and sank away behind us, broadened out to meander across a plain much like the one we had left. For a time we were parallel to another road with occasional traffic on it, but Golly didn't like this and steered us off in a southerly direction round the north east side of one of the largest hills in the area. He had his spear again and to begin with walked well, so again I had a problem keeping up, even though he still insisted on carrying my bag. Oh, yes, and in case you're worrying, before we set off Golly found my hat for me, almost straight away. With the sky clear, and the sun getting lower in it behind us, my brains would have fried without it. But after three hours or so the effects of the gunshot wound were clearly beginning to weaken him, whether from infection or loss of blood I couldn't say. Whatever, he sweated a lot, grunted every now and then, and was clearly using his spear as a support. I insisted on taking ASDA and the mere fact that he let me have my way said a lot. We were, he said, heading for one of the first Maasai villages outside the perimeter of the reserve. Not his own village, but one where he was known.

We didn't talk much although a twister of questions whirled in my head. Eventually I had to ask.

"These friends," I asked. "Who are they?"

"Need to know," he said slyly. "You'll meet them tomorrow."

It was hot, flies were a bother especially when there was water about and the river became just that, shallow, wide with occasional pools. As the day lengthened and the shadows with it we saw most of the more common of the animals: zebra, giraffe, waterbuck, gazelles, antelope, lions and so on. And once another extended family of elephants. But none of them came any nearer and indeed strayed away almost imperceptibly if we appeared to be approaching them. No cheetahs though, or hyenas, which was a relief though Golly may have seen a lot more of everything than I did.

We plodded on. I complained of thirst. Golly stopped, looked around him, tapped his perfect teeth with his thumbnail.

"Hang on for half an hour," he said. We had left

the river bed but now he angled our course back towards another. After twenty minutes we were in it. It was as dry as a bone, dry as the not infrequent animal skulls, mostly wildebeests', that littered the plain. I felt despair. My tongue seemed swollen, the inside of my mouth felt like cardboard, I had a splitting headache and my joints ached. The sweat running down my cheeks had never tasted so salty.

"Not long," Golly murmured, when I stumbled on a loose stone and he caught my elbow.

And of course he was right. The first thing we saw was a clump of reeds, bright green, then we heard the trickle of water. It was a tiny clear spring creating a small pool about ten feet across and only a few inches deep which never seemed quite to fill up and flow over. The upcoming water barely stirred its surface, looked like a sort of shifting swelling near the middle. The area around was broken up by hundreds of footprints, one or two of them the bare feet of humans.

"Spoon it up in your hands as close to the source as you can. It's quite pure there."

I splashed in and did as he suggested. There was a slightly metallic tang to the water, like rust, and indeed it carried a trace of russet colour. I noticed now that the pool's damp edges were coated with a deposit of the same reddish hue.

"Don't you want any?" I asked.

"I can wait."

We stumbled back out of the river bed and resumed our march across the plain. It was not a desert, not even semi-desert, just drought-ridden, waiting for rain that had, in this particular part of the reserve, failed for a year or so.

"Are you hungry?"

"Yes."

"I can find you edible grubs to eat."

"I can wait."

Towards sunset we approached the lower slopes of the quite substantial hill that had been a dominant feature of the horizon for most of the day, higher than any of the other rises we had passed between. The sun behind us lit it with a golden glow and threw deep purple shadows from its ridges and outcrops. You could see that it was volcanic in origin, the now eroded extinct crater tilted towards us so the further rim was above the nearer semi-circle. For a time it so filled our view I thought Golly was going to lead us high over the shoulder, just below the crater, but then quite suddenly, and long before our course would have taken us anywhere near the crest, we were going down and the plain opened out again ahead.

It was not the same as the one we had left on the other side of the hill. For a start it was much lower, in fact it was probably the western side of the Rift. Here the grass was not greener, quite the opposite. In fact there wasn't any, or very little. Although it still had its undulations and was criss-crossed with winding watercourses and even ravines, there was almost no vegetation. Dust devils formed, caught gold fire from the last of the sun, and sank away;

two small herds of skeletal cattle drifted towards a black circle of thorn enclosing saucer-shaped roofs only a mile or so in front of us, black kites wheeled lazily on motionless wings above it, and a couple of thin wisps of blueish smoke climbed towards them. We were leaving the Reserve. A white thread of road, straight as a ruled line, arrowed north east from the village into the lilac-coloured haze.

"This really is desert," I said, as we slithered down a scree of pumice-like stones.

"It is now. Fifteen years ago much of it was grass land and forest." Golly's voice was harsh now, the sentences came with long pauses between them. "Then came the wheat. Bulldozers to root out the trees. Huge ploughs, huge harvesters. Canadian dollars for my grandfather. Nairobi, London and Guy's for me. Three good years, prairie farming as far as you can see, then the harvests got smaller and smaller. Without animals, without our herds or the natural fauna, the surface broke up, the soil was denatured in spite of artificial fertilisers. Eight years ago they gave up. The year I was initiated as moran. Some agronomists reckon it'll take forty more years for the land to recover. If it ever does. Not easy to reverse the onset of desert."

We were welcomed by a couple of scrawny dogs who barked and snarled but did not actually bite, then by half a dozen or so children using the last rays of the sun to play football just outside the gate in the thorn wall. They were barefoot, most in torn shorts, though one had a faded Man United

Beckham shirt. They were thin, but not, as far as I could see, famine-thin. Their ball, which was not as inflated as it should have been, carried the Coca-Cola logo. They broke off their game and three of them crowded round Golly, one taking his hand, another carrying his spear. It may not have been his village but he was certainly known there.

There were some points of correspondence between this village and the one I had visited with Uncle George and his nephews, but not many. From outside the huts looked much the same apart from one with a corrugated roof, built out of shaped mud and dung adobe bricks that had been whitewashed. Its one room served as municipal office, community centre, school-house, and guest room for visitors. And there were three broken-down vehicles – a mini-bus, a Morris Oxford, and a very large Massey-Ferguson tractor with huge flat smooth tyres and a patch of oil beneath it, four wrecked bicycles, and a Chevvy pick-up which was functional. There was a well with a wind pump, but the water table had dropped and, so Golly said, was yielding no more than fifty litres a day for sixty people and about as many head of cattle.

More than these it was the ambience, the atmosphere that was different. This village was bedraggled, used, over-lived-in, yielded too many signs of make-do and mend, mostly with the broken cast-offs of twentieth century industry. There were plastic bottles, scraps of cardboard and polystyrene, old but factory made spades and hoes, the left-overs of government attempts to turn nomadic herdsmen into sons and daughters of Cain. Later I commented on all this to Golly, who laughed at my naivety.

"You didn't think the tourist village was real, did you? No one lives there. They turn up each morning, leave each evening. It's a nine-to-five job."

But before that we were taken to the schoolhouse where Golly was made to sit on the thin mattress of an old bed with a cast-iron frame while his wound was cleaned and bandaged by a thin old man with a straggly white beard. He was one of the few there who wore something like traditional dress, beads, bracelets and so forth, though the four moran who shortly came in having corralled the cattle were got up in much the same way as Golly. Although this old man seemed to be some sort of shaman or witch-doctor, the techniques he used were those of the first world. He had antiseptic ointments, butterfly plasters to pull the edges of the wound together, and he would have given Golly an anti-tetanus jab if Golly hadn't insisted that he'd had the inoculation a year ago in England. His medicine chest was a stout cardboard box labelled Médecins sans Frontières.

"He'd use medicinal herbs if there were any. They all went under the plough," Golly commented.

Next came supper. I'll draw a veil over that apart from telling you that it included just edible tortilla-like pancakes made, I think, from maize flour taken from an Oxfam sack and a cloggy, claggy concoction, brick red in colour, which tasted both yoghurty and metallic. It was only after I had got a couple of mouthfuls down that I realised this was probably what Uncle George's nephew had reckoned is the standard fare of the Maasai – coagulated cow blood mixed with milk and left to thicken. It seemed particularly attractive to flies. We ate outside the school-house, surrounded by four of the elders, with a small fire in front of us and the light from a hissing paraffin pressure lamp. Outside the circle women and children were faces rendered in shifting chiaroscuro by the flames and the harsh light of the lamp. The boy with the Beckham shirt asked me why Man United had failed to win the Premiership. I couldn't say, which surprised him.

I made the mistake of commenting to Golly that this must all be a falling off from the fully tribal days, with decent food, dances, beer, mead and so forth.

"Bollocks, my dear Kit. First, you must remember that all that tribal kitsch seems very romantic and exciting to Europeans, but it was as commonplace to us as an evening in the pub or in front of the telly are to you. And believe me I've had a better time in the Mass at Brixton than I ever had in a tribal knees-up." He was riding a hobby-horse, I could tell. "Lot of rubbish talked and written about the dying away of ancient tribal ways and wisdom. Of course it causes pain and dislocation while it happens, but it's a stage we have to get ourselves through. Believe me, the misery of the English poor for, say, the fifty or so years between 1800 and 1850, as they moved from farming to factory work, was as bad or worse than anything but the unluckiest of us have to put up with –"

"AIDS?"

"Cholera."

"Come on, Golly. Why, if you believe all that, do you go wandering about the savannah in that gear?"

He laughed again.

"I'm Maasai," he said. "You've seen us, you know what we're like. We're poseurs, vain, fancy ourselves. Dandies. Wide boys of the veldt, even. And it's a human trait to be a *laudator temporis acti* is it not? Think of your Morris dancers, your re-enactors of ancient battles, your Disgusted of Tunbridge Wells, your Bewildered of Buxton. Think of the old men who claim it was a better life down the pit or riveting plates in a ship-yard than doing telephone sales or driving a truck. I know they're all pretty horrible jobs but I know which I'd choose to do. And, incidentally, as a doctor I rate penicillin ointment above herbal infusions or poultices made from cobwebs." He touched his arm as he said this.

"And your people are better off now than their grandparents were?"

"There's a lot bad now. But it comes from civil wars to the north, AIDS, corrupt and often brutal officials, and above all the ruthless greed of global corporations, not from the break-down of tribal life. All we need is a good dose of old-fashioned, from the bottom up, workerist socialism, and we'll be living like pigs in shit."

Fat chance of that happening, I thought.

He leant towards me.

"You'd better get some sleep now. They'll still be looking for you. First light we get you out of here and on your way back to Nairobi. Then if you've got any sense you'll be on the first plane back to Blightie. But first, I've got something for you. The chief man here said it was left here for you earlier today, after I had left."

He unfolded his long thin heron-like legs and the flames played over the smooth ebony muscles and shiny shins as his height took his face beyond the light. He was back in a moment or two, annoyingly holding his right hand behind his back.

"Guess what," he said.

"Come on, Golly, don't be silly."

Like a conjurer who knows smooth confidence is more impressive than a showy flourish he brought his spread palm out in front of my face. On it, lying across it so his extended index finger supported the toe, the heel of it on the heel of his hand, a small, black, slip-on shoe. I took it and he melted away into the darkness before I could even begin to put words to the questions that fluttered around the cave of my head like a storm of disturbed bats.

I didn't really need to check it against the one in the bottom of ASDA, but I chucked a sheet of cardboard on the embers of the fire and got enough light. It was a match all right.

* * *

Did this mean Danny was alive and well and living in the next village down that long straight road?

Was it a coincidence that this slipper had turned up or been left in the same village I had fetched up in?

And so on. You get the idea. I tossed and turned on that twangy bed, and eventually, in pitch darkness got off it again, thinking I might look for him. The doorway was a square of lightness in the perfect blank of that small square hot room. I stood in it for a moment, hoping my eyes would adjust to the dark, and slowly they did. There was no moon as yet, but above me in the huge perfect hemisphere of the sky massed constellations swung in unfamiliar patterns around the swathe of stars and galaxies that make up the Milky Way. It wasn't long before I could make out the humped silhouettes of the village in a circle around me. There was not a glimmer from them. The air was not cold, crisp rather than cold, and again I caught that smell of Africa, of dried dung, dead fires, and animals. Slowly I became aware of noises. The scuttle of small mammals or large insects, the chirp-chirp of a cricket, the scuffle of a shifted hoof, the whimper of a sleeping child, the distant call of an owl.

"Golly?" I called, pitching it high but not loud.

I waited, then driven by desperation let go at the top of my voice.

"GOLLEEEE!"

For a second or two I swear even the insects shut up. Then I felt the heat rise up the back of my neck as I asked myself: What will they all be thinking? Has the European done his nut? What should we do about it? And I shambled, groping, back to the bed.

And of course, came the dawn and he wasn't there. He'd gone. He'd left a verbal message which the shaman, whatever, passed on to me over a breakfast of charcoal burnt tortilla and a chipped cup of coffee. There was a small town, anyway a larger village, twenty miles away, from which I could catch a bus to Nairobi, or if I was lucky I might even bum a lift in a plane from the airstrip that was there. A guy called Elisha would take me in the pick-up and I should give him two thousand Kenyan shillings for the fare. That was it. Seemed steep, but I was in no position to argue or bargain.

Meanwhile, I was a wreck. The huge hike of the day before had left every joint in my body aching, my muscles, especially in my calves and hamstrings stiff as well as painful, and a huge heavy weight of tiredness on my shoulders. I was filthy. What was worse, I felt filthy. My head itched, my eyes were gummed up, my teeth and tongue coated, my armpits and groin felt sticky, and I stank. I rummaged listlessly through my bag, but everything in it had already been worn, there was nothing fresh at all, and a heavy damp, musty smell came off it. There seemed no point in putting on clothes slightly less noisome than the ones I had walked and slept in unless I could have a bath or at any rate a good wash first. I thought of asking for water but remembered what Golly had said about the inadequacy of the well. They probably grudged the half cup of coffee.

I stuffed it all back but paused over the slippers. I laid them out together in the patch of bright sunlight that lay like a cloth across the dusty concrete floor. OK, I was very tired, dispirited, confused, and in a general sort of a way rather frightened. I looked at them and as the cold hollowness filled my chest the tears sprang and tipped down my cheeks. They were as much for me as for her. What could I do? What was I going to do? Had I done enough? What more could I do?

I was on my knees. How had I got there: had I knelt because I wanted to surrender, give in, but had no one to surrender to? At all events it was when I was kneeling above them that I pushed my forearm across my eyes, blinked and sniffed. Snorted. And as my vision cleared I saw that there was a small raised square in the insole in the left hand slipper. People often have an insole in the left shoe if their left foot is slightly smaller than the right. I picked up the slipper, got a thumbnail (my nails needed clipping by now) under the edge of the insole and lifted it. Yes. A second memory card like the one I'd sent to Twickenham. I placed it carefully back beneath the insole but this time further in so the upper covered that slight bump that had given it away. Then I put both slippers back in the bag and sat back on my ankles.

I felt better and I knew why. I had a purpose now, something to do. I'd get back to Blightie and I'd go to Twickenham, and deliver it. If I did nothing else for her, I'd do that. That's what I'll do, I said to myself, and gritting my teeth, pressing my lips together so I wouldn't start blubbing again, I repeated: That's what I'll do.

Chapter Twenty

Elisha was a thin old man with thin stick-like arms and a chicken's wrists. He had high cheekbones, a long straight nose and deepset eyes. If he'd had his full ration of teeth he would have been as handsome as all the Maasai are. He was wearing a polo whose little red polo person claimed Ralph Lauren, the usual red robe wound round his waist below it, and sandals whose soles were probably carved from tyres. He was disappointed to learn I had no cigarettes and from then on terrified me by rolling his own from dog-ends, using both hands while his knees kept the steering wheel steady. We didn't say a lot to each other. Possibly because of the noise: the pick-up had a leaky silencer and every screw or bolt in its body was loose, and though his English was OK, his lack of teeth didn't help.

It took nearly two hours to get to the small town he was taking me to and I realised twenty quid was a good deal. It must have cost him most of that in petrol. After the first straight stretch we climbed back out of the Rift and into the highlands, following the escarpment and then dropped back down. In Europe you would have called the place we arrived at a village, but in Maasai-land villages move every five years or so as the grazing gets tired. Towns have adobe houses, some even made out of breeze blocks, several churches, at least one school, a municipal building, a police station, and a Barclays, even though there may be no more than a thousand or so permanent inhabitants. There was also a street market and the last I saw of Elisha he was leaing over one of the stalls trying on a digital watch with an expandable bracelet. I just hoped he wasn't about to be ripped off.

The town, like most, was on a road junction. At the top of the street market a bitumen surface, made briefly into an avenue, Avenue Moi of course, by a double row of tulip trees, had a sign: Narok, 105 kms; Nairobi 275... or thereabouts. I bought a slice of watermelon for five shillings and strolled slowly down the dirt sidewalk, inside the usual grass verge with its trees, towards one of the few two story buildings. This one was marked out by the Kenyan flag hanging listlessly out in front of it and I reckoned it probably indicated the town centre. I was looking out for any sign that might indicate a bus-stop or even the whereabouts of an air strip.

They saw me before I saw them – four caucasians sitting in plastic chairs, the white ones you see all over the world from English garden centres to San Francisco street cafés, in front of a kiosk selling Coca-Cola. Two of them were elderly, thin, skin tanned to a yellowish leathery look, the man wearing a real Panama with the spine across its crown and a slightly grubby linen suit, and, would you believe it? an RAF tie. I know, not because I'm a PI, but because my dad had one. The woman was in a cloth sun-hat and a printed blue dress with a bold white daisy pattern. The other two were youngish men, complexions a reddish oak, fair hair, tan short-sleeve shirts with combat pockets, shorts and safari boots with thick socks. The elderly man was already standing. His lined face wore an expression half-way between a smile and an apology.

"Mr Shovelin?" he called.

I walked over.

"Yes?" I offered, a touch hesitantly. In the previous forty-eight hours or so total strangers had smacked my head, shot at me, dropped bombs on me… and then there had been Golly. Whose side are you on? was the question uppermost in my mind.

"Edward Fitzmaurice, and this is my wife Dorothy. These are James and David. They are from Australia."

I dropped my melon rind in the dust, wiped my hand on my thigh and let them all shake it in turn. I even remembered my manners and let Dorothy have first go. That was the effect Eddie's accent had on me – he spoke the sort of English I haven't heard since Sir Alec Douglas-Home was Prime Minister. One of the Aussies pulled in a chair and told me that he and his mate were really Jimmie and Dave. A kid came from behind the kiosk removing the top from a Coke bottle for me.

"Miss Newman spoke very highly of you." Mrs Fitzmaurices's voice was louder than I had expected, with an authoritative rasp behind it. Much the way I imagine Wooster's Aunt Agatha spoke. "She asked us to try to get her shoe to you, so you can take it back to England with you. I asked N'Goolilah to make sure you received it. Did he reach you? Miss Newman said you would be found at Keekorok."

'N'Goolilah' is my recollection of what she called Golly, and is probably quite inaccurate. But I knew who she meant. Meanwhile she had racketed on, as if I was fifty yards away and not giving me more than an opportunity to nod an affirmative to her question.

"You are a detective we understand so no doubt you found the memory card she had placed under the insole."

Well, I was glad I had. She would have judged me grossly incompetent if I had not.

"She was confident you will know what to do with it when you get back."

Yes. I'd worked that one out already. Twickenham. Garlenda Drive, a Mr Skiros. Her husband now added his pennyworth.

"Miss Newman was anxious that you should get back to GB as soon as you have the memory card. To that end we have arranged that James and David will take you on the first leg as far as Nairobi."

Jimmy, or Dave, leant back in his chair and, looking across at me, shaded his eyes with his left hand.

"We fly a Beaver aircraft. It's out on the airstrip here. We aim to leave within the hour if that suits you."

"That's fine."

"Cool," said Dave or Jimmy, and took a swig from his Coke bottle.

"James and David," Mrs Fitzmaurice remarked, "are in the transportation business. They are very reasonable. My husband and I have a small coffee plantation up in the hills which we run on traditional lines. Half a dozen times over the last couple of years or so we have had occasion to use their services. So much quicker and more reliable than the larger firms."

Mr Fitzmaurice pulled a wrist-watch from his jacket pocket. It was old, gold, and one of the two halves of its strap had disappeared.

"Time we put our skates on if we are to be home for lunch."

Ice skates or roller skates?

He stood up, leant on a walking stick which had been hanging by its handle from the arm of his chair. I realised he was even older than I had thought. Maybe as much as eighty.

"Glad to have met you. I'm sure you'll do the right thing."

"Hang on a sec!" I was up with him pretty sharply. Indeed my seat might have toppled if Jimmy (or Dave) had not steadied it. "Please tell me about Danny... Miss Newman. Do you know what happened to her? Do you know what all this is about?" I was suddenly aware of my heart pumping while embarrassment at my un-British behaviour fought with the desire to know.

Mrs was up too by now, her hand under her husband's elbow.

"Danielle," she rasped, her voice and manner more auntyish than ever, "was very clear in her instructions. It would be much better, she decided, for all concerned if you know as little as possible about her circumstances. Come, Eddie."

Did that mean she could be alive? Not dead?

Perhaps sensing the question that was trying to force itself out of me, Eddie Fitzmaurice smartly lifted his hat to me. They quickly filtered themselves through a small semi-circle of shyly grinning children which had formed between us and the road and he thrust a fifty shilling note at the oldest.

"That's all I've got, young feller-me-lad. You'll have to share a couple of bottles of pop amongst you."

I sat down again, looked at Jimmy and Dave. Words failed me.

"Shit!" I said.

They shrugged. Presently, carving its way through cyclists and pedestrians and causing a large truck to brake savagely with a roar of its horn, a very ancient faded jade green Ford Prefect went by. Dorothy Fitzmaurice was driving. Edward sat next to her, sunk on the broken springs of his seat so the handle of his stick was under his chin. Once they were out of sight I turned back to Jimmy and Dave.

"Is this going to cost?" I asked. "I've bugger all cash on me. But if there's a cash-machine at the airport…"

"No prob. There's a spare seat. Buy us a tube when we get there, OK?"

"Cool," I said. It seemed to be the right thing to say.

"Might as well push off then. The airstrip's on the edge of town, not more than ten minutes walk. OK?"

"Fine." I didn't risk another 'cool', I didn't want them to think I was taking the piss.

"Anyway, seems you travel light," remarked Jim (let's decide this was Jim), nodding at my ASDA bag.

They stood up, and Dave dropped a handful of notes on the table.

"Show on the road," he said.

I damn near got myself dropped out of the Beaver, which turned out to be a high-wing monoplane with fixed landing gear, and a heavy, fat-looking body. They'd cleared out six of the eight passenger seats at the back to make room for freight, and I was sitting up front behind them, looking over their shoulders. Their equipment was an idiosyncratic mixture of the old and new: for instance, they wore leather helmets with goggles framed in spongy rubber pushed up on their foreheads, but also tiny earphones and stalk mikes, as used by the likes of Madonna. They gave me a set so we could chat easily above the racket of the single bull-nosed engine in front of us.

Anyway, once we were up I popped the potentially offensive question.

"Are you friends of Dorothy..." at which point I

realised what I'd done, so the rest came out rather lamely, "… and Edward. Fitzmaurice."

There was a pause while they assessed the possible but unintended sub-text of my question, then Dave answered.

"Yeah, we know them. Not well, but they did take us up their pad one day for a meal. Leg of Tommy. It had got under their fencing and was browsing the coffee bushes, so Eddie bagged it. Dot fixed it up like it was lamb with redcurrant jelly and sprouts, but it was pretty gamey for lamb."

"OK, though," said Jimmy.

"Oh sure, it was OK. Danny was with us on that trip."

Again that lurch in my diaphragm and the stab of loss. I looked out of the window for a moment. We were crossing the Great Rift Valley from west to east, the great escarpments that lay between us and Nairobi were in front of us, green and rocky, but beneath us the plain looked flat with patches of sparse acacia forest and ruler straight roads. The only life I could see in that short glimpse was what I took to be a herd of zebra, wheeling, shifting and coalescing as something, possibly a lion, disturbed them. They looked like tiny ants, their shapes distorted from above by their own shadows. I turned back to peer over the Ozzies' shoulders.

"You knew Danielle, then?"

"Sure. If we were a regular airline we'd have given her frequent flyer status."

We rumbled on through the sky.

"She used you a lot then?"

"Right on. Often as not we could give her a lift dead cheap, because we were headed the way she wanted to go anyway, but that's not the reason she used us."

"No?" I tried to give the word an enquiring, why-don't-you-carry-on sort of an inflection. They responded to it. Turn and turn about.

"As long as the flight was internal there was no documentation necessary, no evidence she had been where she went. And of course if the ground is flat and any big stones have been cleared, we can get down almost anywhere. And that suited her too."

"She did a lot of looking into aid agency fraud, and that meant getting right into the outback so she could check just what was getting through, and what got hijacked on the way."

"None of that made her best friends with every-body. Once when we were carrying her out of an aid distribution centre where she'd been checking man-ifests against what got to the front-line, we got shot at. We'll show you the patches when we land."

"Yeah, but that was up near the Sudanese border where people shoot at you as a matter of course."

The ground below us seemed to soar up towards us as we left the plain. I could see the main Nairobi road hairpinning up what looked like a vertical face though it supported thick vegetation. It was busy – with big trucks spewing black smoke, safari buses and matatus. I hauled in breath to ask the next ques-tion.

"Do you know what happened to her?"

For a brief moment we passed through a patch of rain cloud – streaming droplets streaked across the cockpit windows and a chill grey shadow filled the cabin.

"Nope!"

"No idea."

It was like closing the lid on a box. Then we were in sunlight again.

Five minutes later the wings above our heads tipped to the right as Dave put us on the bearing that would take us to Nairobi and a loop of webbing, no more than ten inches of it, slipped from a rack above my head. I looked up. Dull blueish dark matt steel. A barrel perforated with regular rows of holes, a simple metal butt made by three struts welded in a triangle, a magazine that stuck out at right angles so it protruded and lay against the roof. And the webbing sling. I had no idea at the time, but I've checked since. Sterling sub machinegun. And, as I've already said, like nearly all weapons of its type, nine millimetre.

"The rack for it was already there." Jimmy was peering at me round the back of his seat. "What we're in was used by the SAS in the Yemen. Christ knows how it got on to the open market but it did. We picked the gun up south of Addis from a guy who'd lost his head to a mortar shell. Since we had the place to put it, seemed silly not to take it."

He turned back, but went on speaking.

"You got your passport?"

I patted my jacket. Wallet still there.

"Yes."

"And valid plastic?"

"Yes."

"Righty. Now we can't land at Jomo Kenyatta International because our flight-plan doesn't have us coming in from abroad. So we'll be landing at Wilson. We'll put you in a matatu for Kenyatta. Once you're there try the BA desk first, then, if they're booked out, Kenyan Airlines. Once you've got your ticket stay put. Don't leave the airport. Might even be worth hiding there until boarding time. You know, like lock yourself in the bog."

Dave chipped in.

"We're going down now. ETA ten minutes. Fasten your seat belt. Jimmy, see if you can raise air traffic control at Wilson. Take a look to your left, Kit. Mt Kenya, not often you see her without her clothes on."

No clouds or mist, he meant. And from our height dominating the rolling, hilly plateau, and lesser ranges, surprisingly green after the Rift Valley, like a big woman lying on her side, the thrust of her hip and shoulder forming the peaks, all of a hundred and fifty miles away.

Chapter Twenty One

They thrust a handful of shillings in my hand in case I didn't have enough, and then pushed me into the leading matatu at the head of the queue.

"What about that beer?" I cried.

"Another time, Kit, another time."

"I owe you."

"Don't give it a thought, mate."

The matatu lurched off, side door still open, couple of guys leaning out with their outer arms over their heads, clutching the roof rack.

That was when I learnt a minibus built to seat a maximum of nine people including the driver can carry twenty-seven. I was perched on the edge of a seat, with ASDA in my lap, a big woman in a robe and turban pressing her huge hot thigh against mine, and my knees poking out into the gangway where they knocked the black curly head of a four-year-old urchin. I was in culture shock straight away. The crowds, the rush, above all the noise.

The route was a dog-leg and on the angle twelve people got out and thirteen got in. Somehow a very thin adolescent boy squeezed through between everyone, collecting our fares. He clutched a sheaf of notes in his left hand in a peculiar interweaving, interlocking grip which presumably made it impossible to snatch them. The van half-emptied again as we passed the last of the factories and workshops that lined the dual carriageway to the airport. None of these people were on their way there to fly, I guessed. Flyers go by taxi, hotel shuttle, or chauffered limo.

Why wasn't I in a taxi? The answer came to me and set off a few questions with it. In a taxi I could have changed my mind and headed back into town. At least in a matatu I was sure to get to Kenyatta. And that's where Jimmy and David wanted me. At Kenyatta International and then safe on a plane back to Blighty. Why? Out of concern for my personal safety? Or was there more to it than that? Whose side they were on suddenly became a more complicated question than I had previously thought. How many sides were there? How many conflicting interests involved?

But already the matatu was emptying in a bay on the side of the huge inner circle of the two that make up the main buildings of the airport. These are concentric. In the centre are the main administrative buildings; the departure and arrival areas make up the outer perimeter and are linked to the centre by two enclosed bridges – corridors inside one of which Holly and I had trundled our bags following our arrival from Mombasa. The six-lane carriageway between, a vast roundabout, is edged with parking lots and bays leading out and back on to the main road, giving the whole complex from the air the shape of a giant key-hole. I found my way into the main block, a huge space beneath a girdered

ceiling with the usual banks, offices, check-in points
and so on and found my way to the BA desk. Nice
black lady in the usual dark blue dress filled with
tiny red and white triangles and an accent straight
out of Benenden.

"You are too late for the morning flight, sir, but
there is availability on tonight's flight. Take off is
twenty-two twenty-five, arrival at Heathrow five
fifteen local time. Shall I book you in on that one?
Club class or standard? Will you be paying cash,
cheque or credit card? Visa? That will be fine, sir.
Could I see your passport? Perfect…" And so on.
While she went through it all I caught sight of
myself in an angled strip of mirror glass above her
counter. Christ, I thought. Clothes crumpled, dirty
with a tear in one knee from where I'd tumbled into
a dry riverbed the day before, or maybe it had happened when I was tipped out of the basket of that
bloody balloon, stubbled jaw, and a torn ASDA bag
for luggage. And on top of it all my shapeless fedora. I looked like shit, a Bin Laden hoplite with my
shoes filled with the other sort of plastic. I'd even
picked up enough sun-tan to be taken for an Arab.
Or Indiana Jones? Perhaps not.

"There we are then. Check in at twenty fifty-five.
Have a good flight."

I looked at my watch. I didn't believe what it
said. I checked a digital display at the top of the
departure board. It agreed. Eleven thirty-two. Left
the Maasai village in Elisha's truck at, say, half
seven. Met the Fitzmaurices and Jimmy and Dave at

half eight. In the air by a quarter to ten, maybe earlier. Flying just over an hour. Matatu and messing about here for another forty minutes. OK, eleven thirty-two could, after all be right. So. Was I going to hide in the men's bog for nine hours? No, I was not.

I pushed my wallet and ticket into my inside pocket and looked around for a seat, found one of those high stools at the counter of a functional coffee-bar, ordered a coffee. For a moment I felt dizzy and nearly fell off. Exhausted, still aching in just about every joint and other places too, I suddenly realised I was very hungry. I ordered a cheese roll to go with the coffee. It was like cheese rolls used to be on British Rail back when I was a student. A good honest lump of soft white stodge with a sliver of yellow plastic in the middle. None of your imitation Prêt à Manger with a crust that can damage your denture and sets you back two quid fifty. All the same, coffee and roll took almost my last shillings, or rather Jimmy's, and I looked around for an ACM. Looked like there was one over in a glassed in portakabin sort of an affair in the middle of the concourse with the good old Barclays livery. I ate a little, drank a little, and, since I found I was incapable of thought, let my feelings speak to me instead.

Danny, never ceasing to be an aching loss; Vincey, had he known he was sending me into the arms of Baseball Cap and the AFI hoods? That his apparent effort to save me would have killed me if I had known about the sun, and the equator and all that shit? Golly. Where had he really sprung from? Sent to find me by the Fitzmaurices or Danny herself? And Jimmy and Dave? What was their angle? Who else? Why Holly, of course, Ludwig Holly who apparently had got me into this fine mess in the first place. Holly. Who knew as much about it all as anyone and lived in Nairobi, and I had his address and a good nine hours I could use to find him in. Right. Better than spending the time sitting on a loo seat.

I slid off my stool and headed for the ACM. Out of order. Try window number one. There were three people in line in front of me, and another twenty minutes went by. Passport? Yes. Barclaycard, Visa? Yes. Other form of identification? Would you believe it but I actually had my driving licence in my wallet? How much do you want? Remember you'll have a hell of a job changing shillings back to sterling in the UK. OK. Fifty pounds worth. Five thousand shillings. Sign here and here and here, and take these papers to window six. Again the same three in front of me, one of them just walking away with a grin on his face and a wad of notes in his hand. Another fifteen minutes, and there I was – liquidity restored.

Was I really going to try and find Holly? Put myself back in the firing-line? Risk another thumping or worse? I walked towards the sunlight at the end of the hall, stopped, turned back. That poor cat i' the adage, how I knew how it felt! Then, shit, I thought, I owe myself this much – to know why, even just a little bit of why, I'd been put through all this in what, five? Six days? I was still trying to add up how many nights since Danny and I and the Masters of the Universe had been gorging ourselves on meat at the Carnivore when I reached the taxi rank and joined the queue. It moved quickly, quick enough to prevent me from letting I dare not wait upon I would.

It was an old Merc but the driver had all his bases covered. Hung from his rear-view mirror the beads that tick off the thirty-three Names of Allah jostled with a miniature leaf-shaped shield with two crossed spears behind it. Our Lady of Lourdes waved a hand at us from her little plinth superglued to the top of the dash. His name was Al. A stick-on plastic label fixed just below the statuette read 'Call me Al' (cue for song?). I guessed it didn't apply to the BVM. The fact that Al was in his late fifties, with short-cropped curly white hair and a happy grin, was even more reassuring. No doubt his even, easy-going temperament, as well as sheer skill, was why he had survived in a high risk job. I stuck my head through his window and handed him Holly's card. He scratched his head, frowned. I thought perhaps because he did not know the street, but in fact he had another reason for wondering at the card, which, for the time being, and not wanting to lose a fare, he kept to himself.

"Maybe near Jomo Kenyatta University," I suggested.

"That's what I figured," he said. "Off Thika Road, the A2. Get in. Cost you two thousand."

"That's a lot. How about one big one?"

"I can't do it for less than seventeen and a half."

"Fifteen?"

"Try the guy behind me."

"OK. Seventeen and a half."

I got in beside him. His grin was Cheshire Cat size now.

He cruised at the speed of the traffic, elbow on the sill of his open window, finger-touch control on the power assisted, Sportsman clamped between the nicotine-stained fingers of the other hand. We reached the junction where a left would take us back to Wilson, and went straight on, heading for the centre. Traffic thickened, decibels mounted, driver behaviour went through neurotic until the needle hovered on psychotic. Al chucked his Sportsman – he needed both hands now, one to steer, one to give the finger to matatu drivers who tried to cut him up. He pushed a tape cassette that was sticking out of his player right in. Bouncy Afro pop.

Jambo, jambo bwana,
Habari gani? Mzuri sana
Wageni, mwakaribishwa,
Kenya yetu…

Welcome, welcome man! How are you? Very well thank you. Tourists, you are welcome, To our Kenya.

"National anthem," said Al. "Better than the real one, let me tell you."

I'll bet he plays it to all the new airport arrivals I thought. We stop-started down Uhuru with the Central Park on our left, crossed the big intersection at Kenyatta Avenue, the crossing where I had risked my life a century or so ago, and then been mugged. The groups of thin men chasing out the loneliness of dying with cigarettes and cheap or home-brewed booze still haunted the park and I caught a glimpse of the Serena above its groomed hedges. Al's fingers drummed on the rim of the steering wheel for a moment in time to the beat and then quite suddenly he killed it.

"That guy whose house I'm taking you to. He a friend of yours?"

"Sort of."

"Shame some bad guy offed him." He lobbed a sideways glance at me. "You didn't know, huh?"

"No." Oh, shit!

"It's in the paper. Up behind the visor."

His eyes flicked up.

I pulled the *Daily Nation* down. My hand shook. PROF KILLED IN DRIVE-BY SHOOTING was the headline. I looked at the date. It was two days old, Saturday's edition. OK, so today was Monday and Al hadn't yet cleared out the old paper. There was a column on the front page and more inside. Dr Ludwig Holly had been taking his usual evening walk in the leafy streets near the Jomo Kenyatta University when he was shot four times from a

cruising black car, believed to be a newish Audi. A
gardener in one of the properties bordering the road
saw the incident and gave the alarm. His employers
called for ambulance and police both of which
arrived promptly on the scene. Dr Holly was taken
to the nearby Aga Khan Hospital where he was pronounced dead on arrival.

I fumbled my way through to an inside page
where there was a resumé of his recent work on
genetic engineering and a brief account of his work
at Jomo Kenyatta. And there was a separate piece
that speculated as to possible motives behind the
killing. He had been researching the mycoherbicides genetically modified to attack Cannabis sativa
and it was possible therefore that his murder was
drug-related.

"Snake Park up there on the right."

"Snake Park?"

"Like a zoo, but snakes only."

He took us round a couple of roundabouts and
up a short hill. Suddenly the A2 was clear of the city
and slicing a rather classy suburb instead. Danny
had driven us down this road when we left Nairobi
for Mt Kenya and Samburu. Villas in late colonial
twenties style sat in lush gardens where sprinklers
played and spacious trees carried tropical blossom.
Then again it went slightly down-market with
roads on a grid serving smaller, more modern bungalows in smaller gardens. We passed a sign for
Jomo Kenyatta University, campus, residences,
departments of this and that, and then took a left

into one of the side roads. Al slowed, and watched the numbers go by.

"This is it." And he pulled into the kerb.

I sighed, clenched my fists, unclenched them.

"You know," I said, "I'm not sure there's a lot of point now. It's sure to be all locked up."

"Up to you, boss."

"Maybe I'll just have a look around. Would you mind waiting? I won't be long, and then you can take me back to the airport."

I put the ASDA bag on the floor, swung my feet over it. As I got out Al pushed the cassette back in and lit up a Sportsman.

Hakuna matata
Kenya inchi nzuri
Hakuna matata

No problem. Kenya is the lovely country.

No problem.

Chapter Twenty Two

Holly's road was an upmarket version of the swathe of bungalows that circles Bournemouth like a boa constrictor – his was squat, four sided, had a pyramidal tile roof, meagre metal framed windows, a front door set behind a built-on porch. But this was Africa, a well-watered bit only miles from the equator but high above sea-level, and Africa asserted itself with shrubs whose huge flowers pulsed with colour and the fluttering of butterfly wings as big as the palm of your hand. There was a pair of lemon trees in front of the porch with clumps of star-shaped white flowers and some green fruit too, and a hybrid weeping jacaranda whose last blooms had not quite formed into black pods like the ones down on Uhuru but still trailed swags of fading flowers, pale lilac, like wistaria. A group of sunbirds, probing the lush green grass of the lawn with thin curved beaks, splendid sunbirds (the epithet is part of their proper name), the males with purple masks, green capes, and rich bluey-black underparts, skimmed the top of the shrubbery on flickering wings, and presumably landed next door.

You get a sense, in my line of business, that a house is empty when it is – or you think you do. There's something blind about the windows, the doors give off a sort of dormancy as if they can't be bothered to open. I walked down each side, using a laid path of concrete flags, looking as well as I could through the windows. The first side was utilities, frosted glass for separate bathroom and loo; a smaller high window, also with a ventilator brick near it, which probably indicated a larder or store-room. The next, the back of the house, was two bedrooms with venetian blinds, but the slats half open. Neither large, one with a double bed, the other with a single. The covering on the single had not been pulled back, and the pillow was awry, so I guessed this was the one Holly had used. A dark mirror reflected what I took to be shadows.

Then up the other side: just one room, his study. I found I was looking at the back of an Apple-Mac on the desk under the window, and what was probably a combined fax, telephone and scanner. Filing trays. A small printer. Behind, seen only dimly, bookcases and filing cabinets. I reckoned that was the room I had to get into.

Back now to the front. One window looked into a living room with a zebra pattern sofa, which could, seeing this was Kenya, have been real zebra hide, a faux fireplace with a print above it of the painting you see the world over of elephants coming out of a forest, room-divider with shelves, adding up to the ambience of a room designed and furnished to please no one and offend no one. In short, a residence for transient or visiting professors and the like.

The front door in its porch opened, I guessed,

into the one room I hadn't seen, a kitchen-diner. The door's upper panel was frosted glass, and there was a Yale above a dead-lock mortice. The Yale I could have managed, PIs do have some skills, but not the mortice. There was also a cat-flap. I've used cat-flaps in the past, that is got an arm in and a hand on an inside handle, but again the mortice would defeat me. There was also a yellow band of gaffer tape printed with the words 'Kenya Police, Do NOT Enter', and the same in Swahili, acting as a seal. Not much really, considering the guy had been murdered three days earlier, but then this wasn't the actual SOC.

I gave it all some thought. I remembered Holly. Jolly, even easy-going in his way. Academic. This, I thought, is a guy, living on his own, who could well lose his keys, or close the door leaving them inside, and people like that leave a set hidden outside. There was no garage, just an empty drive-in, but there was a small garden shed at the back. It was padlocked. No it wasn't. There was a standard hasp with a padlock on it, but the two screws securing the hasp were loose, just pushed into their holes. Inside there were a few garden tools and an electric mower. There was also a narrow strip of timber above the door, making a ledge. I ran my hand along it and – bingo! The very two keys I was looking for on a conventional sprung ring, no tag, plus a small one which I reckoned could be for the mail-box at the end of the short drive.

I went back on to the road, round to Al's window.

He had the radio on now: news in English, Dubya and the White House not so much rattling sabres at Saddam as loosening them in their scabbards.

"I think I can get in after all," I said. "Can you give me half an hour?"

He grinned up at me through the smoke of his cigarette.

"With the meter running you can have anything."

"You don't have a meter."

He tapped his forehead with his finger. He had a meter.

I went back to the door. The keys worked all right, the door opened easily. No mail on the mat, the mail-box might bear a look later, I told myself, but there was a small handful of feathers, small ones, bright colours. Cat. Although I'm a birdie, if not an actual twitcher, I'm cool about the hunting habits of domestic cats. I'm as likely to blame a cat for hunting birds as I am to approve shutting birds up in cages. I paused and sniffed, listened too. The air was stale but no unpleasant smells. There was a hum which I took to be a fridge-freezer, and indeed it cut out almost straight away. And almost immediately the cat flap clicked and a lean but healthy looking tabby brushed herself against my shins and miaowed. I know cat language: she was pleased to see me but expected to be fed. I knew I'd get no peace from her until I'd seen to that, so I moved through into the kitchen area. It had the usual appliances but in small, not the family, sizes. I quickly located dried cat food in an eye-level cupboard and an opened but covered tin of Whiskas in the fridge. Like I say, I know cats, so I had to wash up her saucers before putting the food in them. She went on pushing her head against my trousers as I did all this, then, when I put the saucers down, gave each one a sniff without touching them, and was off out again through the flap. Cats. You have to like a man who looks after his cat, and I suddenly felt a stab of loss.

Time now to attend to less important matters. I went to Holly's study, stood on the threshold, and let myself attune to the room before going properly in. Here, partly because it filled quite a large space back from the small window, the ceiling seemed lower, the light darker. I sniffed, detected nothing unusual, not even the slight mustiness of a room where the air had not moved for a day or two. Today was a Monday, Holly had been shot on the Friday. However, I sensed someone had been there since then. Well, you'd expect the police to have at least had a look. I glanced over the carpet, plain oat-meal but with a kilim between the office chair and the bookcases that lined the back wall, to make sure there was nothing visible there I should check out before walking on it. There were scuff marks and a ruck in the kilim that suggested the last thing that had happened there was that it had been cleaned with a vacuum cleaner. Why? Forensic? So they could analyse the dust? I recalled that Komen, and others too no doubt, had been to Henley Police

College. But, as I have already pointed out, this was not a SOC.

A step or two further in so I could look the desk over, and the shelves and surfaces on my side of it, and I began to pick up signs that the whole room had had a very thorough but professional going-over. For instance, there was a pair of soapstone owls on a bookshelf which had been left an inch too close together and off centre. There was a small open cabinet containing small piles of stationery, envelopes in two sizes, a ream of copy paper, a smaller pile of textured letter paper, adhesive labels and so on. All were neatly aligned except for the copy paper which was slightly askew. And so on. No need to itemise but I was sure the room had been searched thoroughly and with everything touched returned to its proper place. I'm a PI. Trust me.

Well, a guy's been murdered, you look through his files and documents for clues. Fair enough. But I got this feeling someone had gone to excessive trouble to make it look as though there had not been a search at all. I went a bit further. There were box-files on the bottom shelf of his bookcase and, lo and behold, they were all empty, I mean emptied, and the hanging files in his filing cabinet, ditto. They would have needed a small van to take it all away assuming they had all been full. But why take the contents as it were, but not the containers? To convince the casual eye at least that it was all as Holly had left it. And why do that? Not because you were looking for clues as to why he had been murdered, but because you didn't want anyone else to find them, or know you'd taken them. And why do that? Because, possibly, you were the murderer.

I pinched myself, metaphorically. Time to get back to what was hard fact and leave speculation to later. Time to get down to the computer. Although it was an Apple Mac the main system was the Microsoft Works Suite 2000. No passwords. Why should there be? Holly lived alone, locked up behind him pretty securely. However, I already knew he was the sort of guy who left a spare set of keys in a fairly obvious hiding place. The sort of guy therefore who might not trust himself not to forget a password. So, via My Documents, getting into his virtual files and folders was as easy as getting into his real ones had been. Personal Correspondence, Household Accounts, Department Accounts, Tax – all that sort of thing seemed normal and as it should be, but it was a different story as soon as I got into files labelled with Roman numerals and small groups of numbers, and three boldly labelled AFI 1, 2, and 3. They were empty. As empty as his hard files.

I pushed back the high-backed black leather executive chair I was by then sitting in and looked out of the window over the top of the monitor. Something much like an English blackbird from the sound of it was repeating ad nauseam its warning cry from a tulip tree. Cat was probably mosying through the herbaceous below. I glanced at my watch. I gave Al

outside a thought. Would I have enough shillings
for him at this rate? Well, tough if I didn't – he'd just
have to accept my fifty quids worth. I doubted if he
made as much on a normal day.

Why empty the files? If the police wanted to go
through the lot they could have, would have, taken
the whole computer, hard disc and all. Or they
could have copied what they thought relevant to
floppies and taken them, but if they had, why wipe
the masters? There was only one explanation that I
could think of. The same as the one I had already
arrived at regarding the paperwork. Whoever done
it did it, not because they thought all of it would
help them in their enquiries, but because they didn't
want the material to be seen by anyone else. From
which, once again, it might not be a wild jump of
the imagination to guess that the same people might
have been responsible for the drive-by shooting.

The real nerds say they can find anything in a
computer that's ever been there, but that's a skill I
sub-contract for. However, I knew a wrinkle or two
yet that might help. Back to Desktop, arrow on
Internet Explorer, give it a moment or two, AOL,
Favourites, the usual, Google, Yahoo, Amazon, and
so forth, and six websites with similar sounding
addresses, like I mean they suggested the same subject area, things like mycoherbicide.net, biotech-
monitor.nl, sunshine-project.org. I noted them
down and then switched to History and got a similar set of pointers. Of course you'd expect a microbi-
ologist to be looking at that sort of stuff, but after I

had accessed three in a row a pattern was emerging. They were not just sites to do with genetic engineering and herbicides, they were anti the whole technology. And there was one which actually quoted a study done in Mexico on a GM corn growing area, by a certain Doctor Ludwig Holly, showing contamination in neighbouring crops. And that gave me an idea.

I went back to Google, typed in Ludwig Holly.

"OK," I said to myself, quietly, but aloud, "let's see what else you got up to."

"I shouldn't, if I were you," a voice behind me murmured.

"Fuck," I said without turning round. And then: "Have a man come in with a gun. It's Vincey, isn't it? Mr Leo Vincey?"

Chapter Twenty Three

And so it was. And he did have a gun. I swung Holly's chair round to face him. He came right into the room, his height making the ceiling look even lower, pulled the spare tubular-framed chair in from the wall against the end of the desk and sat in it. I turned to face him. He put the gun down on the desktop (real, not virtual) and rested his elbow on it with his right hand only inches from the pistol. It was small, black, and I could make out the G logo close to the muzzle which said it was a Glock. Lots of things were bothering me, but for the moment professional chagrin was uppermost.

"How did you get in without my hearing you?" I asked.

He grinned.

"I was here all the time. I heard you arrive, got into the bedroom before you got in, I was standing against the wall with the window in it so you didn't see me when you went past outside. I could see you in the mirror. Which means you should have been able to see me in it too, but I was in pretty deep shadow."

So much for all that guff about sensing a house is empty before going in. I really should have checked the whole place out before committing myself to the study.

"You had your own keys?"

"Ludwig's. The set you found were spares."

I thought about it.

"The police let you have them?"

"OK, Shovelin. That's enough. From now on I'll ask the questions."

"What gives you the right, the authority to do that?"

He sighed and his grey eyes hardened a little. Somewhat awkwardly, because he wasn't going to move his right hand from its place by the gun on the desktop, he used his left to extract a small leather fold from an inside pocket. He pushed it across to me. I picked it up, opened it. On one side, under plastic, a round seal, with a brown and white stylised eagle flying across a blue sky above a green hill. In the top half of the white border U.S. Department of Justice and in the bottom half Drug Enforcement Administration. On the other side an ID, small, but incorporating a hologram of the badge and a scanned photograph of Vincey.

"And this is valid in Kenya?" I asked. Sort of sarcastic, as if I meant it to hurt.

"The local police are co-operating with us." Then his voice hardened. "Don't fuck with me, Shovelin."

I shrugged, broke eye contact, turned back to the screen. Google had come up with seven hundred and eighty-two references to Ludwig Holly. The third or fourth one down had the heading: "American Scientist attacks DEA policy…"

Vincey snaked out a hand, took the mouse, double-clicked on 'close'.

I re-established eye-contact, tried to make myself sound hard.

"Did Ludwig know you were DEA?"

My left forearm and hand were lying, sort of casually, along the desk below the computer keyboard. I was leaning back in the chair trying my damnedest to appear a hell of a lot cooler than I felt. The bastard picked up his Glock by the muzzle and, quick as a snake, smashed the knuckles of my left hand very hard indeed with the butt. I think I've already said somewhere that I wear more rings than most men do. Above my wedding ring, which I keep on, I had a gold ring I had bought at the Turtle Paradise Shoreline Boutique. It had little elephants walking round between two hoops of gold. Vincey smashed it into the metacarpals of my fourth finger, crushing, well anyway splintering, a bone.

I didn't know this at the time but the pain, which came a half second after the blow, had me bent double and howling.

Vincey then got my attention back on him by swiping my cheek with the barrel. Through what followed I could feel blood leaking down my jowl and on to my collar, then inside the collar too.

"I meant it," he said, "when I told you from now on I ask the questions."

"That fucking hurt," I whined eventually, once I'd got the howling under control. "It still fucking hurts."

I felt angry in a fuck-you-too sort of way as well as hurt and frightened. Bugger it if he shoots me, I thought. It will be a mercy-killing if he does. I got myself out of the chair, went back into the kitchen, turned on the cold tap and let it run while I used my right hand to pull an ice tray out of the freezer compartment of the fridge. At this point, I suppose out of impatience rather than sympathy, he took it from me, poured water on the back of the tray, caught the falling cubes and wrapped them in a dish towel which he handed me. I wrapped it round my left hand and then put the whole bundle under the tap. It helped a bit. Not a lot. I sat down on a stool beside the short breakfast counter and looked up at him.

He looked down at me, decided with a twitch of his lips that could have been a sneer that I was not going to cause any more trouble and holstered the Glock in his armpit. He was wearing a lightweight check jacket, the check rather louder and larger than I would have considered tasteful.

"You told us you posted some film cassettes for Danielle Newman," he began. "Those were intercepted. But since then you have met known associates of Miss Newman, particularly a Mr and Mrs Fitzmaurice. They passed on to you more material from Miss Newman. You're going to tell me what you have done with it."

"Oh shit," I said. And the reason why was that though I had received nothing important from the Fitzmaurices, I had from Golly the night before. The memory card in Danny's slipper. And it was in the ASDA bag. And the ASDA bag was still in Call-me-Al's Merc.

He signalled a question mark with his blond eyebrows.

"Neither Mr or Mrs Fitzmaurice gave me anything... No, I tell a lie," I went on. "They bought me a Coke. That's all." I sighed, genuine, deep anxiety welling up from my chest as I contemplated what might happen next. "And you're not going to believe me."

I was right. He did something that was not only very painful, but extremely humilating too. Quite simply his right hand flashed out across the small space between us, and, through my trousers and all, got hold of my dick and my balls and both yanked and squeezed with ferocious determination. Remember, I was sitting on the edge of a small stool, so it wasn't difficult for him to do this.

"You fucking bastard," I squealed, and flailed out at him with both hands. He blocked them neatly with his forearms, then as the twisted rag and ice cubes fell away from my left hand, caught the already very swollen finger and bent it back in such a way that I was forced down on to my knees in front of him.

"I think," he said, "that the Fitzmaurices gave you a memory card compatible with the Fuji digital camera Newman used. And I think you might well still have it on you. Jacket!" And he held out his hand.

No 'please' you notice, so for a second or so I didn't get what he wanted.

"Jacket. Off!"

Now I got it. It wasn't easy. I had to pull the cuff of the left sleeve with my right hand very carefully over my damaged finger.

First he went through the pockets. He found my wallet, my passport and my air-ticket, which he had a good look at. Then he patted my jacket all over, which was silly because it was unlined.

"Trousers."

I hesitated, decided I didn't like the look in his eye, and managed to get them off by loosening the belt, letting them drop, and then doing a sort of grape-crusher's dance till they came clear. A hand-ful of Kenyan shillings in bank notes from the back pocket, some dust and bits of dried grass from where only forty-eight hours earlier I had been rolling about in the Masai Mara, while people who were presuambly this guy's allies were dropping bombs on me, were the total of his catch.

He sighed.

"Shoes and socks."

That left underpants – briefs.

Yes, once he'd drawn a blank with the shoes and socks he wanted those too.

"Oh, come o-o-on!" I cried.

He gave me that grin again, full of the kick he was getting out of the way I hurt, the way I was at his mercy, the way he could do what he liked with me and, as I slipped my underpants down to my ankles and stepped out of them, that anger came back. It was like an electrical surge blowing fuses of

self-preservation, and carrying like a surfer on its
crest the sudden realisation that he really badly
wanted that memory card and what he would do to
me to get it could not include killing me. Not, at any
rate, until after he had got it. In short, I could take
risks. He was preoccupied too. One hand holding
my pants between finger and thumb, the other at
his ear with a tiny cell-phone in his palm.

"Colonel?" he was saying. "I'm at Holly's house.
And just like I said he would, Shovelin turned up.
He doesn't have the memory card, but he does have
an air ticket for the BA flight which leaves JKIA at
twenty-two twenty-five. I guess he knows more
than he's told me so far. Sure. I'll bring him in. Give
me half an hour."

I was standing, bollock-naked, with the fridge
between us. The small freezer compartment was at
eye-level, above the fridge cabinet. Exaggerating the
embarrassment I felt, I sort of twisted away so I was
beyond the fridge and the space in front of it was
empty. As he came forward I got the fingers of my
right hand into the spongy rubber air-tight seal of
the freezer door and swung it into his face as hard as
I could. Which wasn't very hard. But it knocked his
head back while his foot was still leading forward.
His foot landed on the cat's saucer, which shot forward under it, spraying the untouched cat food, and
the combination of door and saucer dumped him on
his backside. From getting out the ice-tray earlier I
already knew there was a small lump of frozen
meat wrapped in cling-film – it turned out to be a

half-shoulder of lamb – in the freezer compartment
and as he came up off the floor I hit his head with it
as hard as I could. He sat down again, shook his
head, pushed with one hand on the floor to get himself up while his other hand brushed blindly along
the breakfast counter behind him, looking for the
Glock. That gave me time to open the fridge door
and take a bottle of South African Chablis by the
neck from the door rack. I hit him with it far harder
than I had hit him with the lamb. The bottle broke,
spilling wine and shards of glass all over him, and
this time he stayed down.

I reached over him and took the Glock. Then I
rescued my clothes from the floor. There was wine
on my knickers, not a lot, and I had to shake them
out carefully to make sure there was no glass as
well, and, keeping an eye on him struggled back
into them, and then all the rest. It took me about ten
minutes, including doing up the shoe-laces more or
less one-handed. Plenty of time for reflection. But it
was all a bit incoherent, unconnected.

Had Ludwig known this guy was in the DEA?
Was there any point in taking the Glock with me to
the airport? No. I put it down again. Was Al still
waiting for me? What the fuck was all this about,
anyway? I was hurting – where had Ludwig kept
his pain-killers? This last of course was the only
question I found an answer to there and then – a
packet of Solpadeine in the bathroom cabinet. I took
four (recommended dose two only, do not exceed)
and put the rest in my pocket. While I was there I

caught sight of my face in the cabinet mirror. Not a pretty sight. I wiped the thickening blood off my cheek and watched it well up again in the gash he'd left. I managed to stem it with a Band-Aid, also taken from the cabinet.

At that moment I heard a crash from the kitchen, a serious crash. A moment or two later I was able to work out that he'd come to, tried to get up, couldn't, opened the fridge door, tried to use it as a crutch and had brought the whole lot down in front of him.

I looked around for a weapon. Fucking Glock was in the kitchen. There was a glass shelf, greenish with bevelled edges, below the cabinet. I tried to lift it off its brackets – it wouldn't come. Fear gave me strength. I struck up at it from below with my right fist wrapped in a towel and one end, one bracket, came loose. I was able then to tear the whole thing off the wall just as he came into the doorway behind me. The first I saw of him was his face in the cabinet mirror.

His face was ashen, his film-star good looks ruined, blood slipped down one cheek from a scalp wound the bottle had made, and was forming a big puce-coloured splash over the checks that covered his padded shoulder. More blood from his nose which I'd hit with the freezer door. He staggered, both arms above his head, crucified in the door frame, the Glock in his right-hand.

It went off.

Plaster from the ceiling fell about my head.

"I'm going to fucking kill you," he croaked and moved towards me.

With a double-handed back-hand I swiped the side of his head with the glass shelf. He toppled towards the small bath and the Glock went off again, but this time his finger must have kept its pressure on the trigger for it went into automatic for at least three shots. I don't know why it didn't kill me. The noise was incredible, the bullets screamed off the side of the bath, passed in front of me and smashed tiles inches from my chest. I lifted the glass shelf above my head and brought it down on his as hard as I could just as he straightened his legs and slid his back up the wall above the bath. This time the glass broke. He caught the shower curtain in a reflexive grip as he went down and that of course fell about him too.

And again he stayed down.

I thought: maybe I've killed him. Or at any rate, since he was breathing in quick, irregular, shallow gasps, maybe he'll die later. At all events, this time he was staying down and I'd make sure he did.

A bit more rooting about turned up a roll of gaffer tape in a kitchen drawer and I used it to make a parcel out of Vincey. But I didn't post him, I just left him where he was. By then his breathing was heavy, sort of effortful. Then I went back into Holly's study, sat down, waited for my own pulse and breathing to become marginally less convulsive, spasmy.

Again I found I was asking myself questions in a moronic, robotic sort of way, like someone doing

automatic writing in a trance. What did it all mean?
Not the riddle of the Universe, but why all this fuss
about testing mycoherbicides genetically modified
to be Cannabis sativa specific? Surely it wasn't that
big a deal? Not even with a specialist like Ludwig
Holly weighing in against the project. I was familiar
enough with the territory to know that for every scientist who speaks out against GM, the people who
are developing it can find five stooges who will say
it's OK, carry on Dr Frankenstein, you're doing a
great job. Then I shook my aching, throbbing head,
and told myself Shovelin, you really do have more
pressing problems right now, like staying alive.

What next? Back to the airport? I walked out the
front door, leaving it on the catch for the moment,
back on to the street and found, of course, that Al
had gone. Where his aging Merc had been there was
now a newish Audi. The one they'd used when they
gunned down Holly? Maybe. Or maybe they had a
fleet of them. They? I shrugged, went back in, thinking to find the car keys on Vincey.

I found them quickly enough in his jacket pocket,
decided again that carrrying a pistol round an international airport was asking for trouble so left it with
him, and then took one last look round the Holly
residence. I felt a touch sad about this. He had been
a nice guy and one of the goodies, I reckoned. It
would be nice, I thought, to find out just why, in particular rather than in a general way, it had been decided that he should be off-ed. Was there anything there
that might tell me, something I had overlooked? I

thought of going back on to the Net, but reckoned that whatever was there wouldn't be specific enough, and anyway would hardly be worth killing for since it was already in the public domain.

I wandered fairly aimlessly through the bungalow and in the spare bedroom cupboard found three travelling cases including the camel-hide combination overnight and document case he'd been carrying when I first met him in the café at Mombasa Departure. The first two, a hold-all and a rigid, were empty, but not the camel-hide. On the top of the main compartment there was a change of clothes, folded neatly but used. At the bottom there was a horizontal panel sheathed in the silk that lined the whole case, but hinged by the cloth so it could be lifted up. And under it there was a spiral-bound notebook, ten inches by six, of lined paper, with a glossy photograph of snow-leopard cubs on the end boards. The small self-adhesive price tag said it had been bought in San Diego Zoo and had cost eleven ninety-five dollars. Half the fifty or so pages were filled with notes, neatly hand-written, interspersed with figures, formulae and sketches, some of which were of plants, others plans of plantations as far as I could judge.

Well, I thought, if I can find someone who understands all this, it might satisfy my curiosity and even be some use. I squeezed it into the side pocket of my jacket, but it was a tight fit and half of it still stuck out. What the hell, I thought, and put it back where I had found it and took the whole case, clothes and all. If nothing else it would give me a bit more cred when it came to check-in time. After all I was now a mess, my own clothes crumpled and dirty, splattered with blood. I was unshaven, wore a plaster on my cheek, and my ring finger was so swollen the two rings had almost disappeared. Given all that and no luggage I would have asked me a question or two before I let me on a long-haul international flight.

One last look around, then I slipped the catch on the Yale, threw the mortice, and out in the street let myself into the Audi, first slinging the camel-hide onto the passenger seat. Just as I was about to get in, pussy brushed up against my shin. I gave her a rub under the chin, thanked her for leaving her saucer where Vincey could take a skid on it, and apologised for not being able to take her with me.

She was cool about that. She'd get by.

Chapter Twenty Four

Driving that Audi back through Nairobi from Jomo Kenyatta University to Jomo Kenyatta International Airport was maybe the scariest hour in the whole trip. Why did I do it? Why didn't I just go back on to the A2 and flag down a cab? Or, for Christ's sake, phone for one from Holly's house? Don't ask me. I just did it, and to begin with with a slight sense of exhilaration. *Vorsprung durch Technik* about summed it up. I was doing well, wasn't I? Got the better of a killer with a gun, nicked his wheels, was on my way home. Not only that but I had the memory card, I could take it to Mr Shapiro in Twickenham, I was a bit of a hero really, wasn't I?

And then I remembered again. The card was in Danny's slipper. Danny's slipper was in the ASDA bag, The ASDA bag was in Call-me-Al's fucking taxi. I was coming off the roundabout above the National Museum and the Snake Zoo when this dawned and I almost missed the left turn for City Centre, just made it by cutting out a packed matatu most of whose passengers were clearly shouting abuse drowned by the discords of fifty car and truck horns. I really was in no state to drive. I was worn out, my left hand was almost useless, the overdose of Solpadeine was kicking in, and if I bothered to think about it I was thirsty and hungry as hell. Five

minutes later I hit a pothole as I pulled away from
the traffic lights on the crossroads by the Central
Park that almost wrenched the steering wheel from
my hand and kicked the base of my spine hard
enough to remind me that it was still less than a
week since I had been beaten up on the pavement
that stretched up the avenue I was crossing.

Still, the route I had to take wasn't complicated
and was tolerably well signposted once I'd sorted
out which airport I was heading for. Soon I was clear
of the city and cruising down that dual carriageway
with its hoardings, its workshops and warehouses,
its small factories, some of which appeared to be
having a lunch break or were on half-time. Men and
women were walking off in groups towards the
shanty towns, others stood around in the wasteland
smoking or eating food they'd brought with them.
Then, on the right, the Nairobi National Park, which,
having see Samburu and the Masai Mara, now
looked more like an unkempt, arid Whipsnade than
real veldt. And finally, seemingly dumped in the
middle of nowhere the citadel-like complex of JKIA.
I slipped into the first parking slot that was available,
hoisted the camel-hide out of the passenger seat, and
headed for the concourse where I had used my Visa
card to draw shillings, what? less than three hours
ago. I left the keys in the Audi's ignition and vaguely
hoped someone who could substantially improve
the quality of his or her life by doing so would nick
it. Stupid thing to do, but the stupidity lay in taking
the car in the first place.

Back in the concourse I looked at my watch. Not yet two o'clock. Seven hours to check-in time. And then I went cold, clammy sick cold like frozen meat just beginning to defrost. I was remembering the cell-phone call Vincey had made to some Colonel or other from Holly's kitchen. He'd told him I was booked on the British Airway flight that left at ten twenty-five. And what else? That he'd be back… where?… in half an hour. And that was an hour ago. How long would this colonel wait before checking out why Vincey hadn't done that? An hour, not more. Round about now, or even earlier, they'd be phoning Holly's bungalow, Vincey's cell-phone. They'd be on their way there to find out why he wasn't answering. They'd find Vincey, the state he was in. Possibly dead.

Then they'd remember I had that fucking air ticket and they'd be down to JKIA as quick as they could with sirens switched on. Worse than that, they only had to turn out the guard at the airport to look for me, they could do that before they got there themselves. By now I was rubber-necking like the girl in The Exorcist, wishing I had eyes in the back of my head. Then I remembered Jimmy's (or was it Dave's?) advice. Lock yourself in the Gents.

It didn't take long to find it. Down a short flight of concrete steps off the concourse, ten yards of corridor with those blank, locked doors one finds in such places, and then the usual: urinals, cubicles, wet tiled floors, strip lighting. By the entrance there was a table, card-table size, with a saucer on it with some coppers in it, and a tiny room, a space marked out with composition walls and a flimsy open door. Inside an attendant, a woman I thought, was smoking and reading a book.

I locked myself in a cubicle, sat on the pedestal without putting the seat up and, well, gave myself up to despair.

What I was doing was, I realised, no more than a temporary measure. Even if I stayed there for eight hours I was going to have to come out eventually. I was going to have to attempt to check in, go through passport control, and somewhere along the line they would pick me up. But what else could I do? How else could I get out of this fix, this bloody country? The airport had been marked exit but it had become the door to a dead-end, a trap, a cul-de-sac.

I was dead meat. I was certainly dead tired, very hungry, and I hurt in more places than I had realised, though that finger was the throbbing nexus of pain. For a moment dizziness swamped me, my vision seemed to close from the sides. I leant forward, over the camel-hide, which was between my feet, put my head between my knees. The dizziness passed, leaving behind a sick headache. Ten minutes later it was compounded with a numb sort of boredom, ennui, too. Almost without thinking I listlessly fumbled at the three straps that held camel-hide shut and pulled out Holly's souvenir of San Diego Zoo. Had it been a present from someone? Had he been there on holiday, perhaps with his family, children? Had he bought it there along with the fridge magnets, the pop-up books, the cuddly soft toy gorillas and pandas? I know San Diego. Zoo and all. Been there, done that, during the three weeks I had to stay while the police and military cleared up the fracas I'd got involved in. I hadn't noticed any family photographs in Holly's bungalow, but then they might well have been in the lounge or his bedroom rather than his study.

I opened his book, began to give it a far closer look than I had before. It was in diary form, but the dates, I realised after a bit, related to the days the entries were made rather than their content. Occasionally the places where he was when he wrote them were included. The technical stuff was beyond me, apart from occasional flashes, since it was written in a personal sort of shorthand that consisted of leaving out most vowels and using abbreviations like $<$ and $>$ and T^0 and others less familiar. And also because, beyond what you read in the *Guardian*, I remain pig-ignorant about the technology of genetic engineering, indeed any sort of engineering at all. Clearly, though, they were summaries of the findings or speculations of other scientists, leading to his own conjectures and hypothesising. One chunk was a resumé, with his added analysis, of Gene Use Restriction Technology (from then on GURT), which seemed to be the means by which a plant could be restricted from using genes in its own genome unless it was fed an inducible promoter gene that would set them going. The dizziness was returning. My interest perked up, however, with a sketch map marked AFI Research Station, Malindi. Irregular plots were shaded in different ways or cross-hatched and there was a key: *Zea mays, Agava sisalana, Cannabis sativa, Anannassa sativa*. Malindi I knew was some hundred kilometres or more up the coast from Mombasa. Had he been on his way back when I first met him?

Another bit was a section on how genes engineered by a global-sized food producer had accidentally 'flowed' from their maize into the maize of Mexican peasants, with some speculation as to the possible bad effects which I could more or less follow. I supposed this was taken from his work quoted on the Net. Then came a couple of pages on transposons which 'generate' chromosome polymorphism via reciprocal translocations, inversions and deletions… Sorry, Ludwig, you just lost me.

Indeed I actually dozed off for five minutes or so. I came to to a repeated banging on the cubicle door to find the note-book on the wet floor between my feet and below my head which I suppose had been between my knees again but came up with a jerk that was painful.

Swahili, or some such, roughened by nicotine and tar, but female. Female? In the gents? Of course. Cleaning out a bog is too low a job for a black male. Just like it is for a Frenchman.

"Speak English," I tried.

"Are you in good health in there or should I use my special key?"

"I'm OK."

"You come out of there then."

"Why?"

"There isn't a thing a man can do in there, on his own, that takes as long as you have been."

Female, yes. Bossy, OK. But Oxbridge educated? That's what the accent said.

Wearily I used toilet paper to wipe down the glossy end-boards of Holly's diary, the effluent seemed to be more or less just water, put the book back at the bottom of the camel-hide, strapped it up, got myself to my feet and the lock slipped over. I hadn't pulled down my trousers or anything like that, no need.

"Sorry," I said as I came out. "Must have dozed off."

She was middle-aged, wearing a blue overall coat which was far too big for her, the sleeves were turned up and it came down to her shins, over black trousers, broken down trainers. Her hair was glossy, black, wiry, three-quarter length, pulled up under a white cloth cap, her shoulders slightly humped. My first impression of her dark face was that it had a past: beautiful, sad, hurt. And that her origins were mixed: mostly African, some Arab. She put the moist cigarette she was holding between apparently arthritic fingers back into the corner of her mouth and reached out, I thought, for a tip. I couldn't be bothered. I picked up camel-hide, went out, up the stairs, into the vast roofed concourse and looked around. It wasn't that busy. Not so busy that I couldn't see a black baseball cap about thirty yards away directing uniformed cops this way and that. I ducked back down into the gents.

"You again!"

I grabbed her shoulder, put down the camel-hide, fumbled in my hip pocket, let go of her, peeled off a five hundred shilling note.

"I'm not here, all right." I picked up the camel-hide, headed back to my cubicle, stopped, turned round. "If I walk out of here on my own, if I'm not found here, I'll give you another five hundred, right?"

She drew herself up to her full height which was still a good six inches smaller than me, and with dark serious brown eyes fixed mine with a severity which would have done credit to a judge. This time I took in the way her top lip had sunk back into the gap where her two front teeth had been. I also registered a slight lisp.

"Your five hundred shillings are of no concern to me at all," she said, "but the reason for your so sudden return is of interest and if I judge it to have merit I may assist you."

"There is a man out there," and I'm afraid I took hold of the lapels of her overall, "who tried to kill me... yesterday."

Was it really as recent as the day before that I and Golly had been shot at and then bombed from an AFI helicopter? Try as I might I could find only one night, the one spent in the village school hut, between then and now... whenever 'now' was.

"I believe," I went on, "that he is some sort of policeman. Anyway, just now, out there, he was directing uniformed policemen. It is not impossible that it is me they are looking for."

"Have you then broken the law? It is not in my interest to help a common criminal."

"No," I raised my voice, for she had turned away from me and was heading for the door. "Only, that is, in self-defence," I called after her, remembering the state I had left Vincey in.

While all this was going on the two or three other users of her convenience were buttoning themselves up and moving quite quickly past her. Maybe they had understood enough from what we had said to guess there was trouble brewing. My tone of voice would have told them as much.

The attendant was now at the door.

"What does your policeman look like?" she called.

"Tall, leather jacket, black NYPD baseball cap."

For a moment she was gone. I looked round the empty room, at the gleaming urinals, the polished brass pipes, the spotless ceramic mosaic of the floor. Clearly she did a good job. I glanced into her cubbyhole, her 'office'. One half of one wall was a window. From the outside it was a mirror. Two-way mirrors are often used in such places so the attendant can keep an eye open for pick-pockets and cottagers. Then she was back.

She took my elbow, very firmly, and pushed me in. There was a small table with the fat hard-covered green book she had been reading on it, an exercise book and a pencil, a deal rush-bottomed chair, a small basin with a single tap, and one of those Camping Gaz domed cans with a burner on top supporting a small tin kettle. And a cupboard at the back. A broom cupboard. She opened it, gave me a shove, then dashed back, picked up the camel-hide and thrust it after me.

"Please to be making no noise at all until I am letting you out again. I'm sorry. I should say 'until I let you out again'."

As the door closed and clicked tight I just had time to see that I was sharing the tiny space with one of those zinc buckets with the top part half covered by a conical sieve arrangement for mop-squeezing, a mop, two brooms, and a shelf loaded with plastic bottles containing a variety of cleaners and disinfectants. Beneath the shelf there was a stack of toilet rolls in plastic wrappings. There was, really, no room for me. Darkness snapped in as she closed the door, just about complete apart from a paper-thin line of dim light framing the door.

She kept me there for, I suppose, about five minutes though it seemed much longer. There was a lot of ambient sound, much of it running water and plumbing noises, not loud but strong enough to drown out any extras that may have occurred, though for a moment or so I thought I could make out her voice, the words indistinguishable but with a negative sort of tone to them. I tried to tell myself she was telling a policeman or two that no one like me had been anywhere near the place.

And so it seemed was the case.

A quiet but firm knock on the door.

"Can you hear me?"

"Yes."

"I am not going to open the door yet in case they come back."

"All right."

"You are right to assume that the man in the baseball cap is a police officer. He is in fact a colonel in the state security police. I am not sympathetic towards him. He is the reason why I lost my teeth and my knuckles are swollen. I should be interested to hear why you are hiding from him."

I too had already had one set of knuckles smashed and I wanted to keep my teeth. I felt we had much to share, that we could be friends.

"It's a long story."

"That is often the case. The briefest of précis will be sufficient for now."

I thought for a moment, searching my mind for the most cogent way of expressing the nub.

"He believes, your police colonel –"

"Colonel Thugu."

"Really? That's pretty apt. He believes that I have in my possession a memory card from a digital camera that will prove that genetic experiments are being conducted, under government auspices, on Associated Food International research sites, which the government and AFI would prefer not to have made public." The cogs of my brain clicked on. I remembered Vincey's phone-call to… a colonel. "He probably knows that I am booked on the BA flight that leaves at ten twenty-five, so if he hasn't picked me up by then, he'll get me when I check in. Or at the boarding gate."

"And do you?"

"Do I what?"

She sighed. I could sense the sigh even though I couldn't see or hear it.

"Do you have the memory card?"

"Yes." Cold in my belly. "Or rather, no. I left it in an English supermarket shopping bag, in a taxi."

There was quite a long pause now. I could imagine she was wondering what sort of a fool it was she was dealing with. Then…

"I don't think they are going to come back. You can be com… you can come out now."

I pushed the broom cupboard door open and stumbled slightly.

"You don't look very good. Here, you have the chair."

She swung it towards me, went into the cupboard, came out with the bucket, upended it and sat on it. Then she shook the kettle to check it had water in it and used a disposable lighter to light the Camping Gaz beneath. Finally, first offering me one which I refused, she shook a Sportsman out of its paper packet, lit it.

"A cup of char, eh?" and she grinned her toothless grin.

Tea-bag, chipped mug with a picture of Nelson Mandela on it, UHT milk, a rectangular block of slightly yellowish sugar. Heaven. While she got all this together, often blinking watery eyes through the smoke of her fag, I took a look at the green cloth-bound volume on her desk. Ulysses by James Joyce, battered, much used, the pages annotated in tiny neatly pencilled writing in an alphabet that could have been Arabic.

"I am preparing an extended monograph with the title 'Ulysses: an Anti-Colonial Text'. That surprises you? It should not." Of course it bloody surprised me. How many lavatory attendants have you come across doing anything like that? But she misconstrued my surprise. "You see, the climax of the whole book is the moment when two English soldiers are knocking Stephen down and Bloom is picking him up. Picks. And dusts him down in true Samaritan fashion. You should not, I think, be catching the flight you are booked on."

"No."

"As you have already suggested, they will be watching for you."

"Yes."

"There is, however, a Kenyan Airways flight, also to Heathrow, which takes off at twenty-three fifty-five. I think I can arrange for you a transfer."

"No. That would be too obvious. But perhaps you could just get me a Kenyan Airways ticket without a transfer."

She thought about it for a minute or two, tapping her pencil on the table.

"No," she said at last, stubbing out her Sportsman and squinting through the smoke, "I have a better idea. There is a shuttle between here and Mombasa. It leaves Nairobi at five'o clock, gets to Mombasa at six, leaves Mombasa at nine, twenty-one hundred, and gets back here at ten." Of course there is, I thought. It was on the second leg of it that I had met Ludwig. She went on: "Back here, you can then catch the Kenyan Airways plane for Heathrow at five to midnight without leaving the transit area."

"What if the planes are late, get delayed."

"They always hold the Heathrow plane until the transit is made of passengers from Mombasa. It's a guaranteed connection."

We refined on the plan. She'd get me a single to Mombasa. At Mombasa I would buy a single to Heathrow via Nairobi. That way the only record on the Nairobi computer would be of a ticket to Mombasa. But it was unlikely Colonel Thugu would even look for me there. Once I'd failed to show for the BA flight, he'd be looking for me on the Kenyan Airways flight. But if I booked that in Mombasa my name shouldn't show on the passenger list in Nairobi. All they'd have would be the number of seats already booked.

"But what if the flights are booked solid from Mombasa and to Heathrow?"

"They won't be," she said, lighting another Sportsman, "since nine eleven they're never full. At the worst you might have to go business class. If you can afford it."

"Frankly…" Suddenly I wanted a name to call her by.

"Vikrama. Doctor Vikrama. D.Litt, that is."

"Chris Shovelin. Frankly Dr Vikrama, right now, if it would get me safely out of Kenya, I would cheerfully sell my house."

Chapter Twenty Five

I finished the tea (since there was only one mug she didn't have any herself, though she continued to smoke) then she put me back in her cupboard as if I were a rag doll she had been told to put away. But first she took my passport and my visa card. She was much longer this time, nearly forty minutes. However, she had locked the outer door of her cubicle so I was not disturbed. I got very hot though and began to feel I might suffocate or at any rate faint. Probably I would have done but she had given me the bucket to sit on and when dizziness threatened I was yet again able to put my head between my knees.

My left hand began to throb and the pain inched back as the Solpadeine wore off. I took two more, breaking the tablets out of the foil in the dark, though it was rather a struggle getting them down without a drink. I was careful not to drop them.

She came back at last, and opened the broom cupboard door.

"Goodness me, you look even less shipshape than you did."

And indeed I almost fell as she gathered me back into the chair.

"Some water perhaps while I prepare another

cup of tea. Perhaps I can find some aspirin. And your hand does not look good at all."

I told her not to worry about aspirin, that I had already taken pain-killers. As I did so I could hear her moving behind me, then came the rasping sound of torn cotton. She was ripping up a drying up cloth.

"It will be better in a sling," she said. And briskly and competently she improvised one that kept my left elbow bent in an acute angle and my hand against the top of my sternum, that is, upright. Rather manically I recalled how I had done much the same for Golly, twenty-four hours earlier. The throbbing eased considerably, almost immediately.

"You should get it seen to as soon as you arrive in Heathrow," she muttered during the whole process, "I am sure they will have a competent first aid post there."

"You've got me a ticket then?"

"Yes and no. I discussed the situation with the lady at the Kenyan Airways desk and she was of the opinion that we should not enter your booking on the computer until the very last moment, that is at half-past four. She will, however, make sure that a seat is kept available for you. Though that should not be a problem. There is, forgive me for using their appalling jargon, 'plenty of availability as of now'. She will take your ticket, passport and credit card to the boarding area where you will pick them up at four-forty just as boarding is getting under way. There is one problem…"

I'd seen it.

"How I get airside without being spotted."

"Precisely. For international departures you must use the overhead covered walkway. But for domestic flights you can simply walk across the car park. They may be watching the entrance to that, and once you are in you still have to go through a ticket, identity and security check to get to airside proper. And even if they are not keeping an eye open for you, which they will be, at that point you will still have no documentation."

"So?"

"There is a sewer."

"Oh shit!"

"Exactly so. I think there is still one in the pot." And she filled me up.

Again the drink pulled me round, for the time being anyway, though her damned Sportsman cigarettes almost undid the good it was doing. I was about half way through when she reached across the tiny space between us and turned my wrist so she could read my watch.

"Oops, sorry. Did that hurt?"

"No. Just a twinge."

"Nearly twenty to three. My shift finishes at three and we will have to leave here. I'll take you to the staff room in the basement where you can wait until it's time to go through the sewer. There will be friends on duty in the boarding areas who will keep an eye open for you and give you your boarding card and ticket and so on."

"You seem to have many friends here at the airport."

"Well yes and no. You know…" and she leant in towards me so our foreheads were almost touching and the smoke from her latest Sportsman drifted up between us, "many sub-cultures exist within the realm of a system like an airport. Consider. There is admin, and ancillary office staff, security liaising with exterior groupings in the police, fire brigades and so forth, paramedics, service personnel providing cleaners, cooks, toilet attendants and so forth. Shopkeepers and bank staff. Then there is the technical side from air traffic control to airplane maintenance, minor repairs, fuelling, and so forth. Aircrew, of course. Now all exist as very separate entities, pocket communities numbering some of them as many as a hundred, others only a dozen or less, many coming and going, just passing through. But there are interfaces, connections. And one thing binds them, gives them a common interest… the enemy. Nothing binds people the way a shared enemy does, though it may also lead to conflicts between them. Dublin in 1904 was such a place, the enemy the English colonial power. But here, the common enemy…?"

"The passengers," I suggested. "The customers?"

"Dear me, no. They are peripheral. They slide by us like ghosts. They are intangible, untouchable, insignificant. No, I mean of course the system itself, partly, but only partly represented by the bosses. The employers. The hirers and firers. But even they, in so far as they are being individuals, are as subject to the system, are its tools or the bits of grit that have to be removed, as any of the rest of us. No, it is the system itself, in our case the airport, that is the enemy – to be feared, placated, served, in much the same way as a theocracy personified as a god is served, like the Jagganath or the Catholic church. But also exploited, mined, robbed, used and abused, but only within the bounds it will itself accept. Go too far and it will spew you out… Dublin, Ireland, spewed out Joyce."

She leant back, sighed with weariness I thought rather than distaste, stubbed her cigarette out in the small brass bowl she kept by her and which now, at the end of an eight, ten, twelve hour shift was over-flowing with noisome noxious ash and dog-ends. A tired smile passed across her tired eyes.

"And so you see, in this underworld, this cel-larage which I inhabit, there is an understanding that you do what a co-citizen of it asks of you, so long as the request will not lead you into more con-frontation with the system than you are prepared to accept. And by knitting together a net or web of tiny collusions, gifts and pay-offs, you can often achieve quite big things." The smile became a grin. "There have been bullion robberies at Heathrow have there not? Imagine how much goes on that is not deemed newsworthy."

Silence settled between us punctuated by a flush pulled, the gush of the urinals. I worked on framing my next question as carefully as I could

"I hope, Doctor Vikaram," I said at last, "that you

won't think it, um, forward of me to wonder why an educated person like yourself is in this situation."

"Educated? We are all educated, my dear. One cannot grow up without being educated. But I imagine you are referring to the western, cultural elements in my intellectual physiognomy. My extended family, of mixed race, we are part Bantu, part Arab, part Sinhalese, are wealthy Mombasa-based merchants. Wealthy enough to send me to a girls' private school in England whence I proceeded to Wadham College, Oxford where I was a student of Professor Terence Eagleton. I am now an assistant professor in European literature at Nairobi University, suspended sine die. The fact that I organised student demonstrations and a petition protesting the shooting of Father Kaiser, a Catholic Priest, by government thugs two years ago, and other activities less obviously noteworthy, none of them actually illegal, brought me to this pass. I am, in fact, lucky to be alive and probably owe my survival and moderately gainful employment to the fact that my professor has the ear of Richard Leakey. I should not complain. It is after all the sort of thing that happened in Czechoslovakia, Hungary and elsewhere behind the Iron Curtain, and it is commonplace in satellite and client states of the United States. At least I am not in a gulag or a chain-gang. Ah. Here comes Miriam…"

A tall thin woman with the even good looks, high cheekbones and straight nose I had come to associate with the Maasai, filled the door. They exchanged

a version of laying on five. Dr Vikaram shrugged
out of her blue overall coat and handed it to the
newcomer, who shrugged herself into it. On her it
was a good fit.

"You come most carefully upon your hour," Dr
Vikaram chanted as she did so, "for this relief, much
thanks."

She turned to me.

"Miriam," she said, "is on a forced sabbatical
from being admissions officer of the Christian
Women's College for Orphans."

Miriam smiled at me.

"I attempted to exclude the bastards of senior
civil servants, on the grounds that they were not
orphans," she said.

Meanwhile Dr Vikaram collected up her copy of
Ulysses, her exercise book, cigarettes, lighter and
tea-bags into a small draw-string bag, and turned to
me.

"Please follow me," she said.

She stopped in front of a door at the foot of the stairs
to the main concourse, pulled out a bunch of keys
and unlocked it. It was one of those featureless
doors you often see in such places but rarely notice.
She waved me through it and locked it behind her.
We were in a long corridor of sweating concrete
with heavy duty pipes and so forth running along
the ceiling. It followed the curve of the building and
we followed it, crossing a long large room the ceiling of which was criss-crossed with machinery –

rollers and ratcheted wheels. Two men on moveable scaffolding were tinkering with part of it.

"The luggage retrieval carousels. They break down. Often for mechanical reasons but sometimes because the handlers have spotted a likely-looking piece."

"Likely?"

"You know. A Gucci with extra locks, that sort of thing."

The long slow curve continued. There were more doors. One was marked Entry Strictly Prohibited.

"This is the one," she said. She unlocked it and left it unlocked. "But you don't want to hang around down there or get to the other side too early. Come back in half an hour."

The corridor ended in a plain double door. Vikaram pushed on one side, held it open.

"Welcome," she cried, "to the fourth circle of hell."

It was a large room, long enough for the far wall to be at a slight angle due to the curve, and almost as deep. Strip lighting glared from the acoustic tiles of the high ceiling and inevitably one of the tubes was on the blink. The walls were lined with small lockers in stacks, like the ones you get in swimming pool changing rooms, and there were three automats selling beers, sodas, crisps. A narrow flight of stairs climbed from a gap between the lockers. There were no chairs, no windows, drinks cans toppled out of the one refuse bin and the floor was filthy with cigarette ends, ash, wrappers. That didn't deter several men and women from sitting on it, or hunkering above it. A couple at the far end played drums made from sections of palm tree trunks and goat skin, while two women swayed to the beat and sang a rhythmically robust but mournful song. Against the far wall two shrouded figures wrapped in patterned blankets appeared to sleep with their cheeks on their arms. Most of the twenty or so people, however, were coming or going, putting personal property into the lockers or taking it out. It was very hot, and the air was stale, a cocktail of rich smells.

A young man spotted Vikaram as we came through the door, pushed his back off the bank of lockers where he had been waiting and came to meet us. He wore a clean white shirt and black trousers and I thought he could be a waiter, or perhaps a clerk from one of the cambio franchises or banks. It turned out he actually serviced one of the two book and newspaper stalls. He had been one of Vikaram's students.

"This is Zephaniah," she said. "But he answers to Zeph. Zeph, this is Christopher."

"I answer to Kit," I said, and shook his warm, moist hand.

"I have to go now, Zeph will look after you," she went on, unlocking a locker and taking from it a small tooled leather purse and a paisley head-scarf. Quickly, using a hand mirror, she dragged a comb through her hair, and painted her lips a very deep carmine, folded one lip over the other to adjust what she'd done, not easy with the gap where her missing teeth had been, put lipstick and mirror into her bag, pulled the scarf over her head and knotted it beneath her chin. I realised her background could have been Islamic. "Just one thing though. If it all goes wrong and they pull you in, they will want to know who helped you and how. They may knock you about a bit. You will want to stop them doing that so you'll have to tell them something. We don't mind what – so long as it is not the truth. Make up names, invent people who look different from us. And when you get to England tell people. Tell them what you know about what is going on here. Right?"

"Right," I said, though my stomach had gone cold again, "and… I can't say how grate –"

"It's nothing. Not a problem. Good luck."

She surprised me with a kiss on my cheek and she was gone, up the mean stairs, while I was still resettling my hat. Gents always remove their lids when embraced. But then I thought it seemed a touch incongruous so I put it on top of the clothes in camel-hide.

"Child-minder," said Zeph.

"Eh?"

"Her child-minder knocks off at half-past three. She has to be back by then."

"Oh, ah."

Long silence. The band played on.

"Long wait, then," I postulated.

"Yeah."

Then, all together: "Perhaps..." "You might be more comfortable..."

"No, you, carry on."

"Perhaps we could sit down."

"Why not?"

Well, there were plenty of reasons why not, see above. Zeph cleared some of them away, made a space, and we sat against the wall, knees up, arms across them, camel-hide beside me. Then he asked me if I'd like a drink. I said I would. But he had no money. He said. In spite of Vikaram's sling I managed to pull a handful of change from my trouser pocket. He took it all over to one of the automats. A Coke tin clanged into the trough below. It left me with the notes I had, still just under fifty quids' worth. He pulled the tab in the can and we shared it.

"What's an Eng Lit graduate doing here?" I asked.

He crushed the can and tossed it in the general direction of the overflowing trash bin. By now the hall or whatever was almost empty, the crowd diminished as the shift changing time passed.

There just weren't jobs for English Literature graduates, he said. Apart from anything else the question he was asked was always: why English? Aren't there enough Kenyan, let alone African authors to study? To which the answer was that almost all of the worthwhile ones were banned and it was an offence to own their books, let alone teach them. His job wasn't a bad one. He got to read the English and American newspapers, or at any rate their airmail editions, which was nice, and it paid almost enough to cover his rent and food. That gave me an idea for passing the time.

"Is your newspaper kiosk still open?" I asked.

"Yep. Until the BA and Kenyan Airways flights to England have checked in."

"Can you get me a paper? *Guardian Weekly* if you've got it?"

"There was one left," he said. "It costs two fifty."

I pulled out my roll, peeled off a five hundred shilling note. He looked at me. He looked at the roll.

"You're loaded," he said.

He took the five hundred and went. I thought maybe I had made a stupid mistake.

Chapter Twenty Six

I was right. The clattering of boots on the concrete stairs alerted me before I saw them. Four uniformed police, peaked caps, belted, armed, old Baseball Hat himself, Colonel Thugu, no less, and behind his shoulder the traitor Zephaniah. Had he struck a bargain? The shillings in my pocket in return for my body? Fucking Judas if he had. I didn't stay to find out, I was off like the electric hare at Poole Greyhound Stadium. I hoped they'd be like the dogs. Fast, but not fast enough.

I went the way I had come and now the gentle curve of the building was a definite asset. I got the lead I wanted, that is they were out of sight behind me, which meant they had to check each blank door as they passed it. I took the sixth, the one Vikaram had unlocked, marked Entry Strictly Prohibited. It presented me with another steep flight of concrete steps down into yet another corridor below the one I had been in. It was hotter and darker, the bulbs set behind small cages in the wall dimmer, less frequent, the ceiling lower. Another junction, I took a right, why not? The passage ran straight to another door. I pushed through it and found I was on a railed gantry which made a diameter about twenty yards long, bisecting a circular space whose floor was a metre lower. Large pipes, shiny with aluminium concertinas, criss-crossed the ceiling or looped down to what I guessed must be heat exchangers, condensers and so forth. There were also heavy cables running in an out of steel grated cabinets, and a console with large switches and dials.

I guessed it must all add up to the engine that drove the whole double building: the water supplies, the electricity, the air-conditioning, and it stank, I mean really pen-and-inked, and not with the smells of hot water, hot metal, oil or whatever that you might expect, but deeply, rottingly, organically stinking – shit, bad food, dead bodies.

There were rats.

I'm not good about rats.

These were grey, slimy, long tailed, and very large, as big as sausage dogs and they were congregated round a thin upright isoceles triangle of dim light in the circumference equidistant from the two ends of the gantry. Later I made guesses as to what had happened. A waste disposal chute dropped wastage from a kitchen into moveable hoppers which presumably were supposed to be emptied or exchanged on a regular basis. But something had gone wrong. Perhaps a waste collection truck had backed too far, I don't really know, but the chute had been pushed askew leaving the triangle of light and a way into the area the rats could use and an inexhaustible supply of their sort of food. A cloud of flies hung above it, dense like a shoal of tiny black fish.

Rats were not the only scavengers. Nor were they the only creatures who had used that gap to get in. As my eyes acclimatised to the gloom I realised that below and beneath the gallery I was on, there were low heaps of material, blankets, split cushions, and the like, old coats. There were bottles too, and in one place a little trickle of cigarette smoke rose until a movement of the fetid air bent and dispersed it.

Shouts from above and behind me. Clattering feet. I ran another ten yards, almost to the middle of the gantry, then I clambered, awkwardly, one-handed, over the railing, dropped to the floor below. Shit, I thought, I've left camel-hide in the staff-room. A squawk and an oath but not in English. I had landed on some part of someone's anatomy. I stumbled, fell to one knee, grabbed up a corner of what felt and looked like a damp tarpaulin, and hauled myself under it, dragging every inch of me in, right down to my feet, as flat as I could be, sprawled on the filthy floor. I had a companion, the guy I'd trodden on. Except that even in the darkness beneath the thing that covered us, I could sense he wasn't a guy: he was a lad, no more than a boy. He squawked a little, said something that sounded like another fuck off or whatever, pulled his legs away from mine. My head bumped against a pillar supporting the walkway I had come over. I pulled back, lifted a corner of the tarpaulin and looked out from under it, keeping it over my head.

Narrowed by perspective I could see the upright rectangle of the doorway I had come through. At that moment two policemen came through, glanced at each other, and set off side by side along the gantry, torch beams swinging across the floor, casting lurching shadows from the pipes and machinery.

A third figure appeared in the doorway, lit dimly at first but then one of the beams spot-lit it for a moment or two as the police turned at the far end and came back. A white bandage circled his head, came down over his ears and supported or was secured under his chin. His eyes were puffed up in huge discoloured bruises. There was a lot of dark dried blood on the shoulders and lapels of his jacket which remained recognisable. Someone had found him an aluminium half crutch which cradled his left forearm. He lifted it, waved it like a cybernetic extension. His voice crackled, screeched like a powered metal-cutter, as if it had been enhanced, his mouth a black hole, the painting of a scream of rage and pain.

"Shovelin? Shovelin! Come out, you fucking bastard. Come out so I can break every bone in your fucking body."

Vincey, Leo Vincey. Back, I must suppose, from the dead.

Silence. The hum of the motors, a steady drip from nearby.

"No sign of him," called one of the policemen.

"Shovelin? Kitty, kitty, Kit, Kit. Be a good pussy and come out. I want to tie a firework to your furry tail, get it?"

Behind the taunting I could detect an uncertain note. I held my breath.

"Oh fuck it. Come on."

The policemen's boots clanged on cast-iron, became muffled, faded. Silence again. But one of the things I'd learnt about Vincey was that he was a cunning bastard. I held my breath, waited. I was right. A shadow fell across the door jamb. Neither of us moved for a full minute. Then a lighter flame distorted the shadow and a thin plume of smoke drifted out of the doorway and hung on the thick poisonous air. Three more minutes passed. What made him so bloody sure I was there? Then a voice from way up the stairs.

"Mr Vincey? Are you still down there? We think we've got him cornered in a storeroom."

"Really?"

And he tossed the Dunhill out over the area. I heard the flurry it caused as two or three of my companions competed for it. He was gone, leaving just the layered smoke in the air behind him.

There were six of them, six I saw, anyway. The one nearest me, the one I'd landed on was the first to sit up, dragging the tarpaulin to one side. The other five faces, heads and shoulders, rose out of the gloom behind him, around us. Their faces were grey rather than black, eyes large and sunken in their sockets, hollows beneath their cheekbones. At least three of them were blotched with ugly sores, and two were losing their hair, in handfuls. The one who had got Vincey's fag gagged on it, broke into a hideous rasping fit of coughing and retching. It sounded terminal. It could have been. And the worst thing of it all was that they were young. The one nearest me no more than five or six, the oldest, the one with the smoke, maybe ten. And three of them were girls. I don't think I worked it out at the time, but I did later. I guess they were AIDS orphans, and themselves HIV positive from birth. And no one wanted to know.

I got to my feet, shuffled through the debris to the oldest, hunkered down in front of him, waited for the coughing to subside.

"Do you speak English?" I asked at last.

He nodded. Sputum, with a streak of red on it, lay across his chin. He wiped it with the back of his hand. He was thin, like a chicken carcass that has been stripped to the internal membrane that covers the ribs. There was fear in his eyes. But maybe there always was.

"What's your name?" I asked him.

"David." He pronounced it Daveed.

"David," I went on. "Those men, bad men, want to catch me and kill me."

He nodded again.

"They bad men." Emphatic agreement. He knew a piece of filth when he saw it.

"I need to get into the other building. The outside one. Where the airplanes are. But without being seen."

"OK," he said and gave a little shrug as if to say, no problem, nothing easier. He dragged himself up on legs like a bird's and reached out a hand. God forgive me I hesitated before taking it – a bundle of twigs, hot and damp, which I was afraid I might crush. He was wearing a rag of a filthy t-shirt above cut-down adult trousers. The t-shirt had a cracked and fading picture of Kanu on it, the Nigerian footballer, in Arsenal strip. He applied pressure through his hand, I followed him and then watched as he shifted blankets or whatever along the floor. A small girl pulled herself out of them, sat above folded legs, her knees like tennis balls, sucked her thumb and batted away the flies that homed in again.

Yes, there was a small circular man-hole with a hand grip. It lifted easily enough. Yes, there was a spiral, functional staircase. Yes, there was a sewer at the bottom. It was a half tube of concrete, three feet deep in the middle, running along the bottom of a semi-circular tunnel five feet high. There was a narrow walkway alongside the sewer which ran steadily away from us, the effluent, untreated sewage, about a foot deep. There was worse. David went first. He had a small cheap torch, which was as well because there was no light down there. The passage, tunnel, took a slow turn about five yards ahead. Caught on the bend was a body, mostly submerged, trapping effluent against it. Rats, as quick as snakes, slipped away from it, from the light, though one paused and gave us a look, its clawed front feet up under its chin. Its black eyes flashed red in the torch light, then it was gone. The body had been a girl, emaciated, wearing the tatters of a shift-like dress. She was face down. The backs of her legs had been gnawed to the bone. The smell was awful. We had to go past her.

This, I thought, is as bad as it gets.

David muttered, "What else can we do with them?"

I followed the light of his torch which got noticeably dimmer as we went, passing beneath the car parks that lay between the two concentric buildings above. Within fifty yards we came to a spiral stair similar to the one that had brought us down.

David turned to me.

"That's it. We're here."

"I can't thank you enough. Can I give you some money?"

"What would we buy with it?"

"I'll tell people... when I get home."

He looked up at me from those eyes like black lamps.

"Why?"

As bad as it gets – when things get so bad there's no point in telling anyone.

Chapter Twenty Seven

This man-hole cover was heavier than the first. It was more than a metal plate, its frame, I soon discovered, filled with ceramic glazed tiles matching the floor around it. I adjusted my footing on the steps, flattened the palm of my right hand above my head against it and straightened knees, back, elbows. No luck. I shrugged my left shoulder and wrist out of the sling. Even to raise my left hand above my head was agony, the effort I willed on it worse, but that extra pound or so of thrust were enough to shift it, lift it an inch or two. Bright light flooded in through the gap I'd made. I heard singing. *I don't want to rock, DJ... 'Cause you're keeping me up all night.* Then it stopped. The singers had clocked the rising floor. The weight was lifted off my hands and the manhole cover rose as if by magic, was laid aside. The sudden relief caught me off balance and I nearly toppled backwards. Uncle George's nephew and one of his mates peered down at me. A hoarse whisper:

"Jesu Christ."

"Tis the geezer went missing."

"Can't be. He were ate by lions."

"Tis."

"Tint."

I intervened.

"Tis," I said.

They hoisted the cover to one side and, with hands in my armpits, lifted me out. I looked around. Yes, a gents toilet. Again.

"Fuck me, but you look a mess. Where you bin?"

"Stinks too."

I swayed. Nephew looked around for something for me to sit on, no chairs. He pushed open a cubicle door, slammed down the top seat, sat me on it. I should say at this point that these airside loos had no attendant.

"Hey, Bri," his mate called, "help me get the cover back on before some silly fucker falls in."

"You're all here, are you?" I asked.

"Just our lot. We're off to a dead smart hotel on the coast for a week," said Bri. Smug as a cat with cream. "Lord and Lady Muck and all the others are on their way home. Couldn't hack the extra week, could they? Not enough dosh. Not like Uncle George."

"Uncle George?"

"'Course, Uncle George."

"Good old Uncle George. Do you think you could ask him to come and have a word with me?"

They looked at each other.

"Don' see why not."

As they went I managed to get off the seat and bolt the door. Then I sat there, and tried to think. But they were back in three minutes and Uncle George turned out to be the complete brick I thought he would be. He had qualities that far outweighed the pallor of his skin (now touched-up with oddly irregular sun-burn), his flabbiness, his bad breath. He'd die, he really would, for anyone he had decided was one of our lot. He was determined to the point of mulishness and beyond. The only authority he respected was that of his own conscience. He was nobody's fool.

Clearly I needed a change of clothes.

"Nobody's going to let you on a plane looking and smelling like what you do."

But all their baggage had been checked in. However, there was a tourist shop open and his nephew was sent to see what he could find. Meanwhile, and ignoring the other travellers who came and went, he got me to strip down and made me give myself a thorough wash at one of the hand-basins, feeding me soap, toilet paper, paper towels. Nephew returned with a full length, long armed robe in cotton printed with a bold jungle pattern in black, green, orange, a round rimless hat embroidered with beads, and a fly whisk made from a bone-in antelope tail. Or maybe it was a Colobus monkey's.

"I'm not wearing that," I said.

"Why not? You're a bloomin tourist aren't you? Tourists do the daftest things."

They left off Vikaram's sling – dead giveaway they said. Without it I might not be recognised. They put my dirty clothes in the duty free shopping bag, and I carried it with me.

"Black you up," grunted Uncle George, "and you'll be the image of old Uncle Jomo hisself. Met him once, back in the early fifties, in the Adelphi, Liverpool. Raising money from the unions he was. I was like deputy shop steward in the old boiler-makers' at the time and unofficial minder to his nibs. Shame he was conned by this bastard who's took over."

I caught a glimpse of myself in a mirror. With baggy eyes, a bit more than a fair share of nose, and a touch of sun-tan, I looked more like Ali Baba.

I explained the ticket situation, and Uncle George went to see to it himself. Meanwhile I went out with the three lads into the departure lounge which was no such thing but a largeish cream painted room with worn vinyl-covered chairs and benches, a couple of scuffed tables, a floor of cracked vinyl tiles and a coffee counter.

Bri, the third of the lads whose name was Tel, and the nephew, who was Tone, played three card brag with me for Kenyan coppers. They used a worn deck of cards Tone had on him. Nudes on the backs, every one different, so I realised after a bit why I always lost. The second lot of Solpadeine had kicked in and I found I could use my left hand without too much agony, though my ring finger still looked like a banana, the rings almost buried by ballooning flesh. I complained of hunger and Tone got me, yes, a cheese roll, getting stale now, and a Sprite.

Half an hour later Uncle was back, waving my passport, credit card and a credit card slip.

"Sign here," he said.

I did.

"Tell you about it once I've delivered this."

This time he was only five minutes.

"OK," he said. "I found the boss Kenyan Airways woman on this side. She knew all about it. Said it was important not to get your ticket on the computer until the very last minute but she promised she'd get it over this side with a boarding card before she let the plane go." He looked at his watch again. He chewed an already bitten down thumbnail.

"I don't know why these lasses are all so dead keen to help you," he went on. "If they were jobsworths you'd be done for. Must be your sex appeal."

"It's Doctor Vikaram," I suggested. "They know who she is, maybe she's helped them in the past or their relations, families, whatever."

"Maybe." He shrugged his big shoulders. "Let's hope so." Then he laughed. "Fine pickle we'll all be in if we're rumbled. Extended holiday at Moi's expense, eh, lads? Chris?"

Time passed. I dozed. I relaxed. The only thing I wasn't happy about were the Kenyatta-type robes. Seemed like laissez-faire. No, I mean lèse-majesté. Draw attention, anyway. Then a shake.

"Wakey, wakeeeey!"

It was the full shout, the way Billy Cotton used to do it on the wireless.

"Twenty-to-five. Here's your ticket and your boarding card."

I looked up at his big, round, beaming, face.

"Uncle George," I said, "you're a genius."

"Not me. The boss woman just brought them over and handed them to me."

Together with about twenty or so other passengers we drifted down to the end of the 'lounge' and through glass doors into more of the same, though this time there was a big glass door, part of the glass frontage, opening straight on to the tarmac. This, apparently, was Gate 2. Tone and Bri went out into the sunlight. No one stopped them, so we joined them. A hundred yards or so away to the left there were two parked Seven Three Sevens. To the right an RAF Hercules, huge, grey-green. Using a stepladder on wheels two sunburnt men in khaki but with dark blue RAF berets were doing something with spanners to one of the engines.

"Support for the SAS," said Uncle George. "They train up near Samburu."

Just the sort of thing he would know.

We waited a further forty minutes. I felt I ought to fidget about it, but I was too tired, too drowsy. After all I'd been through I couldn't get excited about the delay. Inshallah, about summed up my attitude. Eventually another Seven Three Seven rumbled up and did a U-turn which missed clipping the wing-tip of one of the parked ones by no more than six inches. Down came the stairs and a stewardess holding a six-foot post with a simple sign on top and a wooden base at the bottom. The sign had a single word on it: Mombasa. She planted it at the foot of the stairs. It looked like a bus-stop. She gave us a welcoming wave.

"Good enough for me," said Uncle George and we trooped off in an untidy line behind him, across the hot tarmac.

My robe caught on something at the top. The stewardess unhitched me.

"Nice gear," she said. She checked out my boarding card, tore off the tab. "Have a nice trip."

At about five thousand feet, as we banked to get onto a south-east course, I caught a glimpse of JKIA in the armpit where wing joins fuselage. In my head I saw the body of a little girl trapped against a bend in the sewer underneath it. Suddenly I wanted to cry. But instead, I slept. Again.

Chapter Twenty Eight

Not much more to say. It all went according to plan. In President Moi, Mombasa's far more glitzy airport, Uncle George, Bri, Tone, and Tel made a noisy and effusive farewell, full of repeated Mind How You Go's and Look After Yourself's. I tried to pay for the Kenyatta robes but Uncle George wasn't having any of that.

He fixed me with cold, expressionless eyes.

"Can't take it with me," he said.

"What do you mean?"

"Asbestosis. Back from them days in Liverpool. Got the compensation and six months."

"Oh fuck. I am sorry."

And I shook his hand more thoughtfully than I might have done. What else could I do? It explained why he was giving his nephew and his mates the holiday of a lifetime.

Next I bought a through ticket to Heathrow, depart Mombasa at nine o' clock, depart Nairobi five to midnight. Then I climbed the wide chrome and marble stairs to the first floor, checked through security and passport control and wandered into the airside departure area. In the main hall a sprinkling of tourists had already gathered and the two shops were open. I delved into the plastic duty-free bag, dug my shillings out of the back pocket of my trousers, and bought a three-day-old *Telegraph*, a medium-sized bar of Toblerone, and a rhino carved out of something black for my boy back home to go with the seed and pearl bracelet that was still in my jacket pocket, wrapped in a scrap of tissue, waiting for my girl Rosa.

Then I went into the café area. I ordered a coffee. Do you have anything to eat? A cheese roll. No thank you. And I carefully sat ten yards away from where I had sat a week earlier. Lightning doesn't strike twice in the same place, they say, but I wasn't taking chances. Didn't stop the pied crows from gliding in to check out the Toblerone. They weren't interested.

This time there was no plane to watch as it landed since it had already landed and I had been on it. But the sun set just as it had before.

We took off at nine thirty, or thereabouts. Not late enough to worry, which I was inclined to do, even though Dr Vikaram had said they always kept the connection. I missed Kilimanjaro this time. The night was darker, the half moon not yet risen.

We landed back in JKIA at twenty past ten. This time the walk across the concrete apron took me and about six other passengers to the bottom of a flight of cast iron stairs. As we climbed them we could look down through windows into the room the RAF had taken over as an office. It was small, about the size of two cube containers. There were dull green filing cabinets and what I took to be radio stuff, all dials, knobs and switches in the same

colour. A girlie calendar. A St George's flag pinned
to the wall and a framed portrait of Her Madge.
Two men were working there, their big solid faces
the colour of pomegranates when you cut them up,
both wearing combat fatigues with displacement
patterns and RAF blue shoulder flashes. One of
them had three silver chevrons, a Flight Sergeant. If
I get into trouble, I said to myself, I'll give them a
shout. They'll see me right. My dad was a Flight
Lieutenant.

At the top of the stairs a short internal corridor
took us to one of the international departure
'lounges'. Just inside the doors we were passed
through the usual baggage and personal security
checks and got our passports stamped. At this point
a large white man in a white shirt and too clean
jeans, which somehow said policeman, held out a
hand.

"Your passport again, sir, if you don't mind."

Almost every organ between my navel and my
throat did a handstand as I handed it back. My scro-
tum shrank.

He flipped through it. He used a pen-shaped
optical scanner on it.

I thought: this guy is not a Kenyan. Not even a
white Kenyan. He's a Brit. I summoned up the
sinews of the tiger.

"And you are…?" I asked.

He looked up from my little red booklet.

"Her majesty's immmigration officer."

"Shouldn't you be at Heathrow?"

"The Kenyan government recognises that stopping illegal immigrants here is less trouble for everybody, and less expense, than if we wait until they get to London." He returned to the booklet. "Shovelin. French?"

"French five hundred years ago. My ancestors were protestant refugee asylum seekers from Catholic persecution. There were no immigration officers then. Generally speaking, in the half millennium since, we are judged to have made valuable contributions to English civilisation. As you see, we are now English."

I do quite a good posh, thanks to that minor public school, when I think it's called for.

He returned my passport.

"It was the gear that led me to question you," he asserted. "The, whadyacallem, robes."

There were benches against the walls and a few chairs scattered about. A queue had formed behind us as the local check-in had opened by then, so I took a bench further in over on one side, next to a glass partition that separated the main body of the room from the security scanners. Interestingly enough I could see the screen and indeed follow the whole process.

At the door two policemen. One had a black beret, a blue shirt, red sergeant's chevrons, a black lanyard. He had a black cane with a short silver cap. The other had a peaked cap, silver stars on his jacket shoulder. His cane had a silver ball. The woman who examined the screen had a blue shirt and a black jumper. The black jumper had a hole in the arm below her shoulder placed so the number on her shirt, made out of black plastic digits, was visible. She could freeze the images that came before her. For some not obviously apparent reason she could split the screen showing the baggage in monochrome on one side and colour on the other. Then I realised, the colour was not real: it identified materials inside the target – cloth, leather, plastic, metal and so on. A label on the side of the machine read RAPISCAN, Security Products, in italic sans-serif. Sorry about that. Professional interest.

Meanwhile my friend the immigration was having trouble with a very extended Indian family: Mum, in a sari, with five or six gold bangles and gold drop earrings, and at least six children ranging down from six years old to one, was being asked to show proof that all the children were hers. And then I heard voices near me, but over on my right.

"Dad? Will the pilot be a Kenyan, a black man?"

Christ. The Wimbledon lawyer's son, young baggy shorts. "I doubt it. Not many of their chaps are up to that sort of thing, yet."

"We won't be hijacked, will we? What will they crash the plane into if we are? Canary Wharf? St Paul's? That'd be good. Like in that film. Was it *Independence Day*? Near the beginning."

"*Armageddon*?"

"One of those."

There were others, others from the safari, but apart from giving me long and puzzled looks they were, I suppose, deterred by those blessed robes. But they all knew who I was a moment or two later. There was a sudden commotion outside. A woman's voice seemed to be at the centre of it.

"Mr Shovelin. I have two packages for Mr Shovelin."

One of the policeman scanned us.

"Mr Shovelin?"

The bastard immigration officer nodded and then pointed at me.

"Come this way." And at least eight faces jerked up in my direction, then looked away, but generating as they did so a buzz of whispered comment and conversation. Heart banging, I picked up my Mombasa duty free bag and threaded my way through the chairs and people's knees and hand baggage to the airside of the security screens.

"Abandon hope," the father of the Northern Collegiate muttered audibly as I passed him, "it's the Jonah's Return."

On the other side, landside, Miriam, from the loos, Dr Vikaram herself, and behind them, yes, Mr Call-me-Al. And of course they had both the ASDA bag and the camel-hide.

A policewoman took both bags, fed them into the scanner. Dr Vikaram called out.

"You owe Mr Al three thousand shillings. The extra thousand is for the trouble you've caused him."

"Four thousand," he objected. She turned on him.

"Three," she said.

I dug into the Mombasa bag again, found the last of my roll of shillings and handed them, via the policewoman, to Dr Vikaram.

"There should be enough there," I called.

She counted off three thousand. There were a few left. She looked at them, shrugged, gave them all to Call-me-Al. Then with a wave all three turned and were gone.

I now had two changes of clothing. My own, fairly dirty but nothing like as bad as the ones I'd changed for my Kenyatta robes, and Ludwig Holly's, worn, but not dirty, but – nowhere to change them. Oh well.

At ten-to-midnight we were led back down the outside stairs to the tarmac. This time a bus was waiting for us. I managed to get one of the few seats, a single one opposite the door. But also on the tarmac, deep in shadow about twenty yards away, a black Daimler, ministry style, with a green white and orange flag on its wing. Both rear passenger doors opened. Vincey, I thought? With a couple of hoodlums? But no. On one side a tall, thin woman with reddish blonde hair, in a green cotton coat, got out; on the other side an even taller black man, beautifully suited, but with his left arm in a tan leather sling. They kissed each other, rather warmly if, because of the sling, a touch awkwardly. Then the woman walked across the short space and into the light and I could be certain.

The bus doors hissed behind her. Danny reached

up for the grab handle above her and smiled down
at me.

"Hi," she said. "No, don't get up."

Chapter Twenty Nine

I could spin this out. You know, fill in all the details
of the flight, what the stewardesses did and when,
what the supper snack was like, how the lights were
put out, the film (*Legally Blonde*, actually) and so on.
When we slept and for how long. But none of that's
important. What's important is what she told me –
and what she didn't, so I had to guess at it later.

But first, let me explain: she was in business class,
I in economy. But before we took off one of the stewardesses came through the curtain and told me an
upgrade had been paid for and I went through, with
my plastic bags and camel-hide, looking, I suppose,
like the more eccentric sort of dosser or wino.
Anyway I spent the trip with enough room to stretch
my legs, which was nice, and next to Danny, which
was even nicer.

"Hang on," she said, just as I was hoisting the last
of the bags into the lockers above us. "Haven't you
got something for me?"

"Oh, Jesus, yes." I rummaged in good old ASDA.
"Pair of slippers."

"Pair!" she exclaimed.

"One from under a bush near the Polo, the other,
the one with the memory card, Golly gave me."

"Oh no!"

"What?"

"You didn't find the car?"

"Yes."

"You must have thought…"

"You were dead? Yes. I was… upset."

She'd already lifted the insole and found the card.

"Thank God for that."

"Got something else for you," and I extracted Holly's San Diego notebook from the camel-hide. "Found it at Ludwig's."

Well, she was pleased about that too and said so when I finally slid into the seat next to her. I watched her, sort of sideways, the way you do, as she rifled through it, nodding and muttering affirmatives, yes, yes, that's it, this'll help, as she did so. We took off, we climbed. Finally she twisted towards me so our faces were only a foot or so apart.

"You've been wonderful," she said, and her lovely greenish eyes seemed to glisten, "totally wonderful," and she quick as anything dabbed a kiss on my cheek.

"I really did think you were dead. How come you're alive and well and thirty-six thousand feet above Africa?" I asked.

"That's the easy part of the story. We faked it."

"We?"

"The Fitzmaurices, Golly, Jimmy and Dave. Drove the Polo off the track and into the trees, Jimmy used their sub-machine gun on it."

"Why?"

"Ludwig got a message to me. Just one word, one

we'd agreed, because we reckoned most of the places I'd be would be bugged. Certainly the Fitzmaurices' phone, which was where I was. The word was *uhuru* which means freedom, but what it meant for us was it's all gone pear-shaped, get out. Two days later they killed him."

"Who? Vincey?"

"Maybe. It's a long story."

"I'd like to know the gist."

"Of course you would."

And she put her hand on my hand and gave it a squeeze. I have to say I was by now in a state of sublime euphoria, a huge reaction to all that had gone before. It all came together in a warm glow spiced with a sort of ethereal desire: the rhythms of the plane which in the African night seemed so secure and safe, the feeling the nightmare was over, and above all my closeness to her, close enough to sense her warmth, savour the tones of elusive perfume, the caress of her hair on my cheek when we both reached down to pick up a freebie hot towel I'd managed to drop. I hadn't been in love like this since I was fifteen.

Anyway…

"I can't too well remember what I said before, but whatever, it was Ludwig who initially got in touch with us…"

"Us?"

"The news gathering firm I work for."

"Of course."

"You must know a bit about him by now."

"He was taking a sabbatical to set up a GM unit in the microbiology department at JK university. He was looking into a case where a farmer on the coast claimed his hemp crop had suffered through being next door to an AFI research station. Something he discovered led him to contact you." I thought for a moment.

"Go on. You're doing very well." She squeezed my hand. I squeezed hers back.

"Not really. It's mostly stuff you told me anyway. After that it mostly gets to be supposition. Except that he seemed to be on friendly terms with a Drug Enforcement Agent –"

"Really?" She let go my hand, her head came forward so she could look at me. "Leo Vincey? Why do you think that?"

"He showed me his ID."

"When?"

"This afternoon. Then he tried to kill me, but I got away."

"Good for you! And I thought he was a trouble-shooter and occasional hitman, class sophisticated hitman, used by the marketing end of the Columbians. Actually I had no proof of that, it was little more than a hunch, based on some stuff we had on a file back in Jo-burg that our office emailed me while I was hiding out with the Fitzmaurices."

The plane rumbled on through the dark. Danny chewed a nail, looked at or out of the window. After a moment we both realised we were looking at each other in the reflection and grinned.

"If you're going to tell me more," I said, "it had better be now. Before I go to sleep."

"OK. Couple of months ago Ludwig got in touch with us and I met up with him a couple of times in Dar es Salaam. What he told me was hair-raising, needed to be made public, but needed incontrovertible proof to back it. Photographs would help. We arranged that Tim, our picture man, he came to us from Magnum, should do that. Now, we've done this sort of thing before and we've developed a routine. Tim always takes along a courier who will get out at least half of the films by a different route. I was to be the courier. Then just before we were to set out Tim got... immobilised. We asked Ludwig to postpone. He said no, things were getting difficult, it had to be then or never. He was planning to cut and run back to Cambridge within a week. So I said I'd do the pictures, but not unless he could find a third person to act as courier. He found you."

I could think of so many things to say about that I said none of them. Instead...

"And how does Vincey fit into all this?"

"We didn't know anything about him at all until I met them in Nairobi the day after you arrived, the evening of the day I... picked you up. And I didn't learn a lot then. Apparently he turned up at JK Uni about a month ago, as a consultant system analyst helping with the re-organisation of the language faculty, an area Ludwig knew nothing about. But in that month he became Ludwig's buddy. Ludwig

was lonely. He had never been away from his family
for so long. He was dreadfully worried about the
stuff he was uncovering. Vincey, it seemed, was
just what he needed. A younger man, not too much
younger, lively, witty, similar background, East
Coast bourgeois. They were buddies."

"Queer? Like I mean gay?"

"Subliminally perhaps. But I doubt it went
physical. You asked me that already."

"Did I?"

"At Samburu Lodge."

Again she seemed to sink back into herself for a
bit, and it occurred to me she was as tired as I was. I
let it ride for minute or so, then sensing that she
really was dozing off I got going again.

"That limo you were in. At the airport…?"

She laughed.

"Quite the thing, wasn't it? Our consul's."

"Your consul's?" I asked, remembering the green,
white and orange flag.

"Republic of Ireland," she said, and she made the
Irish in her voice sing more than normally. "She's,
the consul that is, she's a sympathetic sort of a person and took us under her wing. Me and Golly." She
sort of centred herself, bit her lip, and looked at me
intently again. "But you want to hear the nut of it
all, don't you?"

"Yes."

"Right then. What Holly found out, and what
my photographs prove, is this. AFI were testing
mycoherbicides genetically engineered to be plant

specific on *Cannabis sativa* on the coast, and on *Erythroxylon coca* in the mountains…"

"Erith… what you said. What's that?"

She patted my knee in a jokingly patronising sort of way.

"Coca, dear boy. Cocaine."

"Oh, ah."

"These mycoherbicides have already been developed and are in wide use under the auspices of US drug agencies like the DEA in both North and South America. And that was the first thing that alerted Ludwig. Why? The work had already been done. But he found plantations where, seemingly, it was still going on. He obtained spore from the areas near them – remember the farmer whose hemp crop had been destroyed – and using the facilities he had put in place at the university, could see nothing new about them. Now, he knew AFI had two research stations in both of the habitats. So he looked at the other two as well. In the mountains, in the Aberdares and on Mt Kenya, and again he found the spores of *Fusarium oxysporum*, GM-ed, just as he expected. Incidentally, the Americans are rather proud of it and call it Agent Green – not a hundred miles from our old friend Agent Orange. Anyway in the Aberdares he found coca bushes sick to death, literally, as a result, but on Mt Kenya…"

It clicked. Partly because I had sudden recall of the one digital image I had seen on her lap-top at the Samburu Lodge: a hillside of healthy bushes.

"They had engineered," I cried, "bushes resistant to the mycoherbicide!"

"God, you're quick!" she exclaimed, and there was, I like to think, a hint of admiration under the mockery. "Catch the stewardess's eye for me, would you, and ask her for a glass of water with ice."

A little later she added a detail or two.

"Remember," she said, "the Masters of the Universe at the Carnivore?"

"Yes."

"I'd been tipped off they would be there which is why I wanted to go. AFI was there, ministries of agriculture and so forth, and one of the banks the Columbians use, the Madrid and Grand Cayman Banco de Corpus Cristi Internacional. OK. So a stage in producing resistant coca bushes, and marijuana seeds too, no doubt, had been reached. Now all they had to do was take samples away to Peru, Bolivia wherever, and grow them for the Columbians to harvest. But I think maybe there was more to it than that. There's lots of habitat in Kenya for both crops. I think they were looking to stage two. Set up plantations here." She looked out of the black window. "Or rather, back there."

And that really was it. Oh, there were questions left unasked and unanswered, but they were obvious enough and it would be easy enough later to come up with viable answers, so I left them unasked. We slept for most of the rest of the way, uneasily, drinking more water, going to the loo, the way you do on a long-haul night-flight. I waggled my feet, hoping to stave off deep vein thrombosis. Some of the time we held hands. Deep inside me the fifteen-year-old told himself to make the very most of it, like all the deepest loves she was illusory, she'd go, she had Golly, but she'd leave the image of perfection intact.

And so it was.

Six o'clockish they woke us with your standard continental, a croissant, a chocolatine, café au lait. The sun poured in from the right, horizontal, hot and eye-searing until the stewardess insisted on pulling down the blind.

"What next then?" I asked.

"As soon as we land I'm going to take all the photos I've got, including the digital you saved of course, to a Dr Shapiro who's a deputy director of the mycological department at Kew." She tapped the leather purse she still carried and which she'd put the memory card into. "He'll confirm what I've told you. Then I consult with my colleagues back at Jo'burg how best to break the story. It's big, you know? Not really because of the drug angle. Crooks will always find ways of getting criminalised drugs on to the street, no matter what anyone does. What makes it big is that it blows AFI as a responsible developer of GM foods. If they can mess about like this, what else can they get up to? And by association they'll contaminate the whole evil GM industry."

"It really is evil?"

"You'd better believe it. Why? It's the main route to patenting seed. To finally getting a monopoly hold on three-quarters of the food the world eats. That'll leave just air and water, and I bet they're working on that."

"Was Vincey really DEA?"

"Probably. And why do you say 'was'?" She turned eyes suddenly cool and serious on me, gave a tiny shrug and then went on. "There are several possible explanations. The most obvious is this. We know that it's been DEA policy for years to get involved in any new development. They argue it's going to happen anyway, best to be in on it, monitor it, until they have the means to bring it down. Or maybe he's part of a scam to siphon drug money into areas where the US government wants things to happen but daren't be seen financing them."

"Irangate. Noriega."

"That sort of thing. Or maybe he's just straightforwardly corrupt and on the make." She shrugged, bit into her chocolatine almost like a little girl enjoying a treat. "Who knows?"

Again I felt lost and frightened. This was all far too big for a not very clever provincial gumshoe, generally down on his luck, if not an actual loser.

"White cliffs," she remarked.

"Isle of Wight. I live down there, over to the left. Bournemouth."

"Home in what, an hour or so?"

"Two or three."

I thought of the bus-stand, number eleven, the

Flight-Link bus in the tunnel of concrete and steel outside terminal four, and felt the cold grip of longing that comes with separation, almost certainly permanent separation.

"Give you my card if…" The robes. I gave a shrug and tried a laugh. Failed. "If… you ever want me to help you again, try private enquiry agents in the Bournemouth Yellow Pages. I've been thinking of setting up a website. Perhaps I will now."

She knew what I was feeling, gave my hand a squeeze. Tears pricked my eyes. Bloody fool. Who did I think I was? Trevor Howard in *Brief Encounter*? She had another film in mind.

"This needn't be the end of a beautiful relationship," she murmured. Then she looked out and down.

"God, doesn't it look green!"

If you haven't guessed what happens next, you're dumber than I thought. I went with her through passport control and customs. Neither of us had baggage to reclaim. We got out onto the pavement in that high roaring grey tunnel of bus-stops and taxi drops and pick-ups. A very quick kiss and I turned away from her, heading for the Bournemouth bus-stop. I reckoned there'd be one along in ten minutes, even though it's an hourly service.

Vincey didn't recognise me. Not in my Kenyatta gear, not without my fedora.

I don't know why I turned back. There had been no noise loud enough to hear above the general traffic, the diesel buses and taxis. Maybe she cried out. She was sitting on the pavement like a broken doll, and the blood slowly filled the two holes beneath her left breast. I ran towards her and her head and shoulders came forward and she slumped over on her side. A grey BMW idled past and, without it stopping, a man got in, carrying her soft leather purse, into the front passenger seat. Vincey was sitting in the back. He had one of those neck things on now, a reversed cone, and a bandage round his head. I guess he'd caught the BA flight half an hour ahead of us.

Maybe she died in my arms, maybe she was dead already.

Bad as it gets.

Author's Note

It is a commonplace error these days to confuse the opinions and even experiences of a fictional character with those of the author. Chris Shovelin is not Julian Rathbone. I mention this particularly with reference to the Kuoni Cheetah Safari Tour. Shovelin's opinion of this may appear critical, even satirical at times. Julian Rathbone, however, together with his family, had a marvellous holiday with them and met no one at all on it who could possibly be identified with characters in the book you have just read. Except Sami, our driver.

Associated Foods International and the Banco de Corpus Cristi Internacional have played parts in at least three earlier novels of mine. Since no one has taken exception to my depiction of them, they too are clearly inventions.

The airline schedules between Mombasa, Nairobi and Heathrow were, however, at the time of writing, accurate.

Some months after *As Bad As It Gets* was finished President Moi surprised the opposition, and probably most of his supporters as well, by stepping down from the Presidency of Kenya. Seventy-one year-old Mwai Kibaki, the compromise opposition candidate, won the election that followed. Mr. Kibaki has pledged that the corruption and institutionalised violence of the Moi regime will cease.

J. R.